THE CURSE OF AMMON

Whispers of Atlantis: BOOK III

Jay Penner

In this anthology:

The Atlantis Papyrus

The Wrath of God

The Curse of Ammon*

Sinister Sands

The Death Pit*

(*) may be read as a standalone

https://jaypenner.com

To my readers, for the faith and support. I am eternally grateful.

Cover designed by Jay Penner.

Printed in the United States of America.

First Printing: March 2020

https://jaypenner.com

5.0 2021.11.09.10.50.26
Produced using publishquickly
https://publishquickly.com

JAY PENNER
HISTORY AND FANTASY

Choose your interest! A gritty and treacherous journey with Cleopatra in the Last Pharaoh trilogy, or thrilling stories full of intrigue and conflict in the Whispers of Atlantis anthology set in the ancient world.

THE LAST PHARAOH

WHISPERS OF ATLANTIS

https://jaypenner.com

AUTHOR'S NOTES

Writing ancient historical fiction poses its own interesting challenges. How do you describe concepts that did not exist at that time (*be pedantic or accept anachronisms*)? How close do you stay to history (*go academic or take liberties*)? Do you stay true to ancient sensibilities (*e.g., treatment of women*)? Can your hero be flawed, or should he be perfect? How much violence do you depict (*too much for some, too little for some others*)? I have tried to navigate these waters, and I hope that you will enjoy the book. If you notice any editing gremlins that have still escaped watchful eyes, please let me know.

ONCE YOU FINISH

I ask for your kindness and support through a few words (or even just ratings) after reading. I've provided review links in the end, and it will only take a few seconds (or minutes). Thank you in advance!

ΛNΛCHRONISMS

**an act of attributing customs, events, or objects
to a period to which they do not belong**

Writing in the ancient past sometimes makes it difficult to explain everyday terms. Therefore, I have taken certain liberties so that the reading is not burdened by linguistic gymnastics or forcing a reader to do mental math (how far is 60 stadia again?). My usage is meant to convey the meaning behind the term, rather than striving for historical accuracy. I hope that you, reader, will come along for the ride, even as you notice that certain concepts may not have existed during the period of the book. For example:

Directions—North, South, East, West.

Time—Years, Minutes, Hours...

Distance—Miles.

Other concepts—Imperial, Stoic.

CONVENTIONS

The names largely follow Greek convention. In specific circumstances, I have used *(Old Persian and Egyptian names.)*

PERSIANS

Cambyses (*Khambujia*)—King of Kings, *Shahanshah*

Aberis (*Abrahasa*)—Nobleman

Eribaeus—Greek Nobleman

Ritapates (*Ritapata*)—Advisor

Babak—Advisor

EGYPTIANS

Psamtik—Pharaoh

Jabari—Advisor to Cambyses

Petubastis (the 3rd)—Pharaoh in Exile

Amunperre—Chief Priest of the Oracle of Ammon

LOCATIONS

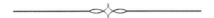

Locations and *modern equivalents*. All are in modern Egypt.

Memphis—*Mit Rahina*

Thebes—*Luxor*

Aostris—*Kharga*

Horosis—*Dakhla*

Farrasis—*Farafra*

Ammon—*Siwa*

At the end of this book, in the notes section, you will find a link to a Google maps flyby that will take you to many of the locations in this book. It's a must for history enthusiasts, give it a try!

WATER AND THE DESERT

---◇---

Scientists estimate than an adult can survive 3 – 5 days without water. This is under moderate, unsupervised conditions (some can last more and some less). However, one would be disabled long before death. Adults need about 3 – 4 liters of water *per day* for healthy operation, and this is under normal circumstances. Dehydration manifests itself in thirst, nausea, dry skin, headache and cramps, lethargy and confusion, fever, coma, and death following organ failure. There are documented cases of people dying *within hours* when lost in a desert under hot conditions and without adequate water.

An army of fifty-thousand, planning for, say, a twenty-day trek through a desert, would have to ensure availability of at least **1.1 million gallons, or 4,000 tons of water.** This excludes food, protection, and soldiers' belongings, and one can only imagine the immense and incredible undertaking of moving an army of fifty thousand through a hostile desert.

"…That the Persians set forth from Oasis across the sand, and had reached about half way between that place and themselves when, as they were at their midday meal, a wind arose from the south, strong and deadly, bringing with it vast columns of whirling sand, which entirely covered up the troops and caused them wholly to disappear. Thus, according to the Ammonians, did it fare with this army."

Herodotus, 440 B.C.

The Histories by Herodotus.

Translated by George Rawlinson

PROLOGUE

ESΗΛΝΝΛ, 527 B.C.

BABAK

———

Babak sat in his courtyard, drinking a strong herbal brew—water, salt, honey, rose extract—that his wife made. It rejuvenated him for the drudgery of the day—dealing with complainants, mediating disputes, auditing tax records, writing property deeds, dealing with requests for the governor and king, managing town budget, adjudicating criminal mischief, taking stock of town granaries, overseeing military assignments—his duties were many as Eshanna's administrator. His position was appointed by the elders of the town and ratified by the governor.

Babak had been the administrator for the last ten years—widely respected for his acumen, cunning, and fairness. He had proved himself on the battlefield for The King of Kings Cyrus and had retired after an injury. He was proud of his job, protecting his town from the whims of the Royal Court and the greed of the governors.

"Where are the boys?" he asked his wife.

His two sons were ten and twelve. His lovely wife had borne him the two boys he was immensely proud of. He hoped that one day they would grow to be magnificent warriors. They were the light of his life. Not that he did not love his daughter, but she would be gone in a few years as someone's wife—hopefully a good man. But his legacy would live on with his sons.

"Out in the northwest grain fields, helping their uncle," Roxana said, wiping her lustrous black hair away from her forehead as she squatted by the fire pit, boiling grain. He watched her affectionately. She had grown older, of course, having given him three children, and she still carried that gentle beauty and dignity. He remembered her in the initial days of their courtship—she was thin, but she had honey-smooth skin, dark and pretty eyes that shined, curly hair that fell all the way to her waist. She had a heart-skipping smile. It brought fond memories. *How shy she was!*

It did take Babak a while to get used to her ways. Unlike the women of his province, who were deferential to their husbands and offered no opinion of their own, Roxana made sure to let him know what was in her mind. Her mouth had sometimes embarrassed him in front of the elders, but over the years they had found ways to make her acceptable in public while retaining her ways in private.

Babak smiled. Helping their wealthy uncle in the fields earned the boys some barter, and they learned valuable farm skills. *I would rather them wield the wheat than hold the sword*, Babak thought. But the boys would be called to serve the empire when they reached twenty. They would also soon learn to tame a horse and ride one. He took a deep sip and let the bitter-sweet taste spread through his mouth. Then he walked to his wife and tickled her waist. She giggled and swatted his hands.

"Where is Amastri?" she asked.

Babak returned to the courtyard and silently walked behind his daughter. There she was, his pretty little princess, her head bobbing up and down as she played with her makeshift clay doll. Amastri was five—she would soon need to start helping her mother around the house. Babak hoped that one day his daughter would catch the eye of a senior official and be wedded to their family. While Babak had greater comfort than most others in this town, it was still a far cry from the luxuries of those that received the King's patronage. But that patronage came after years of servitude, backstabbing, sycophancy, and sometimes murderous conduct—something Babak had never mastered.

"What are you doing?" He asked her gently. She looked up; her beautiful black eyes shone at the sight of her affectionate father. It was rare for him to hold or cuddle her—it was frowned upon, lest the girl grows without fear of the father. But sometimes, when no one looked, he hugged her tightly and smothered her with kisses. He knew she longed for those. Sometimes when no one was around, she would intentionally come and stand by him.

And he knew why.

He smiled at her. "Is that a dog?" He asked, looking at the clay figurine she had fashioned.

She shook her head. "It's the King of Kings Cyrus!"

He threw his head back and laughed. "Well, you need more practice to make it look like a King," he said, pinching her cheeks.

And just then a figure peeked through the courtyard gate.

Angash.

The recently appointed town chief—a delegate of the governor, and technically the man Babak reported to. Angash was a political animal—not from this town, and he had no love for its people. It was a punishment posting as far as he was concerned, and Babak knew that the unctuous man had set his sights on being transferred and getting into the good graces of the Royal Court.

But why was he here?

It was rare for Angash to come by Babak's house. The Chief lived on the opposite side of the dusty citadel, and he would have to walk the dirty, cramped, dusty walkways to get here. *Not something his implied royalty usually did,* thought Babak.

"Angash! What brings you here? I would have come to you if you summoned me."

Angash gestured him to come out. Babak told his Roxana that he would be back soon and stepped onto the busy street.

It was a calm and humid morning. Eshanna's people went about their work—harvesting by the river, preparing meats, working in the metal shops, selling fruit, cleaning houses—and nothing foretold them what the day would bring. Babak walked with Angash until they reached a small open area near the west of the citadel. The man looked nervous and fidgety, but there was sickly excitement in his eyes.

"You look anxious," Babak said, eyeing Angash's restless fingers.

"There is something important to discuss," Angash said.

But Babak knew better.

These were not normal days. The town had defied the new King of Kings who had imposed additional levies. In a frenzy the people had killed the tax collector and hung his body on city walls. The previous chief had sent emissaries to the Royal court for reconsideration. Such acts rarely went unpunished, and while Babak had not supported the murder, he was supportive of the town's resistance. No king in their history had impinged on their freedom like *Khambujia*, the one Greeks called Cambyses. Cambyses, in his desire to show the empire that he was in charge now, had made many unreasonable demands and sometimes met resistance with brutal force. They had not heard from the emissaries and there was no news from Babylon on how their resistance was perceived. The only change was that the governor had demanded the dismissal of the previous chief and appointed a new man, Angash, in his place. Angash's eyes darted to the people around, going about their work. He looked quite like Babak—lean, of similar height and stock, a sharp, long face with a generous mustache and beard. His fingers drummed incessantly.

"What is it, Angash?"

Angash's voice began to crack. "They're coming," he said.

"Who is coming?"

"Who do you think?" he said, sharply. He was missing two teeth in the front, and it gave him an odd, clownish look.

"I don't know, Angash," said Babak, anxiously. "What have you done?"

"I've done what we should have long ago!" he said. "How foolish were you all to kill the tax collector? That too when the new King was flexing his muscles!"

"What have you done, Angash?" Babak shook the man's shoulder.

Angash's nervous look changed to a sly smile.

"Aberis is coming here with his Greek mercenaries."

"Today?"

"Yes."

"Why are they coming?" Babak's voice rose an octave. A noble of The Royal Court never came to a town with the intention to deliver a lecture. *What had this scoundrel done?*

"They want those responsible for the murder, and then they want promises for the town to pay what the King demands."

Babak leaned back on the muddy wall. Angash had deliberately sold them out. On this day, and for the next three, four hundred of the most able-bodied town men, former and current soldiers, were on leave. They were away to partake in a ceremony organized by Angash.

He deliberately sent them away to prevent organized resistance, leaving the town at the mercy of the forces.

"We will be fine, Babak," he said. "Only a few need to fear."

How wrong you are!

The Empire rarely relented—it responded to resistance through ruthless suppression and then pardoning or absorbing the best into the forces.

What a stupid man, Babak cursed inwardly, and now his own family, a wife, two sons, and a daughter, were in terrible danger.

He had to act quickly.

"Who else in the town knows?"

"No one," he said, proudly. "Only you."

"With whom did you discuss the terms?"

"With two messengers from the court."

"You have not met Aberis or any other commander from the siege force?"

Angash gave him an irritated look. "I used a messenger. He conveyed my words. And when Aberis sees that my words were true and the town surrendered with not an arrow shot or a man dead, you and I will receive

our awards."

"Where is the messenger?"

Angash sniggered. "At the bottom of the river. He knew too much. Keep your mouth shut and help me make arrangements."

"Who meets His Excellency when he is here?"

"I will."

"You said you never met him."

"Yes, but my name is known, and my messenger has conveyed whom to look for."

Babak eyed Angash. *What a treasonous bastard.*

"This was foolish. We should warm the people and let them run," Babak said, still thinking through the situation.

"Are you mad? There is no running. Aberis' men have already circled our citadel—we just don't see them yet. They have us on the three sides, and we have the river on the fourth. Why would you run when we have the chance for reward and peace?"

"You should have talked to us!"

"Talk to fools who thought it best to hang a King's man on the walls?"

Babak sighed. His mind churned like angry waters— trying to see the future.

Their fates.

He paused to think.

Then he decided what to do next.

"Come with me to the river, there is something I must share."

Angash looked at him suspiciously. "Share what?"

"Not here, you fool. People are already eyeing us. Once they know what happened, do you think they will spare us?

Do you think they will let the town chief and the administrator live amongst them peacefully?"

"Why would we live in this backwater? We will move to Babylon or Susa under the noble's influence."

"That's what you think. That is not what they plan. I want you to meet someone, but first let us go away someplace quiet."

"Who is not planning what?" Angash asked, and this time it was his voice that pitched higher.

You are the one surprised now, aren't you? You bastard.

"You are not the only one in touch with them, idiot!" Babak said. "But we shall speak no more of it here!"

Angash was aghast. "What—"

"Not here!" Babak hissed. He then grabbed the man by his shoulder and pushed him. "Come with me."

They walked the narrow, dusty paths of the town. The light-yellow mud-baked citadel wall loomed ahead. It was a pathetic wall, but good enough to keep bandits and casual robbers away from the town. The walls protected the town on three sides, with the river and its marshy banks forming a barrier on the fourth.

They had covered their faces with their turbans and looked like busy farmers on the way to something urgent. The few who recognized them paid no heed—after all, the new chief and the respected administrative officer often conferred with each other on official matters. Babak had served them since Cyrus' time.

They walked out of a narrow opening and a shallow bridge on to the marshy area. It was a broad dirty marsh, a mix of flowing rivers of open sewage from the town, thick mud, dry tree stumps, tall reed grass, thorny bushes, and rocky protrusions. The townspeople had access to a relatively clean section much further north than where they were now. At this time of the day there was no one in this section—*for there was nothing to do here, except to fuck, get drunk, or fight,* thought Babak.

"His Excellency has other plans for the town," Babak said. "Clearly he was clever enough to shield your name from me, and likewise."

Angash's curiosity was piqued. He walked briskly with Babak—the men wore flimsy sandals and had to be careful here, lest they pierce their foot with the innumerable dry stumps that jutted from the ground. People had died when the wound suppurated and sucked sickness from the air into the body.

They reached a thick, bushy area. Reed grew abundant here, rising almost as tall as the men.

"We don't need to go this far—" started Angash, who was now ahead of Babak, walking down a narrow path surrounded by bushes.

And that was when Babak swiftly grabbed the greedy chief by his throat and stabbed him from behind, just below the rib cage. Angash grunted and gasped, but his voice died in his throat, and this far away there was no one to hear him shout.

Angash collapsed. Babak leaned forward and stabbed him in the heart. The Chief struggled briefly before his eyes went cold and life left his body.

Babak took Angash's sword and scabbard. Satisfied that no one was looking, he dragged the body to the edge of a watery area. He tied a large rock to the feet, fashioning Angash's gown as rope, and then pushed him into the water.

Angash's body sank into the marshy river.

When he rushed back to the citadel, people were already chattering and running around—the guards had spotted Aberis' men converging from all sides. Some rushed to him, asking anxiously what was happening. Babak sent word: The King of King's forces are here, and he has been summoned to talk. *Do not attempt to run,* he cautioned, *and do not exit the citadel with weapons in hand.* That would be a certain death sentence, unless the noble had already decided to storm the citadel, raze the town, and kill everyone inside it.

Soon, one of the soldiers from Aberis' forces walked up to the gates. "Tell every villager within these walls to come out, unarmed. All of them. Children included."

Somehow, Babak knew that his world would be very different from that day, as he watched the frightened villagers walk out, one by one.

PART I

THREE YEARS LATER

EGYPT

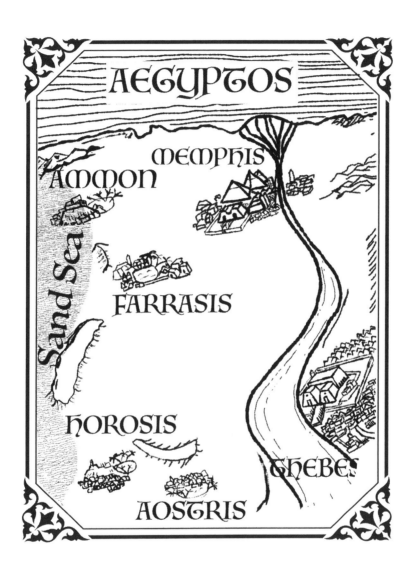

CHAPTER 1
THEBES, 524 B.C.

ABERIS

Behind the magnificent temple of Amun-Re, on the eastern bank of the Great River, in the city of Thebes, there was once a vast empty field, stretching miles in every direction before the eastern deserts began. It was forbidden to occupy this land that was reserved for the temple administration. But now it was dotted with thousands and thousands of tents, men, and animals, all part of a vast invasion force under *Shahanshah Khambujia*, King of Kings Cambyses, of Persia. On the southern edge of this hive of frenetic activity lay a ring of tents belonging to the senior men of the expedition, with the King of King's tent in the middle. It was no grand tent, and one might even be surprised by its modest size, for Cambyses was no stranger to a hard life and military living. He had governed rough areas in Babylonia and quelled many a rebellion on behalf of his father, Cyrus. Cambyses had traveled far from Babylon to Thebes. He shunned the Palace of Thebes, instead preferring to stay with his men as they prepared to travel south to invade the Ethiopian lands.

This afternoon the King's tent was busy. He sat in the sweltering heat, tolerating the fine dust that coated everything in sight. The servants swung the fans as hard as they could, but all they did was circulate the warm air and sprinkle sand on the sweaty men. But the heat in the tent was not what worried those that seated near the King of Kings—it was the news that a messenger had brought him.

Cambyses was livid. He sat on a simple highchair, wearing his customary gem-studded tiara and blue flowing robes. He rocked back and forth, rubbing his thick, black beard. He massaged his temple and wiped the sweat off his eyelids. The messenger was still on the floor—prostrate and too afraid to look up. "Stand up," he ordered.

The man scrambled to his feet and wiped his face to remove the dust.

"Tell it to me once more. You shall leave no detail," the King of Kings said softly, but his barely contained rage was palpable. The court shivered even in the heat.

"Yes, Your Majesty," the messenger said, his voice barely a whisper. The courtiers were all silent, terrified of what the King of Kings might do next. He had already had a minister of the court whipped for suggesting that they send a negotiating party.

"Everything."

"Yes, Your Majesty. Where do I start?" He asked, nervously, fidgeting.

"From the beginning!" Cambyses screamed, spittle flying from his mouth. The messenger flinched. The King of Kings had executed more than one man with unwelcome news in recent months.

"Forgive me, Your Majesty. Yes. I reached the—"

"What did you tell them? How many priests?"

"I conveyed your message to them, Your Majesty. There are three priests and a Sybil, but the head priest is Amunperre. He is the only one allowed to confer with the Oracle of Ammon."

"What did you tell them?" Cambyses asked.

"That you, *Shahanshah Khambujia*, the King of Kings, mighty King, Ruler of the World, King of Akkad, Sumer, Babylon, and all four corners, beloved of all gods, brighter than the sun, light of the Achaemenids, now the ruler of all of Egypt, appointed by the priests of Memphis, blessed by Her Divine Majesty, Goddess Neith, must be proclaimed legitimate heir to the Egyptian throne after the defeat of Psamtik.

"That you have preserved their temples, worshipped their gods, and allowed Egyptian nobles to continue in their posts and collect tax. And that it is time for them to accept His Majesty as Pharaoh."

Cambyses grunted. "And?"

The messenger fidgeted again and earned a strike from the guard behind him. "But they say it is too early to proclaim you Pharaoh. And that the Egyptian spirit is not yet extinguished."

Cambyses tugged on his beard. "Do these bastards not know that I have taken their Pharaoh captive? That by the grace of Ahuramazda and Marduk, I have defeated them, and most of their noblemen's sons are dead?"

The messenger said nothing, haplessly looking at others for help.

"What else did they say?" asked Cambyses.

"They say that the role of the Pharaoh extends beyond the realm of the living and that the Pharaoh must prove to be a great patron of the temples and the priests, beyond just praying to the gods of Egypt and making symbolic sacrifices."

Cambyses slapped his hands together, causing the messenger to flinch. "What does that even mean?" he asked, rhetorically, staring at the terrified man.

"I do not know—"

"What else did they say?"

The messenger began to dance on his feet, his nervousness and fear palpable. Finally, general Artapharnes spoke. "There was something else, speak," he ordered, his voice stern.

The messenger looked helplessly at the people around, and receiving no help, he started again. "They heaped curses on you, Your Majesty."

Cambyses leaned forward. His eyes burning into the man. "What curses?"

"They say that the Oracle foretells that the curse of Ammon will bury your soldiers."

"Bury us with what? Cow dung?" Cambyses shouted. His face had taken a ruddy complexion. "Who do these Ammonians think they are!"

"I do not know, I–" the messenger stammered.

"What else?"

"Not much else, Your Majesty. They heaped insults on me for daring to bring the request, and they would not allow me an audience with the Oracle. I told them— I demanded—"

"Wretches. They will change their tune when blood flows from their bellies," Cambyses retorted. "What does Amunperre really want?"

"I do not know—"

"Useless," Cambyses shouted. "Get out of my sight before I have your head!"

The messenger scurried away, relieved at the dismissal. Cambyses turned to his trusted general, Artapharnes. "*Artapharna*, what do you make of it?"

Artapharnes bowed to the King of Kings. "They are stubborn. The priests have too much power and hold great sway over their people."

"But do I not have a claim over the land after defeating the Pharaoh?" asked Cambyses.

Artapharnes nodded. "That may be so, Your Majesty. But the priests are driven by the same desire for power and pleasure as everyone else. They fear that you will put an end to their influence and sever the heads of the corrupt."

"What do you think, *Abrahasa*?" he said, turning to a nobleman by his side.

Aberis always welcomed the moments when the *Shahanshah* sought his opinion. It elevated him in the court. He puffed up with pride. "They wish to protect their greed, and they see you as the wolf out to eat their meat, Your Majesty," he said.

Cambyses shook his head, mollified by the thought that the resistance came from their fear. Aberis knew of the insidious rumors spread by the Egyptians about Cambyses.

That he was mad and was losing his mind each day.

That he spoke ill of their gods and conspired to destroy every temple.

That he wished to kill the sacred Apis bull with his own hands and eat

its flesh.

That he would enslave every Egyptian man and relegate the women to

brothels.

Lies. All lies!

Cambyses had done no such thing and had no desire to. He wished to bring Egypt to his dominion and was even willing to imbibe their ways. His father, Cyrus, had brought so many peoples under the Achaemenid empire and ruled them justly. Aberis recognized that *Shahanshah* Cambyses only sought to expand the empire to include Egypt. All they had to do was recognize his rule, pay him taxes and tributes, and accept certain administrative reforms.

The King of Kings rose from the wooden chair and walked outside the tent, followed by Artapharnes, Aberis, and other members of the court. All around them was the energy of a powerful force. The Persian army was preparing for its invasion of Ethiopia. It was hot, and the fine dust kicked up by the hundreds of thousands of feet and wheels had created a yellow haze. The air was thick with the smell of sweat, dirt, river water, palm trees, cow and pig manure, hay, rose and lilac perfumes, and running sewers. Cambyses relished the sights and smells—no Persian, not even his great father, had ever set foot in Egypt as a conqueror, and he had done it. He watched quietly for some time and then flicked his finger towards Aberis. The nobleman walked next to the King of Kings.

"Subduing the Ethiopian savages under the title of a Pharaoh would have been easier."

"Yes, Your Majesty."

"The Priests of Ammon think they can dictate terms to the *Shahanshah* of Persia," Cambyses said and spat on the ground. "They think that the powers conferred upon them long ago by their Pharaohs give them the authority to defy me, the one blessed by Ahuramazda."

"They are arrogant," Aberis concurred. "And their hubris is intolerable."

Cambyses walked on the rough-cut path as his guards cleared the way. He coughed as the dust irritated his lungs. "A lion does not negotiate with hyenas."

"Yes, Your Majesty."

"Do they realize what foe they make of me? Do they not know what I did to them at Memphis?"

After the defeat of Egyptians at the battle of Pelusium and emerging victorious at the siege of Memphis, Cambyses had sent off two thousand young Egyptians, including defeated Pharaoh Psamtik's sons, to death.

"They sit in their temple and think of themselves as invincible, Your Majesty," said Aberis.

Cambyses was quiet for some time. He rubbed the scabbard of his long royal sword, tapping on the gold-inlaid luxurious leather to loosen the dust that stubbornly clung to it.

"How many men do we have here?" he said, turning to General Artapharnes this time.

"About two-hundred thousand, Your Majesty."

"How many do you think the Ammonians have?"

"If I were to guess, Your Majesty, no more than a few thousand," Artapharnes said.

"And yet, they stand against me."

"They rely on the desert between them and us, Your Majesty. They think their land will protect them. They do not know the King of King's resolve, and nor do they understand the depth of his servant's desire to prove his worth to the glorious *Shahanshah*," Aberis said, referring to himself. Cambyses knew that Aberis saw an opportunity. The noble had waited patiently for years.

Cambyses nodded. He knelt on the ground and gently rubbed his palm on the coarse rock and sand. He then stood and kicked the ground, raising a cloud. "Let us teach them that the sons of Ahuramazda do not fear a few grains of the earth!"

"Yes, Your Majesty."

Cambyses turned to Aberis. "You are a faithful servant, *Abrahasa*."

Aberis knelt in front of his *Shahanshah*. "And I will always be, Your Majesty."

"Then I might have a mission for you," Cambyses said as he slapped his palms together, creating a small cloud of fine yellow dust.

CHAPTER 2

THEBES

BABAK

Babak gently lifted his daughter to a sitting position and placed a clay cup of water to her lips. She was frail, and her skin felt like aged leather. The sickness that entered her a year ago, at the onset of his King's invasion of Egypt, appeared to have only strengthened in its destructive power. His beautiful girl, just eight years old, no longer exuded the energy and joy of a child of her age. Her hair was falling off in clumps, her ribs and collar bones showed prominently, and there was no light in her eyes.

Babak wondered if his softness towards his daughter was a result of his past, for it was certainly unusual, and his wife had often teased him about it. "She will get married and go away," his wife had said, "don't get too affectionate."

"Amastri," he told her gently. "You must drink."

She turned her head away, protesting feebly. It was just weeks ago when she would still engage in more boisterous arguments, but those days had ended. All she did now is grunt, say a few words, or cry silently. Babak's heart hurt.

I have prayed to Ahuramazda. I have prayed to Amun. To Isis. To Angramainyu.

Nothing had worked. He wondered many times if the gods of Egypt were angry at the incursion of Persians—but why his daughter? She was innocent of any wrongdoing. Babak himself had never struck an Egyptian. His advice may have led to the death of the enemy, but such was the nature of war. Surely, if anyone was to be afflicted, it should have been him—not an innocent child. *Not again.*

"You must drink," he said, more firmly this time. His wife was away to buy bread and vegetables, and it was Babak's turn to deal with their daughter. He reached around her face and pushed her cheeks towards him. This time she did not protest, and he made her gulp the water infused with some herbs that the Royal Physician said could cure the illness. They had been doing this for two months now, along with regular prayers to the many gods, but not much had changed. After she drank the medicated water, he laid her back on the reed bed and caressed her face. "You will be better soon," he said, "and you will climb trees again like a monkey." She smiled. Evil had taken away her strength but not her ability to smile.

Babak left her side and sat by the side of his humble home, leaning on the worn muddy wall. For the last three weeks, he had been struggling with a powerful conflict in his mind. The Royal Physician had told Babak that the cure to his daughter's ailment could be found with the Oracle of Ammon. The physician said that Amastri's illness was a type known to the temple priests who had the concoctions and incantations to heal the sufferer. The news infused some hope in him, and he was desperate to find a way to convince the King's Court to release him from duty. But that hope had been dashed once the King of Kings, *Shahanshah Khambujia,* Cambyses, declared the invasion of Ethiopia, and Babak was included in the expedition. There was no question of seeking exemption—such requests were treated harshly, especially with those who were in the employ of the King's inner circle. The army was preparing for the march, and Babak, as one of the administrative advisors, would accompany the King deep into the unknown land with hostile tribes.

Babak felt a deep sadness—he wondered if it would be the last time he saw his daughter alive when he left for Ethiopia. At her rate of deterioration, he had little hope that she would survive many more months. He had explored the idea of sending someone to the Ammonians and engaged a man who promised to bring the cure. But he had vanished with the money and never returned. Besides, there was little guarantee that the Egyptian priests would do anything to save a Persian advisor's child even if he chose to make the journey himself.

He heard the door open and he quickly hardened his face, lest she see his glistening eyes.

It was his wife.

She rushed in, and there was a strange excitement in her face. "My husband! My husband!" she called out loudly, and it was rare for her address him that way. The strain of war and her daughter's condition had sapped her life too.

"What is it?" Babak asked.

"Ahuramazda smiles on us! Perhaps he is watching over us, he the all-powerful," she said, as she knelt and placed her hands on his knee. Her deep black eyes blazed with an intensity that Babak had not seen in a long time. Roxana may have aged due to the hard life and as a mother of three, but her almond-shaped eyes and angular face still captivated him.

Babak scoffed with irritation. "Enough with the mystery, woman! Did he make me King of Kings? Is Cambyses dead in a Thebes ditch?"

His wife glared at him. "Say no such thing. You never know who may be listening. It is something else."

"Well, speak."

She whispered urgently and Babak's eyes opened wide. He hugged his wife tightly, almost surprising her. Ahuramazda had given him an opening to save his daughter's life and let him and his wife pursue an ambition they long harbored.

But he had to act now.

And be brave.

Very brave.

CHAPTER 3

THEBES

ABERIS

The royal tent smelled of anger and impatience. The King of Kings sat in the middle, surrounded by his courtiers, advisors, and senior officers. Ambitious men who tread hard ground and struck fear in their enemies' bellies.

General Artapharnes sat by the King.

Next to Artapharnes was Aberis, the nobleman in the King of King's inner circle and his companion in this journey.

Jabari, the Egyptian advisor, was in the tent as well.

Cambyses clenched his jaws and turned to Aberis. The second messenger had returned with the same news. "And yet they refuse to heed my demand. They refuse to grant me what is mine."

"I do not yet understand if it is their greed or hubris, or if there are other forces at work that undermine your authority, Your Majesty," Aberis said.

The King narrowed his eyes in contemplation. *He is a hawk with the heart of a lion,* Aberis thought. Cambyses was an intimidating man. He was taller than most, muscular, with a hooked nose like an eagle's. When restless, his cheeks twitched, and he tapped his knuckles on any hard object nearby.

"Beating the Ethiopians and controlling the god-fearing Egyptians requires that I bear the mantle of Pharaoh—

what say you, Jabari?" Cambyses said, turning his attention to the Egyptian advisor. Jabari was a senior man, and the King had grown to value his words, for Jabari knew much about the practices of the people of this land. The Egyptian was once a priest in one of the prominent temples in Memphis, up north. He had provided valuable advice against his own countrymen during and after the battle of Pelusium. But Jabari and Aberis went back even further—the Egyptian had accompanied Aberis in some of his minor campaigns in the marshlands south of Babylonia.

"Your Majesty knows the ways of his new dominion," Jabari said, bowing his oil-polished skull.

Unctuous and servile traitor, Aberis thought to himself. While they went back years, he did not trust the Egyptian.

"The Ammonians will fare poorly against us, Your Majesty," Aberis said. "Your angry breath will blow the sands away and expose their treacherous hearts to our arrows."

Cambyses nodded approvingly. "But we must address the matter now. Bringing Egypt to heel quickly is necessary to prevent sparks of rebellion anywhere else in the empire. The Priests of Memphis have declared me Pharaoh, but that is not enough."

The senior men of the court knew that Cambyses' ways had drawn the ire of many other nobles back home, and the King always had to project strength and expansion. Aberis and other advisors nodded in agreement. The Persian empire was vast—and any news of weakness would cause many restless souls to raise their hand against the King.

"We cannot wait to deal with them, even as we prepare to launch ourselves against the foolhardy Ethiopians."

Aberis frowned. "Should we not wait to subdue the Ethiopians first, Your Majesty? This land is hostile and our forces—"

"Waiting will only cause our troubles to exacerbate, Your Glorious Majesty, and most respected noble," came a sudden voice.

Aberis shot an irritated glance at the man kneeling before the King. *The insolence of some of these advisors!*

"Did I ask you—" Aberis started, desiring to put this man in his place. The King of King's court was not a place for any man to open his mouth unless asked. *Cambyses has grown softer,* Aberis thought, for otherwise, no one would dare speak out of turn in front of him. The King of Kings had even spared Psamtik, the disgraced and deposed Pharaoh, and had sent him off to Babylon to live in luxury.

Should have cut off his head and paraded it on the streets of Memphis.

"Let him speak," Cambyses said. Campaign discussions were almost the only time that the King of Kings listened much to anyone, even if he rarely heeded their words.

The man—Aberis was vaguely familiar with him—had made valuable suggestions at Pelusium and before. He was an often-seen advisor and administrative officer who floated among senior ranks. But his name eluded him. "Tell His Majesty your name," Aberis said. "Do not forget where you are."

The customs of the court were sometimes ignored in the heat and stench of battle tents, Aberis thought, but such exceptions were reserved only for the inner circle of the King of Kings, and this man was no part of the inner circle.

The man prostrated before the King of Kings. "Babak. Your Majesty. I served you in Pelusium, and I will serve you till my breath becomes one with Ahuramazda."

"Rise. Speak." Cambyses ordered.

Babak rose to his feet. He was a wiry man; his limbs sinewy like knotted rope, his face gaunt and the texture of worn, beaten leather. A thick silver-specked beard hung like a honey-bee hive. But his dark eyes shined with clarity and peered under bushy eyebrows. Aberis guessed that this man was surely of the stock of people from the marshes south of Babylon, and judging by the scar on his temple and the imprints of a blade on his neck, this man had either wielded a weapon at some point in his life or had been at the receiving end of punishment.

Wise with the word but weak with the sword.

"The Egyptian High Priest cares about three things, Your Majesty," Babak said. His voice was soft and firm with a fine timbre, and his sunken cheeks and eyes gave him a grave and wise look. But his words caught the attention of the hard men.

"He cares for the preservation of his power. He cares for the sanctity of his ways to appease his gods. And then he perennially conspires to enrich himself and those that derive power from him."

Jabari cast a hostile look at Babak who ignored him. Babak continued. "But his power is immense. There are many tales of misfortunes for the Pharaohs that confronted the power of their priests. When the priest refuses to acquiesce, then he is certainly conspiring for something greater than what he has or will soon have."

"And what is that?" Cambyses asked, now curious.

Babak paused. He looked around the room, knowing that all eyes were upon him.

"Control of the Pharaoh," Babak said, his every word carrying the weight of a rock. "They may get your patronage, Your Majesty. They may be showered with gold, silver, and grain from your vast coffers. They may even be accorded the same stature and respect as the temple masters of Ahuramazda. But they know they will never control the will of a foreign King, especially a *Shahanshah*."

Cambyses tugged on his beard and looked at Aberis. The Noble felt compelled to offer his words. "That has been made noticeably clear. Let them sit on their cold stones and wait, so why not turn our attention to them and smite them when it is time?" Aberis said, and he turned to Artapharnes who was uncharacteristically quiet.

Babak leaned forward and spread his arms. His dusty and dirty gown spread loosely on his frame. *It is like having a beggar advise the King*, thought Aberis.

We should give him some clothing befitting the court!

Babak continued. "We have never set foot in Ethiopia. We know little of the land. But we know it is far away from the River. And the further we go from the River, the freer the Egyptian feels. When we stalk the canyons and ridges far away, the Priests will get plenty of time to raise a rebellion. They stall us so they can rile up their people to rise against us. The more we wait, and farther we go, the stronger the resistance will build here in Thebes, in Memphis, in Ammon, in Pelusium—"

"Babak," said Artapharnes, finally speaking, his voice firm but warm. "You lecture us as if we are children in the theater of war and politics."

Babak bowed his head. "I meant no disrespect, Great General. It is only my duty."

Aberis had to put this man in place. "And yet your voice—"

The King laid his hand on Aberis' forearm. "He speaks for I have allowed him to."

"Yes, Your Majesty."

He will pay for his insolence, Aberis thought. Babak had made him feel small. But on the other hand, going to Ammon had many benefits.

Cambyses reached for a bronze cup of water and took a long sip. He then wiped his hands on his shimmering gown. Aberis knew that it was the sign of the ruler ready to rule. He knew to show his obeisance and readiness to accept orders. Aberis stood and bowed to the King of Kings. Other courtiers stood as well.

"I have decided," Cambyses said. He turned to Aberis. "You will command a detachment of fifty-thousand men and march to Ammon. Bring me every Ammonian—man, woman, and child, in chains. I shall teach them a lesson they will never forget. Burn their temple and raze their homes—may the city of the Ammonians cease to exist!"

Aberis feigned protest. "I long to be by the side of the King of Kings, Your Majesty. Why do you send me away? Let me fight by your side in Ethiopia!" Everyone knew by then that Cambyses had chosen Aberis—it was known for days. The King saw this expedition as an irritation that must be dealt with.

Cambyses touched his gold-studded scepter to Aberis' head. "I know you wish to be at my side, *Abrahasa,* but I cannot have you in both places. *Artapharna* will accompany me to Ethiopia for that will be a larger campaign. But you, my loyal servant, must put an end to a Kingdom-wide rebellion or any other mischief before I return from Ethiopia. This will also be your first experience in leading a major campaign."

"Your word is my guide, Your Majesty," Aberis said. It was true—he had led small forces to quash rebellions and put down revolts. But none with a large army.

"Bring me favorable news and I shall grant you one of Egypt's nomes to rule. Perhaps Ammon."

Aberis was elated at the news. *A Governor!* He had long desired the chance to be a satrap. Like a shrub that never grows under the shade of a mighty tree, Aberis knew that for him to make greater his name and fortunes, he must have his own province. From there he would forge his destiny. It was as if the gods had smiled on him and brought this opportunity—and he even begrudgingly acknowledged, in his mind, Babak's contribution to this fortuitous change of events.

"Your generosity exceeds all men's deeds, Your Majesty. I will bring them to you in chains and Ammon will only be a footnote in history!" he declared, now excited at his prospects. *The destruction of Ammon is paramount.*

Cambyses turned to Babak. "I remember you now, Babak. Are you not the man that suggested we use cats to subdue the Egyptians in Pelusium without much bloodshed?"

"I am, Your Majesty," Babak said.

"Very well. You will be a worthy companion during our campaign in Ethiopia."

Aberis was quietly pleased that he would not have to bear this man.

But Babak looked unhappy. He dropped to his knees again and raised his hands to the King of Kings. "I beg you to listen to me just once more, Your Majesty!"

Artapharnes laughed.

Aberis was flummoxed. *What now?*

Cambyses looked perplexed. "Speak," he said.

CHAPTER 4

THEBES

BABAK

Babak felt his heart fight his ribs. What he had just done, asking the *Shahanshah* to listen to him again, could lead to his execution. Aberis had already expressed impatience with his behavior—but how far could he test the mercy of those greater than him?

But it had to be done.

"I beg you to allow me to accompany the detachment to Ammon," Babak said.

"Insolent swine! How dare you turn away the King's patronage?" said Eribaeus, the pale Greek nobleman who had accompanied the King of Kings to Egypt and had supplied a great many Greek mercenaries in service of the Persian Empire. Eribaeus was another fixture in the court—in service of the ruler and making a corrupt fortune along the way.

The Greek dog curries favor at every given opportunity.

Jabari, the Egyptian who shot piercing glances all this while, joined. "How dare, and how shameful, for one to turn down the opportunity to go with the King!"

"Let him speak. He has something in his mind," said Cambyses, smiling, once again displaying an unusual kindness. *Perhaps the King of Kings knows of my personal pain*, thought Babak. *The eyes and ears of the King are everywhere.*

Babak composed himself. He removed his turban and held it in his shaking hands. "The land far west from Thebes and north until to the temple of Ammon is unkind to any living being, Your Majesty. They call it the Great Sand Sea. Many a caravan has been reduced to bones, and many a trader has vanished beneath the waves of sand."

Cambyses nodded. "Go on."

"They say deserters and exiled nobles vanish there, only to lay low and to foment trouble, for they are so far and so inaccessible to invasion by large armies."

Jabari scoffed loudly. "Not every story that floats in the air is true, just as not every man with a crown is King."

Babak stood his ground. *I know you do not want me there.*

"Your words are wise, Your Excellency, but I beg you to listen to me," said Babak, addressing Jabari. "If we must send an army of fifty-thousand under the command of a noble favored by the King of Kings, I think it is better to hear the stories than to dismiss them all."

Every man was intrigued by this debate and Aberis recognized this. "I agree with Babak. Let us hear him."

"And what is your interest then?" Cambyses asked.

"To bring you glory and to serve the noble ably where I am best able to. I know the lands beyond Thebes and the oases on the way to Ammon."

Cambyses looked surprised.

Aberis leaned forward. "You have walked those sands?"

"Years ago, Your Excellency. As a merchant I have thrice traveled the paths with water sprouts and oases, from Thebes and Memphis, all the way to the Ammonian lands."

"Why would I not use Egyptian guides?" The King of Kings asked. "Besides, two of our messengers have traversed a road from Thebes to Ammon."

Babak glanced at Jabari, and the Egyptian's furrowed brows conveyed great displeasure, as if already reading Babak's mind.

Babak continued. "The messenger path is completely unsuitable for an army, Your Majesty, and that will be established soon as we plan. Besides, you seek to enslave the Ammonians. The priests hold great sway over the people that dwell in the sands and many other Egyptians. And in their pursuit, there must be Persian guides, lest there be a betrayal or abandonment of any sorts, whether by design or by accident."

Jabari protested loudly. "How dare this man place in question my loyalty? What right does he have!"

The Egyptian flexed his chest like a rude wrestler in the pits. *I am not intimidated by a bald peacock,* Babak thought.

Cambyses turned to Jabari. "You are a faithful servant Jabari. But one must pay heed to the influence of your gods and shamans, and that even without your desire they may compel you in these hostile lands. And therefore, a Persian advisor that knows the lands as well might not be imprudent."

Jabari bowed and sulked.

Cambyses turned to Babak. "You will be another pair of watchful eyes."

"Yes, Your Majesty. Along with His Excellency Jabari of course."

Aberis snorted. "It seems I must suffer you, Babak," he said, but the yellow-toothed smile told Babak that the noble had accepted Babak's company and perhaps even relieved to have a Persian guide in unforgiving lands.

"My only desire is our victory and the service of the King."

Cambyses raised his hand and the tent went silent. "It is decided then. *Abrahasa* will command a contingent of fifty-thousand against the Ammonians. Prepare for your departure. Eribaeus, as previously decided, you will go with *Abrahasa.* Your Greeks will follow you more willingly than this gruff Persian," he said, smiling at Aberis. "Babak, you will act as a guide and advisor along with Jabari. *Abrahasa,* choose your army after consultation with *Artapharna* and prepare to leave."

The named men all prostrated before the King. A warm wind blew into the tent, bringing a thin veil of golden dust and blanketed them all. Aberis stood and shook his body. He said quietly, "The Ammonians welcome us."

CHAPTER 5

THEBES

BABAK

So began the preparation for the attack on Ammon. Aberis was no fool, he had sent discreet inquiries regarding Babak's trustworthiness and honesty of his experience. While it was true that Babak had traversed the vast plains of nothingness to the temple of the Ammonians, he had only done so once and not thrice as he bragged. But with no way to prove otherwise, and yet finding scattering affirmations of Babak's experiences in Egypt, Aberis accepted that Babak could have a say in the expedition ahead. *What of fantastical tales of hands emerging from the sand and drawing soldiers underneath, and desert hawks as big as bulls descending from skies to snatch men and asses alike,* Aberis had asked. *Nonsense,* Babak had said, assuring the noble that there were no more fantastical beasts and dangers lurking here than there were anywhere else. Jabari had agreed, rather reluctantly, but was petulant like a child for Aberis had sought Babak's counsel rather than his own.

The King of Kings was true to his word. A contingent of fifty-thousand men, including a vast baggage train, but no concubines or family, was assembled. While this was no ragtag army of the unwanted, it was forged hastily, and the logisticians had made quick and hopeful calculations for water and food. General Artapharnes and the King himself were unwilling to part with experienced commanders. *This should be a quick and relatively uncontested expedition,* they had said. There were many arguments as to how much to carry. If they carried too much water, the exertion might cause the animals and the men to consume more, thereby destroying the very argument to carry more. Even food was controversial—the Egyptians, mostly in the baggage train, complained about beef. But the Persians, much larger in number, complained about pig. The commanders had to be scolded that this was not a leisurely jaunt to a friend's marriage and that they had to make do with what they had. Besides, not much meat accompanied the detachment— most of the food was hard bread clumps, salted fish, some quail and preserved lentils. There was a very limited quantity of beer and wine reserved for the senior men. *Heady drinks are dangerous in the desert,* the commanders were told to tell their troops. The Greeks and Scythians made much ruckus about it, joined by the Syrians, until they were threatened with

latrine duties.

Eribaeus had second thoughts about accompanying the detachment, until Babak convinced Aberis that the Greek contingent would not behave without their noble, and that the Greeks were important to the journey. Eribaeus cursed Babak who feigned innocence. *I was only pointing out to the noble that the Greeks bring strength and wisdom to the journey,* he said, causing Eribaeus to curse him some more.

Since almost the entire force was infantry, they were ordered to travel light, conducive for the march in dry and arid climes. *Leave your heavy shields, heavy armor, thick leather corsets, and any metal helmets behind. Travel light to the extent possible,* they were ordered. But Babak knew many paid no heed to these rules.

Babak paid little attention to these arguments but only opined that the forces carry as much as needed for the next supply station. The army comprised of every element of the

Persian force except the cavalry. *The horses will fare poorly,* Babak and Jabari counseled Aberis, and he acquiesced. The beasts were expensive to maintain and there was no clarity on how they would fare in the desert with little water. There were archers, axemen, swordsmen, and spearmen. There were no battering rams or siege weaponry as it was considered impractical to drag heavy machinery in the sandy desert on a less-traveled path.

In the end, with counsel from Jabari, Babak, and Eribaeus, Aberis assembled seven thousand Syrians, five-thousand Medians, five-thousand Scythians, three-thousand Indians, ten-thousand Greeks, fifteen-thousand Persians, and five-thousand men in the baggage train. Aberis had grumbled that he would have preferred more Persian troops, but Artapharnes was unwilling to part with more. Most of the men in this detachment were known to Aberis who had used parts of them in the past conquests. Babak played a major role in identifying potential groups that could go with Aberis.

Now, they were all cobbled together to this force. *Like putting hyenas, monkeys, peacocks, pigs, and cats together for an excursion under the leadership of a jackal,* thought Babak. Babak also knew that Aberis had done something that showed the mind of the man. He had provisioned greater comfort, water, and bread rations for the Persians and the Greeks.

What Babak recognized, which neither Aberis or Eribaeus had not appreciated yet, was how different the western deserts of Egypt and the Great Sand Sea were to anything they had ever experienced. No one in the empire had sent an army of even five thousand, let alone fifty thousand, through an inhospitable desert with barely a supply station for days. They had no idea what lay before them or what travails they may face. To them, this was a short campaign that would bring glory and pillage—and an unwavering belief that numerical superiority would bring them victory.

A thought and fear for the land between them and their enemy mattered not one bit.

A thought for the powerful gods and their anger at this sacrilegious mission mattered not one bit.

Then there was the matter of guides. There were heated arguments on who to employ and how many. Babak held firm to his view; *few guides who know the area—if you have too many then it leads to confusion.* Ritapates, an advisor to Aberis, concurred. Eribaeus wanted more Egyptian guides but Aberis distrusted Egyptians. They were going to burn Ammon and enslave its people—how could they possibly trust the locals to take them there? Who would they even believe? And so they went on, until it was finalized that three Bedouins, Babak's knowledge, a few maps provided by the Memphis temple guardians, along with a some of Jabari's wisdom, would suffice. Not many were happy with the decision, but Babak and others also argued that they could find more guides, if needed, during the water stops in Aostris, Horosis, or Farrasis. In any case, they had little time to go scouting the city for more guides. Aberis had to rush with preparation. The King of Kings had ordered them to leave immediately.

Babak held his daughter close to his chest and smelled her lily and cinnamon scented hair. He turned to his wife. "We leave in six days."

"It is a most unholy mission, my husband," Roxana said fearfully. But they knew what they were aiming to do. "You must stop it. You must stop the men from destroying what the Egyptians hold dear. From defiling the women and children. You must."

"It is. I will. Which is why I must be there. And the gods have given us the perfect opportunity."

Roxana's eyes filled with concern and devotion. It was not just Babak that had suffered; they had lost two of their sons long ago, in greatly unjust ways, and yet they had persevered. "Do you think your idea to convince the Ammonians to help us will work?"

"Ahuramazda will guide me," Babak said. "Have you not known me to find ways? The world is full of possibilities."

Her eyes sparkled. "A mind as bright as the sun hides beneath that thinning hair and mottled skull."

"And an Elephant's strength behind those lovely braids," Babak said. His wife had weathered the hardships and the losses and yet her resolve remained unbroken.

A fire burned in them that no man outside knew.

Babak cuddled his soporific daughter, caressing her hair. "I will be back in less than a month, my little cherub," he said. Surely no gods would be cruel to take their only remaining child after all the years of devotion to them and the land. But Babak knew that the mission was likely an idiot's fancy. And that great odds lay between him and his quest—they had to conquer the terrain, they had to subdue the stubborn Ammonians, he had to find those that had the cure, he had to convince them to give it to him, and then he had to make his way back, his daughter would still have to be alive, and then the cure had to work. Lesser men would despair at the thought, for the task was akin to a village fool attempting to build a mountain by hand or drain a river by his mouth. Besides, bringing the cure to his daughter was only one of the missions that his wife and he had resolved to complete. Babak had no doubts that every man in that detachment had his personal mission.

"Keep her breathing until I return," he implored his wife. Roxana nodded and gingerly took possession of the child. Babak then discussed how they should live and survive. Then they spoke of the dangers, of the fact that Jabari would be there, plotting, conspiring.

"Do not think that there are no scorpions around you," Babak warned her. "Be wary of your surroundings. I am not well-liked, and there will be much interest in our lives. There will be those who seek to harm me through you, so be on your guard."

They prayed together one last time as he prepared to leave.

Babak bade them a tearful farewell. His daughter's eyes remained downcast and her limbs remained limp as he kissed her goodbye. Babak held his wife and sternly told her to conduct her duties and care for their child until his return. He then walked out to a blast of heat and an unknown future.

CHAPTER 6

THEBES

JABARI

Jabari stood beside his wife who held a small polished bronze lamp and moved it in a circular motion around the golden statuette of Amun. The little prayer room was filled with smoke, aroma of melting wax, and heady fragrance of lotus and jasmine. It was an important occasion, one that could bring great fortune and power. They had sought the blessings of their gods, sacrificed two goats, and donated three bags of grain to the temple of Amun, visible from their courtyard and awe-inspiring every time they looked at it. In return, they nervously sought success in the mission. It was an anxiety-inducing situation—after all, Jabari, who was once a priest, was now on an invasion whose entire purpose was to burn a sacred temple of none other than the all-powerful Amun. Did they really want this to be successful?

Once they completed their prayers, they retired to their comfortable living room. They lived in a relatively luxurious house, much nicer than the huts and basic homes of peasants and soldiers. It had a big living room, three bedrooms, a courtyard, a small room for prayers, a bathroom, a granary room, and a guard room. The sunburnt brick villa was coated white with limestone, giving it a brilliant look. The plaster was cracking in places, a source of argument between him and his wife. Nevertheless, Jabari had done well, and he felt he was now finally on the cusp of greatness. Rising from a lowly temple orderly, he had risen to be a priest, an advisor to a Pharaoh, a trader, and then even ingratiated himself to a Persian nobleman. All that led to his close involvement in Cambyses' Egyptian incursion where Jabari had abandoned Pharaoh Psamtik, with whose people he had a falling out. The victory in Pelusium and Jabari's advice to Cambyses' men was what helped strengthen the King of King's hand as he moved south towards Thebes from Memphis.

But that he was now bowing to a Persian King, and a Persian noble nagged him, like a fly in one's ear, or a worm in a wound. What came from becoming a high priest again? Was that the extent of what he could get?

Jabari wanted more.

A lot more.

He looked at his dutiful wife as she held his hand. She was a clever woman, one that knew Jabari's ambitions, for she harbored much of the same herself. But Sekhet was not just clever and ambitious, she was as if Amun had personally bestowed beauty upon her at birth. Sekhet had a beautiful oval face, almond eyes, full red lips, like pomegranates, that she made sure to color every day, a gentle broad nose, and the most supple skin that felt like butter had been spread on it. Her hair fell gently on her shoulders, and she often tied it with a luxurious ribbon. She was every bit a royal even if not born as one. When she walked into a room, it was as if a full moon had lit the space, for such was her power on those around her. But he also knew she would discard him like aged papyrus if he abandoned their ambition. But so far, she had brought light to his life, stayed by his side, and kept his blood flowing.

"Do you think you will succeed in your mission, husband?" she asked, her voice fearful now that the hour of departure was near. "Will our gods forgive us for what Cambyses is about to do?"

"All the signs from our gods are clear. No competent general heads this army. Aberis is no commander—the arrogant idiot is bound to make mistakes. God willing, we will never have to raze the temple."

Sekhet looked unsure. Jabari knew she worried what this sacrilege might bring upon them. "But you are in that march through lands that you have never seen. They say great dangers lurk far from the river."

"Have I not served Amun all this time? Have we not made necessary sacrifices? The god's eyes will guide me."

Sekhet nodded. They had discussed their strategy at length, and now was not the time to question or be indecisive. He pulled her closer. The rose-scented perfume on her bare arms and sensual torso was distracting. "We must act now, or your husband will forever kneel in front of a Persian. Is that what you want?"

She shook her head vigorously. "Do you think the senior men trust you?"

"You know that Aberis and Eribaeus have known us for years. Ritapates—I do not know him too well. He seems a dullard. A village idiot who has somehow made his way to the court, but Aberis trusts him."

Jabari contemplated for a while. There was something he had so far not shared with his wife. "But the one I worry about is Babak."

Sekhet's eyes widened. "Is that the Persian advisor you do not like?"

Sekhet was aware of the tension between Jabari and Babak—they had often clashed on matters of advice, and it endlessly irritated Jabari that Babak's words received weight, even in the matters of Egypt, *his land!*

"Yes. He is the one that I do not know well. He has inserted himself into the campaign for some reason. I know his wife is here," he said.

"Yes, I have seen her. Roxana. She has a strange look for a Persian, that woman."

"Maybe you should strike a friendship. Find out more about them. If you find anything alarming, then—" Jabari made a sign of slashing one's throat. "But be careful about what you do. Be guarded until the mission is complete and I return."

Sekhet passed a beer cup to Jabari who drank from it. He then inventoried the belongings he would take with him. It was not wise to leave it all behind with his wife when he was away. As much as they were of high status, crime had increased in Thebes and one had to be careful. He would take most of the valuable ornaments and jewelry, and she would hold on to some just in case of emergency barter. Jabari was expected to return in no more than a month or at most two.

When it was all done, he stood by the door and embraced her. She wished him safety. He brushed her curled hair and caressed her cheeks. She was gorgeous, and she deserved more than what they had. He whispered into her ear, "One day you will be queen."

CHAPTER 7

THEBES

ABERIS

Aberis admired himself in the reflection of his fine courtyard pool. The noble had finagled a spectacular villa by the river, a home that once belonged to an Egyptian high born who had been led to his death after the defeat of Psamtik in Pelusium. But the place felt empty—for it was just him, a few whores and mistresses visiting once in a while, and many servants.

Finally, a commander of an entire army! It was a pity his family could not be here with him to revel in his glory. His wives and children were far away in Susa, and he had not seen them in over a year. Not that he missed them much—except maybe his youngest wife. She was a fire in bed and outside. The children were annoying, and he hoped they would all stop sucking his wealth and bleeding him dry. Egypt was a chance to replenish those personal coffers. He had spent years in the service of King of Kings Cyrus and now his son, Cambyses. He had hinted to the Kings that perhaps he deserved a fine province of his own, one where he could retire and profit from the produce of the land. But until now, no such benevolence was forthcoming. Either the Kings were blind to his service, or perhaps they waited for the right opportunity.

And now, *finally!*

The order was to raze Ammon and enslave its citizens. He did worry about the mission–what if the Oracle was truly powerful? How would this act of impunity against a house of god be seen by the gods and people of Egypt? Was the *Shahanshah* making a mistake? Aberis cast aside those seeds of doubt. He would have to find out a way to not lose the entire population, for what would he have to govern otherwise? A desert? Mute rocks and sand? It all depended on how the town fought. If they gave up quietly and complied, he might choose to let them live and convince the King to spare them. He could make a handsome bounty by selling them as slaves to various needs of the empire. The women could resupply the homes and brothels, the children could do delicate work at the mines, though of course they died quickly, which was a pity. In any case, towns could be built, and people would come back. A few thousand dead or enslaved meant little in the greater purpose of the empire.

He would lord over all Northern Egypt. With luck, he would control the ports by the sea, the trading routes from the Levant and Babylonia, and even the western edges of the fertile delta. All he had to do was finish this pesky mission. He was aware that he was no general, and he hoped that even this hastily assembled detachment and the rag-tag team of advisors would be more than enough. Many had warned him about the hostile nature of the desert— but he had seen deserts before and was not too worried. After all, there were supply points, and who would dare attack an army of fifty thousand? Where would they appear from? The Scythian archers were talented, even if they were to act without their horses. The Syrians were good with the Ax. He still had fifteen thousand of the Persians, better equipped and rationed, and no doubt they would handle anything that came their way. The Greeks could be annoying, but they were vicious and talented.

Their leader, Eribaeus, had some influence with the King, but nothing Aberis could not handle.

In his journey he would take with him some of his most prized possessions—a full cart with incredible treasures gathered since his departure for Susa. He could not risk leaving it here. But he would have to guard it during the expedition—no one would need to know of it.

He straightened his back and let his assistant fuss over him.

A nobleman today.

An influential governor and lord of an entire portion of Egypt in twenty days.

Aberis smiled to himself.

It would be a glorious campaign.

Once they dealt with the temple, they would compensate the priests in Memphis and elsewhere to pacify the gods.

CHAPTER 8

THEBES

ERIBAEUS

Eribaeus grunted and heaved half-heartedly on the girl who lay below his sweaty and flapping belly. She seemed disinterested in the act, laying almost lifelessly as her soft brown eyes remained fixed on a carving of a bull on the orange-dye wall of the room. After a few more thrusts and a failing erection, he finally rolled off, annoyed with her and himself for being distracted. He poked her on the waist and gave a guttural order for her to leave. She got up, wrapped herself in a gown and left quietly, without a word. Eribaeus watched as she walked out–she was pretty. He was suddenly filled with rage. He had endured much from these haughty women growing up. Eribaeus was a short man, stout with an ample belly, a broad and powerful chest, a pudgy face that looked like poorly kneaded dough, and a thick nose that looked like a squashed orange. His only redeeming feature, his brothers often told him, was his thick mop of golden hair that one might get lost in. He had long accepted that few women were inspired to disrobe for him willingly–some said it was for his nature and not his features, but he did not believe that to be true. That did not matter anymore, he smiled, for his riches, influence, and power had afforded him the ability to use and discard them at will. He was almost tempted to get up and chase the girl to beat her, but he was distracted.

His mind switched to the next day. It was almost time to leave Thebes on the journey to that wretched, miserable little town somewhere in the desert. Eribaeus cursed Aberis and Cambyses for the situation. He could have just stayed here, guarding this city, enriching himself and fucking when he wanted. But no, his majesty *not-in-his-right-mind* Cambyses had to order him to leave for Ammon.

Why? Why even attack a holy site? Why, after already being blessed by a goddess and accepted by the Priests in Memphis and Sais? How did it matter what some Oracle in a dusty old town said? Did it not occur to his out-of-his-mind highness that angering the gods would do little to help him? And this was not just any little god—it was the God of Gods Ammon. Not just that, it was also holy to the Greeks as the temple of Ammon-Zeus. Did he really want to anger Zeus? *Idiots.* The whole lot of these Persians were just idiots! And then there was Aberis. Yes, he and Aberis had a few good campaigns, but it did not give that idiot noble the right to drag him like a street dog through the desert. His mercenaries were among the best, and their loyalty was firm only as long as he guaranteed the loot, plunder, women, and slaves. They weren't going to get much in Ammon, not with Cambyses' stupid order that every denizen be brought back in chains. In the end, all he and his Greeks would be left with was holding their cocks and waving it in the hot wind. *Idiots!* He had to make sure to negotiate a good many of the captives for himself and his men to be sold for a fat profit.

And what about that Persian advisor, reedy thin goat-fucker with the ugly beard, Babak? He had definitely played a part in trapping Eribaeus into this mission. Oh, how nice it would be to break his neck. He wished he was in Babak's village at some point in the past where he could have wiped him out. Him and his entire miserable family. Eribaeus got strangely excited when he remembered dealing with rebelling populations—the frantic people, all that crying and begging, the glorious slaughter, blood on the streets, the screaming and struggling women and girls.... All his riches had come from someone's tears, but such was the world built by the gods. He was glad he was amongst the strong.

He revisited the positives of the mission. He had played this over and over again in his mind... it was the only way to raise his spirits.

First, it would be a short campaign. A short few weeks of trek through the desert and they would be at the destination. And then a few days to raze and burn the town, round up the townspeople, arrest the priests, and arrange for return. But a successful mission significantly increased his stature with Cambyses and Aberis. Who knew where the King of Kings would turn to, next?

Greece?

The situation back home was not perfect. The Greek King had aligned himself with Cambyses, supporting the Persian's incursion to Egypt. But these equations changed by the day and how the winds blew. An improved standing meant Eribaeus could have Cambyses ask the Greek King to elevate him to a high position. If Cambyses attacked Greece instead, then Eribaeus might be able to finagle a position as the satrap on behalf of the Persian empire. One thing was sure, glory would be muted if he went to Ethiopia with Cambyses—there were too many important people on that expedition. But to Ammon? It was Aberis and himself. And that oily Egyptian Jabari—no doubt that pig fucker had some agenda too. He knew Jabari. He would have loved to know his incredible wife a lot more, but that had not happened. Jabari had known Eribaeus for a while now, but it was never clear what that man wanted. Could he even be trusted? He was, after all, on a mission to destroy something sacred to him. Babak had made sense that they not rely on Egyptians alone on this mission. Maybe that reedy goat-fucker wasn't the idiot. The rest certainly were.

He just wanted to be done with it all and rest. A month or two and glory would be his.

Eribaeus closed his eyes and stared at the limestone white ceiling. The warm stifling air had caused his sweaty buttocks to itch on the fine fabric. He put his hand on his flaccid penis and cursed the Persians and the Egyptians some more.

CHAPTER 9

WEST OF THEBES

BABAK

Babak looked behind him from the head of the march. The vast column seemed to stretch forever. The fifty thousand walked to a four per row and extended more than three miles in length. Interspersed were baggage camels and asses, burdened with food, water, and protective tents. The scene always brought a certain thrill to Babak—there was something about thousands of armed men walking in discipline and kicking up dust on their way to the next mission. Not to mention that thick, unyielding smell of unwashed bodies. Besides the Egyptians and some Persians, the rest had little interest in cleansing their skin. So, to anyone that neared the area, it was the smell that struck most—sweat, piss, shit, animal odor, perfumes. To the Egyptian it may have seemed a strange scene—an army walking away from the life-sustaining river. Few Egyptians had yet committed themselves to the service of the Persian army, and even fewer were asked to be part of this detachment on a sacrilegious mission.

Babak mused on the various elements of the army.

The Persians, mainly those from regions around Susa and Pasargadae and close to the Achaemenid family, were the best equipped. These men were favored by the ruler and they walked proudly in a disciplined manner. Their crisp gray and white gowns, fine deep-red, rich leather belts, well-tied turbans and caps were a contrast to the rowdy

Scythians, who wore all manner of colorful garments like they were out to quarrel and flirt in a market. The Scythians had tattoos on them, covering their arms and legs with fantastical drawings of deer, cows, birds, lions, strange six-legged hyenas, two-trunk elephants, naked women, and other assortments. These men were master archers, much like the Parthians—who stayed with Cambyses. The Greeks—they were a strange bunch. These mercenaries strutted like proud peacocks with their plumed helmets, striped skirts, and towels hanging from their backs. They wore little on their upper body, as if to show the world their powerful chests, no matter how fat or thin the man was, and whether their breasts were hollow or pointed to the ground like an old woman's. It was said that their Sparta hoplite fought naked with only light breastplates, though here they chose a more modest path, for who would want to see thousands of dangling penises in the desert wind. They also mingled little with others, preferring their own company. They irritated everyone with their condescending manner and belief in their superior tactics. Aberis had Eribaeus accompany him for he knew that the Greek noble would be the only one who could control these men whose only aim was plunder and rape.

The Indians—they were few but known for their longbows. They were skilled in directing elephants, but there were no elephants on this expedition. These men, who wore simple waistcloths and turbans, kept to themselves. It was said that some ate no meat. But there were also rumors that some ate human flesh. There were many strange tales about the land they came from, but Babak paid little interest in these fantastical stories. Monkeys larger than men, ants as big as horses, women with three breasts. Where these stories came from, Babak did not know.

Aberis sat on an ass, an unusual position for the noble who had no cavalry on which to parade himself. Senior men followed close behind—Eribaeus, Jabari, Ritapates, and a few military officials. But on this expedition, it was finally decided that the advisors—Jabari, Babak, and Ritapates— would be the ones guiding the military and making expedition decisions with final approval of the noble. Since there was no general, each ethnic unit had a captain. This detachment did not follow the customary structure of the main army. Every soldier was aware that their commander was no career military-man. But then every soldier hoped that this campaign was a simple march and siege. A raid party. The captains of the units, all foreign to this land, had no experience in the Egyptian deserts. Their experience in Egypt was a comfortable march down the fertile river valley and staying close to the source of water.

Ritapates was unknown to Babak. He was supposedly a confidant of Aberis. Three Bedouin elders had joined the army on recommendation from local guides and after an interview by Babak and Jabari. Knowledgeable, trustworthy, and with no allegiance to a Pharaoh nor any other King. The desert was their life, and their gods lay in the sand temples. A promise of camels, grain, and a few coins of gold secured their loyalty—such were the simple ways of these men.

Curious villagers looked on. Some even dared to throw clumps of sand and run away with no fear of pursuit. The instructions to the army were clear—do not engage the locals unless a life is threatened. The King of Kings had issued orders to prevent any measure by this dispatch that might enrage the people while he was away to Ethiopia.

"Not too bad, so far," Danofis said. He was the commander of the Greek mercenaries. Babak had encountered Danofis before, years ago. He knew him to be a capable fighter and, unusual among Eribaeus' Greeks, kindhearted too. Danofis looked every bit a warrior–fit, purposeful, measured. Babak squinted in the evening sun, for the glowing orange orb was directly in their eyes as it set in the far unknown.

"It is still the first day," Babak said. He knew of the hardships ahead of them—like any excursion to the unknown, the first day lulls one to complacence before fate bares its claws and rips the flesh. "You Greeks have not experienced much of the desert."

Danofis shrugged. "We are hardy souls, Babak. We have seen mountains of Macedon, forests in Cappadocia, turbulent seas of the Aegean, ridges of Syria, and marshes of Babylonia. The desert is just another obstacle for us to leap."

Not just another obstacle. Babak mused. Danofis' mercenaries were experienced in pillaging villages, killing the men and raping the women. They had not been on an expedition like this. And now he rode next to Babak as if it was all a stroll in a market. There was some tussle behind them—a few hot-blooded young village men had tangled with some soldiers. Babak could not see how it ended— whether with decapitated heads in the dunes or just bruised egos.

Babak caught up with Danofis again. "Family?"

"Far away. A little town two days north of Athens. Wife, two sons and a daughter. Lost two sons years ago."

Babak nodded. "War?" though Danofis did not look old enough to have his sons in battle, but one never knew.

"No. Disease. A sickness came to the older and spread to the younger. Our prayers to Zeus and offerings at Delphi bore no fruit. But the other two will grow to be fine warriors!" he said, his face reflecting the pride in his sons. Babak felt a sharp twinge of sorrow.

"Yours?" Danofis asked.

"Wife is in Thebes. Daughter. I lost my sons years ago in war."

Danofis shook his head in sympathy. "Is she a good cook?"

"Who? My wife or daughter?"

"Either! My wife is quite terrible, but the girl is better. Persians make the most delectable food!" he said, already dreaming of good food.

Babak laughed. "My wife is excellent. My daughter is recovering from an illness and I hope she will be a fine cook that can please her husband."

"That is important," Danofis concurred. "We fathers must ensure they go to a good house worthy of a good alliance."

Babak agreed. But did Danofis know the tumult in his mind, Babak mused. Danofis seemed to be struggling to ask something else. "Does something bother you, Danofis?"

Danofis shook his head but furrowed his brows. He finally sighed. "Do you think your *Shahanshah* is doing right by going after a holy site of Ammon-Zeus?"

Babak considered his answer. He took a while. "Who are we to question the orders of emperors and pharaohs, Danofis. They do what the divine winds tell them, we follow. Whether his orders are blessed, we will find out."

"Indeed," Danofis said, his voice betraying the lack of confidence in that assertion.

Babak once again looked at Danofis. He was a good man. If such a time came, Babak would seek the gods' blessings to protect him. This army was on an unholy mission.

And then they fell silent.

The march was quiet as the feet tread the gravelly ground. Everywhere they looked they saw a vast expanse of orange and yellow earth—with sandy bluffs on one side and rough, rocky desert on the other. The landscape would change in a few days, but for now there was beauty in the starkness. The tens of thousands of feet kicked up fine dust, irritating the eyes and lungs. Captains had to be told to tell the men not to kick the ground as they walked. *Walk like a dainty dancer*, they were told, *as if you float on the ground*. Of course, the rascally Scythians made good use of this instruction to kick as much dust and dirt in the air to heap misery on those behind them.

The day, and the next, ended with no event worthy of gossip except a few tussles and usual arguments when many feisty men are together. Babak had walked silently and only briefly conferred with Aberis and the others on the path. The Bedouins told them that the next stop, Oasis of Aostris, was three more days away at this pace. The soldiers were in a merry mood—making lewd jokes on what they would do to the Ammonians and their gods and behaving like merry bandits with no worries. It was clear to Babak that many paid no heed to the rationing orders—especially the water. It was like boatmen cutting their boat for wood while in an open sea. The army usually began its march as the first hint of light on the horizon and then stopped as the sun rose high. For a few hours they rested until they began their march after lunch, walking all the way late into the evening and until the path was pitch black and the skies were ablaze with a million shining diamonds.

They usually conferred in the night and that night was no different. It is the nature of the desert that while the skin burns in the day under the angry sun, the air descends to a chill at night. They halted to set up campfires by the sand ridge.

Aberis was comfortably attired with a loose linen gown, allowing for enough circulation of air. The men sat around on a higher rocky outcrop with a view of the miles of the troops behind. The silence of the desert was cut harshly by the din of thousands and the braying of the beasts, and the thick darkness sliced by thousands of little light pricks from oil lamps.

"No signs of any activity?" Aberis asked, turning to one of his intelligence officers whose name Babak did not know.

"Nothing, Your Excellency. We are already far away from the nearest villages."

"It is not the villagers I worry about."

"Yes, Your Excellency. No, no signs of any other miscreants."

"Keep the perimeter guards on duty at all times. Send out your scouts once every few hours to survey the surroundings."

"Yes, Your Excellency." The man bowed and left.

"Why is it that we walk further west from Thebes instead of staying closer to the river and heading north?" asked Aberis. The path was kept a close secret from all but the very few—this was intentional to avoid leaks and ambushes. Aberis often forgot the details and had to be reminded more than once.

Ritapates started to speak but Babak cut him off. "The path we take is an ancient aquifer route. Along this route are multiple oases where we can replenish before we enter the Great Sand Sea for the final leg. The other route, while it certainly appears more logical, is bereft of large enough supply points and has a much harsher terrain, making it exceedingly difficult to take an army."

Aberis nodded. "This route was your suggestion, Babak. Pray that it leads us to our destination."

Ritapates, who was glaring at Babak for taking his minute of glory away, interrupted Babak. "Well, not entirely true. There are smaller supply points along—"

"Then why did you not argue for that route?" The noble asked Ritapates, shutting him up. *I have won this round*, Babak thought, for they were always in a contest to please their master.

The fire reflected off their faces. *Each man hides a desire he does not share with the other*, Babak thought. Aberis sought glory and power. Eribaeus sought riches and a comfortable retirement back home. Babak did not know yet what Ritapates or Danofis wanted, but surely no man in his right mind would willingly be on this expedition. He suspected what Jabari wanted. The Egyptian snake was the most dangerous one here.

Babak knew what he wanted.

And it was certainly not what any other man by the fire wanted.

CHAPTER 10

WEST OF THEBES

ABERIS

Aberis leaned forward and warmed his hands on the fire. His back felt cold against the desert wind, but his face and arms felt comforted by the gentle heat. He pondered his past and his future. A past full of conflict and hardship in service of the empire; much blood and tears had been shed, not much mercy shown, and he had amassed much wealth that he had little time to enjoy. He looked forward to beating the Ammonians and securing his place as a governor—certainly a far plusher job than going around with the King and leading men to battle.

The wood seeds exploded in the heat and the fire crackled. The sounds of the army began to quieten as soldiers went to sleep. Aberis looked at the men before him—he wondered what they hoped to get from this expedition. Some had willingly put themselves here—like Babak, and Jabari. Even Ritapates was keen to be by Aberis' side. When men placed themselves in harm's way, as this expedition across the unknown certainly was, Aberis knew that something lurked in those men's minds. It was a matter of time when their nature sprang from their bodies and displayed itself.

There was Babak, who spoke of duty. But Aberis had heard of some difficulties with his daughter. Then there was Jabari, a willing servant since Pelusium—but the Egyptian had lost many a loved one to Persian swords—

including his brother who was led away to his death after the capture of the fort. Besides, a native who turns his own back to his people was never to be fully trusted. And then Eribaeus and Danofis; the Greeks had no allegiance or loyalty. They saw no master in the Persian or the Egyptian. Their heart sang for the brighter gold and the sturdier slave, and where it came from mattered none. And Ritapates—*Ritapata*—he was an enigma. He had stuck with Aberis for years, but Aberis knew that he had ambitions of his own. Not once, but twice, Aberis had heard of Ritapates plotting to ingratiate himself to the King and finagle a satrapy. But Aberis had spared the man, for his secretarial duties could be useful, and sometimes it was better to keep such men closer to the ear than at the tip of a sword.

There were snakes in the pit, he was sure. *But which one was the viper?*

"How much farther to Aostris?" he asked to no one in particular.

"Just a day," said both Ritapates and Jabari. Aberis smiled—his men were eager for his approval, and that was always a good thing. The Egyptian was a loyal servant who had proved his worth in Pelusium, but Babak's advice had merits in that it was better to not just rely on the Egyptians leading the way. This, of course, had the effect of angering Jabari but such was the complexity of the time.

Aberis received another report of peace from the scouts and dismissed the men around him. And then he sat quietly observing the silence around him. His solitude helped him think. On one side was the sand ridge and the other side was a plain, though not much was visible currently. As he dreamed of victory, his eyes began to droop with the fingers of sleep pulling down his eyelids. He thought he saw two men, shadows in the wind, scurry across the gentle dunes, away from the column, and vanish. He wondered what that was but banished the thought of demanding an explanation—who except perhaps a pair of men buggering each other would seek to find a hiding place in this empty wilderness? And then darkness came over him.

CHAPTER 11

HOROSIS

The two stood bowed in front of two other figures—one dressed in a

Pharaoh's garb and another a priest. The sandstone walls of the chapel

of Medu-Nefer reflected the flickering candles.

"Speak," the man in the Pharaoh's garb ordered the two. One was an older

man, but the other was still a boy.

"They were last camped a day from Aostris, Your Majesty," said the older

man. He still wore his turban, which somewhat irked the man in the

Pharaoh's dress.

"Is it true that they are fifty-thousand strong?"

"It is, Your Majesty. The detachment is an army on its own with the full

complement of fighting units."

The Pharaoh conferred quietly with the priest. Then he addressed the men

again. "What is their pace? When will they cross Aostris?"

"They make satisfactory progress, Your Majesty. Their expedition has

only just begun. They should have crossed Aostris by now after having

supplied themselves with water and fruit."

"You two were slow, then," the priest observed.

"No, Your Holiness. It took us a day for your men to grant access to

your presence."

The Pharaoh nodded. "We must take precautions. What is it that Cambyses

seeks?"

The man hesitated but gathered his courage to speak. "He wishes to

enslave all the Ammonians and burn the Oracle's temple."

The priest took a sharp breath. "And that is his response to our not

declaring him Pharaoh?"

"Yes, Your Holiness."

The Pharaoh and the Priest looked at each other. The Pharaoh whispered

to the Priest. "Not even a negotiation."

The Priest nodded. He then turned his piercing gaze to the men. "This

King is mad. What does your master seek?"

And then they conferred quietly under the watchful eyes of ancient gods.

The Pharaoh was secretly pleased—what these men were telling him matched

with what someone else had also told him just a few hours earlier.

So many spies, he thought with a smile.

CHAPTER 12

ΛOSTRIS

ABERIS

The column departed the oasis of Aostris two hours after the mid-day meals. Aberis was back on the saddle followed by his usual retinue. He had sent Danofis, the Greek mercenary commander, to the middle of the column to guard the most valuable section of the baggage train, which itself was broken to three different areas within the column. *There is always a risk of sudden attacks, especially on baggage trains,* Aberis thought. The people that surrounded the oasis may not care for the empire or titles, but they certainly would for food and goods. But there was no attack as they trudged further west. The desert was endless. The orange-yellow landscape stretched as far as the eye could see, with not a hint of green. While the path had no dunes, it was still a difficult walk, and the towering rock and sand buttes offered no respite.

The pace of the column had slowed—the jest and camaraderie of the initial days had slowly evaporated in the heat. Aberis could see trudging feet and downcast looks—and he knew that they were not even an eighth of the way. Aberis decided to halt the march after dinner. Messengers went along the column to convey the order, and the great train of men, materials, and animals, ground to a halt. Aberis received reports from the unit commanders.

"What is the mood of the men?" he asked them.

"Upbeat, even if a little tired from trudging in this desert. Egypt wears them down a little more than Syria," said one of the commanders, and others concurred. The scouts had returned too with no news to tell.

A day with no news is a wonderful day, thought Aberis as he looked at the dying light outside. He soon drifted off to sleep, dreaming of sitting on a throne with bowed nobles and priests around him.

It was a strange and violent dream. A bull had appeared out of nowhere and was goring him. But his hands were tied, and he was—

"Wake up, Your Excellency! Wake up! We're under attack!" one of his attendants shouted, shaking Aberis to reality. He sprang to his feet and swiftly donned his battle-gear—a leather cuirass, belt, scabbard and sword, and a light helmet. His men and bodyguards had already surrounded the tent. Aberis quickly noted that there was no action near the head of the column, but he could hear the noises much farther down—so it was clear that the attack was on a specific section. Aberis rushed outside and was soon met by Babak and Eribaeus. One of the commanders gave a quick report.

"There are two sections under attack, sir. One near the baggage train, and the other near the Syrian unit near the rear."

"Who is it? Do we know?" asked Aberis.

"We do not know yet sir. I rushed to give you an update."

"Ask the units to hold where they are and not rush down, let only those closest to the unit react," he ordered. He then mounted a camel, a very uncomfortable experience, followed by his contingent. Aberis rushed down the column and squinted in the low light. The light orange sky was darkening, and a cloud of dust was prominent further near a baggage train. The animals were throwing a ruckus, and the sounds told Aberis that the wretched attackers were not just targeting the men, but also the beasts. *A deliberate attack to cripple the march!*

It took them a few minutes to get to the first point of attack, and Aberis was astonished at what he saw. The center was in disarray. Heaps of camels and asses lay injured, pierced in their bellies and chests by spears and arrows, their limbs hacked, or their necks broken. Many were free of their harnesses and ran around with men chasing to control them. Many lay dead on the ground. Knowing the attack was over and there was little they could do, Aberis summoned the unit commanders for a report.

"What happened?" he asked Asmana, a tall bearded leader of the baggage train. Asmana was haggard and bleeding, but he still stood proud.

"We were attacked by a wave of men who appear to have hidden behind the low-lying hills by the side, Your Excellency," he said.

"How did our scouts not find them?" Aberis asked, angry and irritated.

"We do not know, Your Excellency," Asmana responded. "I have already ordered two of them flogged for their failure to notice."

Aberis nodded. He looked around. Order had returned to the units. The captains had asked their men to return to their stations and be vigilant. Guards stood looking out from the edges of the column, with many clambering over the low-lying hills on one side.

"Losses?"

"We lost a hundred and five so far, sir. Most to an initial wave of arrows."

Aberis walked to the body of one of the dead attackers, rolling the man's head with his feet. The man was unmistakably Egyptian, as evidenced by his shaved head, kohl-drawn eyebrows, and the waistcloth. There were no ornaments on the man.

Asmana continued. "Losses were not terrible. But we were clearly not the target of the attack."

"I noticed that. Impact on the baggage train? What do we have in this section?" Aberis asked, not remembering what was held in this section of the train.

"Water. Bread. The attackers did not take any of the soldiers' belongings—they were repelled before that."

"Or perhaps they cared not for it and only wanted to inflict damage on our supplies," said Babak, who was quiet so far.

"What of the water?" Aberis asked.

Asmana looked distressed. "They smashed the pots and tore sheepskins. We lost most of the water in this section of the train."

Aberis grunted. Whatever the reason, loss of water and food, even if in small quantities, could have a significant demoralizing effect on the troops. But what was more concerning was that the attackers knew where to attack.

In this wilderness. In this vast column. They knew when to attack and where.

"They knew where to attack, Your Excellency," said Babak. Then he looked around and asked. "Where is Jabari?"

The Egyptian was nowhere to be found.

CHAPTER 13

ΛOSTRIS

BABAK

Babak, Aberis, and a few others waited for Jabari to arrive. The remnants of light had long since vanished, leaving the men huddling in the cold. Jabari finally arrived. He was sweating profusely even in the chill. He saluted Aberis and then took several breaths and a swig of his rationed water before he was able to speak.

"Where were you?" asked Aberis.

"At the rear, Your Excellency. I had gone there to check on the state of the troops."

"Your place was closer to the center, was it not, Jabari?" asked Babak.

Jabari turned sharply to Babak. "No, it was not. What are you

insinuating?"

Aberis addressed Jabari. "Look at me, Jabari."

"Yes, Your Excellency," said Jabari, chastised.

"Do you recognize the attackers?"

Babak noticed Jabari's face flush even in the darkness and the light of the torches. "I grieve at your words, Your Excellency. I knew nothing of this."

Aberis took a deep breath, puffed his chest, and stepped back. *Here come the threats.* Thought Babak. He knew the noble's ways.

"If I find out that anyone had anything to do with this," Aberis said, addressing no one in particular, "I will have him flayed and left in the open desert to die."

"And they would deserve such a death, Your Excellency!" declared Jabari, though Babak noticed the false enthusiasm in his voice.

Eribaeus finally arrived with Danofis.

"We pursued them briefly into the desert, Your Excellency, but they knew the ways, and we risked getting lost," Danofis said. The Greek was smeared head to toe in the sand that clung to his glistening, sweaty body. *At least they tried something,* Babak thought, *unlike Jabari.*

Aberis turned to Babak and Jabari. "Should we send a contingent to Aostris to resupply water?"

"If we send a small detachment, then we risk exposing them to attacks—" started Babak.

"And also hold up the column," said Jabari, completing the sentence. Eribaeus agreed with the assessment.

"We take the losses and march faster to Horosis," said Danofis, referring to the next town about four days away.

Aberis fumed and fretted for some time, but there was little they could do. It was dark and the desolation offered no comfort. The noble sent messengers up and down the column to let the alarmed troops know that the losses were minimal and had no impact on the journey. And that they would be victorious and rich, and not to heed to rumors.

The dead were cast aside. Their bodies were stripped of supplies. Priests offered prayers and the officers finally dispersed to their tents. As Babak began to walk back to his tent, Jabari caught up with him.

"That was deliberate!" Jabari shouted, pointing at Babak.

"I meant no disrespect," Babak said, adjusting his turban and covering his mouth from drying in the chilly wind.

"You put doubts in his head," Jabari said, his voice bitter as the Arnak tree sap.

"Maybe the doubt is in your heart, Jabari," Babak said. "I was calling for your name for you would be the best to assess the attack! But why were you in the back, anyway?"

Jabari calmed down. "Do not do that again. My loyalty is not in question. I went to the back because a relative works in the rear train."

"An Egyptian soldier?"

"Not a soldier. Cleaner. Still fifteen years of age. I went there to infuse some encouragement."

Everyone needs encouragement in a death march, thought Babak.

Danofis caught up with them. "Is it really four more days to Horosis?"

"Three, if we increase our pace. And we must, before we run out of water. Rationing is in effect now," Babak said.

"If the Ammonians have any sense, they should surrender and proclaim Cambyses Pharaoh," Danofis said.

"The Oracle bemoans that they do not have you to advise them," Babak said, drawing laughs from the others. Danofis pretended to be offended, but Babak knew the hardy soldier had the skin of a Hippopotamus. The Greek commander shouted at a slouching guard to stay alert, and the Median responded with what sounded like expletives but most likely respectful responses knowing how the Medians spoke. Babak's mind drifted again. He thought of his wife and daughter. *Roxana, care for Amastri until I am back. And if I die here, may Ahuramazda protect you all.*

They walked quietly and the only sounds were the crunching of the gravel underneath their feet and the faint swish of the flames that danced in the cold desert wind.

CHAPTER 14

THEBES

ROXANA

Roxana watched her daughter with worry. Amastri had not improved. There would be no messengers from the detachment to Ammon until they completed their mission and returned. Vultures circled the vast and deserted camp area after Cambyses had left for Ethiopia. In their haste to leave, the army had simply abandoned the dead and left them to rot. The stench wafted to the eastern edges of the city and mixed with every other aroma and bad smells. Roxana looked at the birds circling at a distance. *They seek the dead and their souls,* Roxana thought, *but they shall not have my daughter.*

What worried Roxana was that her daughter had begun to bleed from her gums and there was blood in her urine. The girl was far from reaching her womanhood, and therefore the bleeding was an indication of a sickness that was eating her insides. There was little Roxana could do except care for her as best as she could while she cleaned and performed other camp duties for the administrative quarters of the King. The pay was enough to fend for themselves, and Babak had left some barter for their use. Amastri stirred in her sleep and Roxana gently wiped her sweaty forehead.

Fever.

What life have you confined us to? She asked her god. Her faith had been shaken. She had willingly accepted Babak's ways after her marriage, and she had even accepted praying to his god. Could that have angered her own? She wondered. The circumstances in Egypt had put her in great conflict, for the lips that once showed obeisance to one god could now bring the anger of the other. Like the helpless ants that scurry under marching men only for some to die for no fault of theirs, she was feeling inexorably tied to the powerful currents of destiny and loyalty.

She had succeeded in making Babak see the unfairness of their lives, and like a boat slow to turn in a turbulent sea, Babak had begun to see her arguments. It was perhaps divine providence that Cambyses had ordered an army to assault Ammon.

Under noble Aberis.

Aberis. Cruel tyrant. Unjust.

She cursed the man inwardly. But she had told no one, except her husband, that she was elated that Aberis had been chosen to lead the expedition. But she worried each night and hoped Babak would return unscathed.

And today a strange peace descended on her like gentle leaves under a strong breeze.

She folded her feet beneath her thighs and bowed. It was time for her to beg the forgiveness of her gods—gods that had blessed her in her birth. Gods that held their ancestors' hands and helped them walk the path of life. She felt remorse for abandoning them in favor of another. She would set it right.

She whispered her apologies to Ahuramazda—perhaps the Persian God did not favor her and her family, and would not find fault in her return to her roots. And then Roxana, born Nedjem Merytamun, *Sweet and Beloved of Amun*, prayed to Amun-Ra, The all-powerful.

PART II

CHAPTER 15

TO HOROSIS

BABAK

Babak stood with the others as they looked at the sight ahead, bewildered. The seemingly flat path had not only turned rocky and uneven, but it had also suddenly ended in a sharp drop with steep ridges on both sides. It would be challenging for the men to go down, let alone the animals that would panic and cause a great ruckus.

Aberis turned to Babak. "Why did you not know this? You suggested this path! Why did the Bedouins not know this?"

Babak looked into the noble's eyes, knowing that he would draw further ire if he showed weakness. "The sands shift in the desert, Your Excellency. In these parts, there can sometimes be great flashes of water that cut the ground and open gashes."

I hope no one refutes what I just made up.

The Bedouins looked too frightened to answer and nodded along as Babak explained the strange phenomena and the mischief by none other than the Egyptian gods. Jabari kept his mouth shut, for no sheep willingly bites

a lion's tail.

"They say that an extra day's march will get us back to a benign path," Babak said, as they stared into the bleak nothingness. It was late morning, time to break for lunch. There were already reports of some unrest and arguments over water rationing in various parts of the column. It had been just six days, but many more had already died on the way from ailments and thirst. Weak of heart, stomach, or mind, their bodies had given up and they were left as they lay; such were the cruel rules of the march.

"How much longer to Horosis?" Aberis asked.

"Three more days," Jabari opined.

"Assuming we can maintain the pace of the march," said Eribaeus, echoing

what was certainly weighing on every man's mind.

They were silent for a while as they waited for the noble to decide what to do next. *Accelerate or perish*, thought Babak. The desert was a harsh mistress and she offered no easy answers.

Aberis walked around for a while—looking out and muttering to himself. Babak wondered what the noble thought—*how is this so different than the marches from Babylon*? Babak knew that the marches through the often-populated paths of Persia, Babylonia and Syria were far easier than the sandy emptiness of Egypt where almost all life lived by the Great River. Gedrosia, farther east from Pasargadae and Persepolis, was the only other region that ground men to dust.

"We pick up the pace. Set the units to walk late into the night and begin early in the morning. We reach Horosis in two and replenish," Aberis said, finally.

Babak translated to the Bedouins who nodded and offered no resistance. That was no surprise, for those hardy men who breathed and tamed the desert could reach such distances with not more sweat than any other day. But for the army it would be a different matter.

"That might pose some dangers to march, Your Excellency," began Jabari. The Egyptian looked genuinely worried.

Aberis turned on him. "Do you want the men to die on the way? Can our men fly? Are they camels?"

"No, Your Excellency, that's not—"

"I have ordered, and the units will make it happen. Get back to your stations," he said dismissing them all.

A chastised Jabari trudged back slowly to his position with Babak following closely. Eribaeus stayed with Aberis. *No doubt trying to ingratiate himself*, thought Babak.

"He will cause the death of many," complained Jabari. "The sun has already beaten the will of many men."

"That is the burden of a leader, Jabari. A roaring river does not ask permission from the bank or the pebbles for the path it charts," said Babak. *And you should know when to shut up and when to speak.* "It is not the pace of the march I worry about, but the plan to walk through the center of the Horosis."

Jabari looked at Babak quizzically. The Egyptian was taller, and his black eyes glistened under the brightness. "How so?"

"Do you think the attackers came out of nowhere? No. They had their base somewhere—Aostris, or the next habitable area. And that is Horosis. If we walk through it, then we risk much greater violence."

Jabari thought for some time. "Whoever attacks us again is only a fool. We will not be without our guard this time."

"Think, Jabari. We are not up just against sneak attacks. We have nature against us. Every chance we give them, they take. The hyenas kill a lion with a thousand little bites, not with one single battle."

Jabari said nothing as he wiped the sweat off his broad forehead. His bald pate shined.

Babak continued. "Ritapates had an idea. That we go around Horosis, with a heavily armed detachment sent for supplies. Send a second armed contingent at a distance, hidden, as a backup. We will trap any ambushers and destroy them. The main column can continue to march, and the smaller detachments can catch up. It is the best thing we can do."

Jabari turned to Babak. "The two of you have many ideas."

Babak smiled. "I will not bring this up with His Excellency."

"Has Ritapates?"

"Do you think that coward would?"

Jabari smiled. "Let us hope someone else will."

The scorching pace set by the march to Horosis tested the hardiest souls. The army moved with purpose on the day of the obstacle and with a little less purpose the next. But the day after the second told a more difficult tale. The column stretched, now over six miles long and clumped in places due to the different speeds of each group, moving like a long snake in the deathly stillness of the desert. Strange dark brown and black buttes and little rock mountains sprang in the unlikeliest of places, like fretful sentinels guarding the great land against impious invaders. In places, the ground was littered with thousands and thousands of fractured flat orange and black stone, as if an invisible army of the past had littered the place after a tantrum. Not a plant grew anywhere, and no life sprang from the earth. Messengers, entrusted with passing news along the column, struggled under the blistering sun that poured fire on their backs until it was time to set in the far corners of the earth.

Many messengers, walking or running back and forth, collapsed with no energy. Aberis had only allowed nominal extra water to the messengers, far below what such burden demands, and the men began to deliberately slow their pace. Babak intervened twice with the noble to increase water allowance to the messengers, and his request was only partially met. Several scouts died on the march and Babak knew they were discarded by the side, with not a tear for them. They watched out for the army, and now mute rocks and sand would watch over them. As the feet trod the dusty ground and the afternoon wore them, they arrived at an area where the rock outcrops, small mountains, sandy bumps, and other features vanished. In front was a vast field of ribbed and patterned sandy ground, with only the smallest of rocky outcrops, and Babak knew then that this segment of the journey would bring great pain. Not long after, there was much clamor from somewhere behind them, and a messenger, along with a captain, walked hurriedly towards them.

"The men are raising hell, sir. We seek advice," the captain said. He had dried blood on his shoulder and chest—not his own—and he had taken his turban off as he spoke. "Put your turban back," Babak commanded. With the noble not intending to be bothered by the squabbles of lesser men, he had assigned Babak, Jabari, and Danofis to mediate and quell any unrest. The man shuffled on his feet.

"Two hundred men from the Scythian unit have grown very unruly and are demanding water from the cart. They've run out of their water and are holding up the units behind them."

Babak cursed. "The Scythians should have known better. I've seen that merry bunch drinking water as if it sprouts from every spring in the sand. What action have you taken?"

"I ordered them to march on, but that lasted only briefly. I had ten rabble-rousers arrested and beaten, and I executed four instigators. But now the unrest has spread, and more are angrily demanding additional water—some are clearly in distress, but many other mischief-mongers seek to take advantage of the situation."

Eribaeus, who was nearby and relaxing by the side, yelled at Babak. "Order all of them executed. We have no time for such quarrels."

A march where death appears to be the only solution to any problem, Babak thought. He turned to Danofis. "We cannot have this spiral out of control," Babak said. "Take us there. Bring two contingents along."

They rushed to the location of conflict, now with over five hundred soldiers forming a cordon around the rebellious Scythian unit, after separating the rest of the Scythian contingent. Babak and Danofis approached about thirty men, hardened soldiers with their swords out and desperation writ large on their faces.

"Put your swords down. You know what your fates will be if the noble finds out," Babak said.

"We know what our fate will be even if he does not find out," said the man. His voice was raspy and hoarse—the dry lips struggled to pronounce the words from the parched throat.

"What is your name?"

"Ishpaka," he said.

"Stand down and tell your men, Ishpaka. Many before you who have mutinied have died."

Ishpaka's wild eyes looked around desperately. Babak knew that the man meant no harm and what he desired was a drop to let him live.

"We will die. We will all die if we do not get a drink," Ishpaka said.

"You knew the rules," Babak said, his voice harder. "And you and your men disregarded the instructions in the beginning."

"No one said that these wretched lands would have ambushers," he complained, not answering Babak's accusation.

"It does not matter. Most of the army has followed what the noble commanded, and why must you be an exception? You are slowing us down, endangering a lot more."

Ishpaka's followers began to yell. "Just some water! Or we will create more trouble!"

The soldiers in the cordon began to advance on the rioters, and the constricting ring became smaller. Many onlookers had gathered on the periphery, and captains had to labor to keep the rest where they were.

This will get ugly. Babak thought. But he wished no harm on these unruly, but poor bastards. Only if they listened. His mind desired to condemn them, but he would try one last time.

"Ishpaka. Men. You have no escape from this. March for a few more hours until evening, and you will be eligible for your next gulp and piece of bread. You know that you will be punished—perhaps with a flogging or a further reduction in rations for a while—but you will be allowed to live. Make your choice."

There was stillness. The harsh and hot climate magnified the desperation and fear that reeked from every pore. The Scythians grew restless as the cordon got closer. Danofis, commanding his Greek contingent, waited for Babak's word. He too shouted at the rioters. "Give up, men. Save yourselves. Do not lay down your lives in vain!"

Ishpaka stared at Danofis and spat on the ground. It was no secret that the Scythians had no affection for the Greeks.

"Make your choice, Ishpaka," Babak said.

For a while no one moved, but the Scythians did not put down their sword. *The stubbornness of a mule combined with the indiscipline of a street dog,* Babak thought.

And then, inexplicably, the man beside Ishpaka lunged at Babak, swinging his sword, and screaming, "We will die anyway!"

In an instant the scene erupted in violence. Babak escaped the sword but felt the warm air brush his shoulder as the blade swung. He jumped to the side and reached out for his knife. As he regained his balance, he saw Danofis rush forward and engage the Scythian. Danofis was a brilliant fighter–he moved with the grace of a dancer but with the lethal bite of a viper. The Greek soldier saved Babak twice, protecting him and beheading another Scythian who rushed at them. Quickly, the entire contingent had devolved into close combat. The Greeks, outnumbering the stupid Scythians almost five-to-one, began to cut them down one by one. Blades sang in the stifling air, spears pierced bellies, and warm blood cooled the burning ground. The acrid smell of bodily fluids and feces permeated the air. Quickly, no man was visible in the rising dust, and hacked off limbs piled on the ground, making a distinguishable soft sound when men stepped on them instead of the flat sandy stones. The screams rose in the air, with no one to heed or care, and died in the empty blue dome above their heads. Babak twice avoided a rushing soldier, and once narrowly escaped being struck down by one of the Greek guards. He rushed to Danofis' side, "Tell your men to watch who they plan to kill!", he said, spitting sand from his mouth. Babak knew he was no fighter as he was years ago—and he stood no chance in front of a younger trained soldier.

It did not take long for the skirmish to die down. Most of the Scythians were dead, and so were some Greeks. A few rolled on the ground, wounded, bleeding into the earth. Danofis ordered a swift end to them, and guards walked on the dusty, body-strewn narrow stretch, plunging their blades into chests, or slicing the necks deep enough to cause a quick end. They arrested twenty of the rabble-rousers.

The men, indistinguishable from each other, covered in sand and blood, were lined up with their hands tied behind their backs. Danofis waited for Babak to decide the next step, in the absence of His Excellency Aberis. By then Ritapates had arrived.

As the men contemplated their fate, Babak placed a hand on Danofis' shoulder. "You saved my life twice today."

Danofis smiled. "May the gods bless me for it!"

Babak came to the front of the prisoner line. He shook some sand and sheathed his knife on his belt. "There is not much to say. I hereby condemn you to death. Say your prayers."

They turned their attention to the men in front. And then Babak heard a ruffle behind him. The sound of parting men.

"Not just yet," said the voice.

His Excellency, Aberis.

CHAPTER 16

HOROSIS

The man in the Pharaoh's garb walked with purpose. On this day he wore the double crown of Egypt, held a Pharaoh's crook and flail, wore a crisp tunic embroidered with golden threads. He had anointed his body with scented oils—causing him to glisten in the early morning sun. He walked slowly and deliberately up the steps of the great temple complex; one he knew as the Palace of the Governors. This large structure dominated the oasis and was known to be the residence of governors since the time of the great Pharaohs of the past. The complex had chapels, storage granaries, weapons storage, living quarters, open courtyards, administrative rooms, hidden rooms and even an extensive underground tunnel. With the looming walls of the outer precinct behind him, he faced the many thousands before him. Four priests from the temple of the Oracle of Ammon stood with him to show their solidarity. Amunperre, the Chief Priest of the Temple of the Oracle of Ammon, was right beside him, his long cap, kohl-lined eyes, gold and lapis-lazuli necklace radiating holiness to the audience.

The Pharaoh then expanded his chest to breathe in the crisp morning air. He cleared his throat. His most trusted lieutenants stood near him, and he had announcers in the front lines who could convey his words to the men out of earshot. After the customary greetings and platitudes, he delved into the topic that mattered most.

"The Persian army marches towards us. The bearded ones think that a single battle, where they preyed upon our piety and benefited from the treachery of our admiral who now sits on comfortable couches in Memphis, is enough to break our will. The shameful priests at Memphis may have crowned Cambyses King—" he paused for effect. Many men shouted "Shame!" and the thundering reproaches scared the birds on the palm trees that surrounded the complex. Once the crowd settled, the Pharaoh continued. "This traitor even took Cambyses to Sais to seek blessings of Neith, Her Majesty mother of all-powerful Re, and thinks that a few sacrifices will make Cambyses Pharaoh of all Egypt."

The men shouted.

"Never!"

"Not while you are still here, our beloved Pharaoh!"

"The hubris of the foreigner!"

He looked fondly upon his warriors; some no older than thirteen, and some reaching sixty years of age. All willing to carry the bow, the ax, the sword, the spear, the stone, the oil drum, the burning sand. All for the glory and prestige of Egypt.

"No foreign King shall proclaim himself Pharaoh. Have we not forgotten the shame of a hundred years under the *Hyk-Khase* that defiled our temples, molested our women, drank our water and made our men slaves?" He said, causing shouts of outrage. The Pharaoh knew some history of those men that occupied the lands in Lower Egypt, a thousand years ago, and a great Pharaoh named Ahmose had fought them. He knew not whether these invaders had defiled the temples or molested any women, but such embellishments were necessary to spark the right flames in angry hearts.

"And now the Persians seek to make Ahuramazda rule over Ammon. What man or woman of this glorious land would accept bowing their heads to gods not their own?" he asked.

"None!" came the shouts amidst raised spears and swinging swords that glinted in the beautiful morning sun, often blinding the Pharaoh.

He smiled. "Today we prepare to inflict another wound on the snake that slithers through the desert. Your commanders will send instructions. Go home, those who have your homes in this magnificent oasis, and others, embrace your fathers, your sons, your brothers, your fellow-man, for we will embark on a march like no other!"

A great roar rose from the crowd. "May the gods bless Pharaoh Petubastis! May you wear the double-crown for eternity!"

Petubastis nodded and acknowledged the adoring men. The stocky Pharaoh then turned to his general Senwosret. "Make sure half the army is ready. The others stay."

Senwosret looked puzzled. "Your Majesty. We are up against fifty-thousand."

"Prepare them for a march," the Pharaoh said, not answering the General's remark.

Senwosret's eyes narrowed again. "A march? Is that army not walking through the oasis, ripe for an ambush?"

"We have much to talk," the Pharaoh said and smiled. Amunperre, who stood nearby, caught the Pharaoh's eyes and his lips curled up.

"There is much you do not know," Petubastis said to Senwosret's puzzled face.

CHAPTER 17

TO HOROSIS

BABAK

"You swore a duty to the King. And yet here you are, rabble-rousers, putting an army of fifty thousand to risk because you could not control your greedy throats," said Aberis. He stood on a small rock placing him at a height compared to the men around. He had ordered all the Scythian units to witness his speech and punishment of the offenders. The Scythian units themselves had been disarmed, all two-thousand, and surrounded by Persian special guard under the command of the noble. A selection of men from all other units had been summoned as well as spectators. Babak stood next to Eribaeus and Ritapates.

"My hand swings to the wishes of the King of Kings. Let this be an example to everyone here; whether Scythian, Median, Greek, Persian, Syrian, Indian, or Egyptian. No matter your land, your ways, or your gods, here on this mission your god is the King of Kings and I am his messenger. Today is a shameful day, for the wound inflicted was neither by marauders, nor by ambushers. It was by our own! We shall not let our own hands turn on us again!"

Aberis removed his noble's turban—embroidered with green and dusty feathers. He smoothed his beard and let his silence weigh like a heavy blanket on the anxious men. He turned to his guards.

"Dig pits in the earth," he said, as he pointed to the barren path by the side. The implications were clear to all—some of the condemned men began to pray, some swooned and fell, some began to shout and beg for mercy, with their voices barely heard due to lack of water. As the audience watched, the guards worked swiftly to dig shallow pits. The earth would not lend easily—the rocky, hard ground challenged the shovels and picks—but it finally yielded to stubborn men who worked in teams.

As their work came to completion, Aberis ordered each man caned in full view. Angry red welts rose on their backs and thighs, but the Scythians, brutish men that had grown with little but violence in their lands, cried not once. To each man they had accepted their fate. Once the work was complete, without a word, another set of guards dragged each resisting man to the pit and pushed him in it. And then they covered the man to his neck in sand and rock. But it was not over.

There were five additional rows of empty pits next to the buried men.

Cruel and unforgiving, thought Babak. Just like how the noble had dealt with a rioting population. The marshes brought bad memories. Aberis had forced many men to run barefoot in the deadly marshes, and they had screamed and wailed as sharp roots pierced their feet and thorns ripped their flesh. And then they were left in the water to die of exhaustion.

Aberis turned to the unarmed Scythians. And then he pointed to a man at random. "Him."

Guards rushed to the man and grabbed him the arm. The man began to shout. "I have done nothing, Your Excellency! May you have mercy!"

But even as he resisted and pushed, Aberis turned and pointed to another. And so on it went.

"Him."

"Him."

"Him."

"Him."

"Him."

"Him."

"Him."

"Him."

"Him."

"Him."

The fifty innocents, all protesting, wailing, crying, were dragged to the pits. But there were only forty-nine open. Each man was pushed in on the orders, except the last.

"You will live," Aberis said. And the man collapsed to his knees and began to sob. "You will tell every man you see that your life was spared, and that no one should ever take his chance on defying orders."

The man nodded vigorously. Babak watched as the heads protruded from the pits—squirming, some gasping already, some with their eyes wide open in fear, some already with their heads on their chest having fainted, and others praying as their lips quivered.

Babak knew their death would be slow and horrible.

With that, Aberis made final remarks and ordered all to return to station. They would march again in an hour.

Babak would hear soon after that some men in the marching columns, unidentified, had surreptitiously thrown heavy stones at the men's heads to end their misery.

Mercy in its most brutal form, thought Babak.

The army's progress had slowed considerably, and for the rest of the day there were sporadic reports of fighting, news of men bribing water guards for sips, stealing another man's waterskins—and in each case the situation was resolved quickly and harshly with summary executions by the side of the path. Captains who struggled to enforce discipline were stripped of their possessions in the baggage train—a terrible punishment in its own way, for the men had procured their rewards after years of hard life.

Babak wondered if the men secretly cherished these deaths, for it meant more ration for others, even if it only meant only a few grains of bread and a few more drops of water.

That night, as the noises died down, Babak went out for a walk. The chilly air provided a welcome departure from the blistering heat of the day. As he walked quietly around the flimsy canvases fluttering in the wind, he was puzzled by the shadows cast by the lamp in the noble's tent. Babak casually strolled by without drawing the guards' attention, but the silhouettes of the figures hunched in Aberis' tent were unmistakable—Jabari and Ritapates.

The scoundrels were conferring with the noble in his absence.

What do they plot? He wondered.

CHAPTER 18

THEBES

NEDJEM

Nedjem was at the market for her supplies. It was a routine every few days. She walked about a mile from her house to the path to the great temple of Amun. The road was lined with magnificent Sphinxes, a thousand of them, they said, watching them on both sides. The path was lined with hawkers selling their wares. Everything from vegetables (*the freshest, straight from the riverbank*), clothes (*the finest silk from Persia. You are beautiful but this will make you queen!*), pottery (*imagine how happy your husband will feel if you serve him with this cup!*), beer (*will make your evenings heady and glorious*), cake (*the tastiest in all of Thebes, the type our Pharaoh used to eat! Now cheap!*), wine (*they say the Greek nobles only drink this!*), perfumes (*from the most exotic lands, madam!*), magic potions (*will bear you many children and strengthen your man's seed!*), slaves (*the sturdiest from Nubia, look at his muscles*), whores (*perhaps not for the dear lady, but could we interest you in this trade?*), workers (*we can build your home and paint the walls, very cheap*), maids (*you look like you could use some help*), building materials (*the best quality bricks of course*), worship goods (*these are dear to Amun and Isis*), protection (*in these uncertain days you need someone to watch your back*) and jewelry (*just imagine yourself wearing these beautiful pendants! Even the Persian King will want to marry you right away*).

She knew how to handle the aggressive ones and haggle with the others. It was simply the way of life. She had things she could exchange, and they had things she wanted. There were some rumors of something called currency that the Persian administrators were proposing but it was not implemented yet.

Nedjem found who she was looking for—a friendly vegetable vendor with dates, olive, pomegranates, lentils. She stood there to haggle when she heard a soft voice.

"Roxana?"

Nedjem turned. It took her a while to register who the woman was. She was younger than Nedjem, beautiful, and dressed like someone who had better means.

"We've seen each other occassionally, and perhaps spoken some time ago. Remember me? Sekhet."

Jabari's wife.

"Ah, yes, of course. The respected High Priest's wife. Sekhet?"

"Yes, indeed," Sekhet said, with a dazzling smile. She wore fine jewelry and a glamorous gown that accentuated her looks. Her hair was perfectly oiled, straightened, and fell on her shoulders. She tied it with a fine thin golden ribbon that matched the necklace and the bangles. Her orange-gold gown matched the rest of her fashion. Nedjem felt a tinge of envy–this woman had it all, youth, beauty, money. It was rare to see highborn at this time of the day in a common market. They usually sent someone on their behalf.

"What brings you here?"

"Well, sometimes I like to walk these markets. It gets boring at home when everything is taken care of."

"Of course. I did not think you would recognize me."

"Well, your dress is very Persian, and not many Persian women walk around here. So, I was just curious who you were, and then recognized you."

Nedjem was unsure where this conversation was headed. Sekhet leaned and held Nedjem's elbow. "How is your daughter? I heard she has taken ill." The woman exuded fake concern, all mixed with the heady aroma of the rose perfume.

Nedjem was surprised. "She is still recovering. I pray to our gods every day."

"Ahuramazadha, is it not?" Sekhet asked, almost deliberately mispronouncing the Persian divinity. Her eyes had no twinkle in them.

"Yes. Ahuramazda. One who blesses us all, just as Amun."

Sekhet eyed her for a while. "I hope your daughter gets well. Poor thing. Well, was it difficult to convert to Persian customs?"

Nedjem was caught by surprise again and she stammered. She realized that to lie would only make matters worse. "It took a while. Their customs are quite different."

Sekhet smiled, but there was no mirth in her expression. She played with her hair. "But you could almost pass off as a Persian now."

"One might say so."

"Isn't your husband on the expedition as well?"

"He is. Isn't yours too?"

"Yes. A great responsibility falls on them. I'm so glad they are together!" Sekhet said, and she rubbed Nedjem's arm in camaraderie.

Dripping fakeness.

"Of course! It is a difficult journey and they must watch out. Your husband is a learned man, and he knows the ways and means," Nedjem said, insincerely herself.

Sekhet nodded enthusiastically. "Jabari is blessed by Amun. He has made my life glorious."

"I am sure," Nedjem said.

Sekhet appeared to be in no hurry to leave. She leaned forward conspiratorially. "How did you marry a Persian? It is unusual. Not that there is anything wrong with them, of course."

Nedjem smiled. Her lips were beginning to hurt from all this insincere smiling. She knew what Egyptians thought of the Persians. "He came on a trade visit. I found out that Persian men are not too bad. In fact, in some cases they may be even more cultured than some of our own!"

There was awkward silence as the two women appraised each other. Sekhet drummed her fingers and looked around the market, while Nedjem stood frozen unsure what to do. They smiled at each other time to time.

It appeared that all the false enthusiasm tired Sekhet as well. She fanned her face and pouted. "Well, it was nice seeing you. What was your birth name? It would be nice to call you by that!"

Nedjem had had enough. "I am only known as Roxana now. I wish you good health and safe return of your husband."

Sekhet seemed annoyed at the rebuff. "And yours as well. Praise to Amun and your new god," she said, wanting to have the last word.

Nedjem did not respond. She thought it was odd for Sekhet to seek her, and that there must be a reason—but she was unsure.

Perhaps Sekhet just noticed her and wanted to say hello.
And maybe show
her high status.
Maybe.

CHAPTER 19
Horosis

PETUBASTIS

As the night flames flickered, Pharaoh Petubastis, accompanied by Senwosret and Amunperre, walked quietly to the chapel of Medu-Nefer. There, under the eyes of the gods, they sat to discuss.

"Preparations?" Petubastis asked.

"Excellent, Your Majesty," Senwosret said. "The men are eager to take their swords to the invaders' necks."

"Very well. What of food and water?"

"We are adequately stocked. We can mount an offensive or we can wait out a siege for at least thirty days."

Petubastis turned to the High Priest. "And you are certain the Ammonians will send a contingent."

"I will make sure of that," Amunperre said. "We will begin dispatch preparations as soon as I return."

"When are you leaving?"

"Tonight, Your Majesty."

"Good. Await news before you act."

"Of course."

With that Amunperre sought Petubastis' permission to leave to prepare for his difficult journey back to Ammon—five to six days by a fast camel through another oasis. Once Amunperre left, Petubastis and Senwosret strolled through the expansive courtyard and columned inner sections of the temple. The Pharaoh then turned to Senwosret again. "I have new instructions for you."

Senwosret looked puzzled. The General, who had served this Pharaoh in exile since the death of great Pharaoh Amasis and capture of Psamtik, was rarely left out of decisions. "Yes, Your Majesty."

"Split the army in two. Prepare one with two thousand men to ambush points along the town and around the oasis."

Senwosret nodded, unsure of what the Pharaoh was planning. *Why splinter the army of ten thousand against the overwhelming odds of fifty thousand?* He wondered.

"And then prepare the other of eight-thousand for a rapid march, towards the salt flats and black rocks in the north."

Senwosret adjusted his kilt. He bowed to the Pharaoh. "It seems you have something in your mind, Your Majesty," he said, knowing that the Pharaoh sometimes toyed with him. They had grown up almost like brothers and knew each other better than most boys of the same mother.

"I was waiting to see when you would ask," smiled Petubastis. "But wait until I explain."

Senwosret nodded, satisfied. "The rapid march—the salt flats are more than five days in length until they turn to the Great Sand Sea. So how far are we planning to go?"

"Midway," said the Pharaoh. "Prepare for a three-day march and no more. But we also need twenty scouts to leave tonight to begin tracking the army."

Senwosret agreed. The benefit of tracking a large column was that the dust they raised and the glints off their metals were visible for miles, making it remarkably easy to find their position and project their trajectory.

"If I must infer from your words, Your Majesty, we must send men that are quick on their feet, nimble with light weapons, and masters in the craft of attack-and-run," said Senwosret.

Petubastis smiled. "You read my mind, *Senawe*," he said, referring to his General with an affectionate term he used when they were alone, as friends rather than a Pharaoh and his General. "Lions by heart, deer by feet, wild dogs by the tactic. No camels or asses with them. They must move swiftly."

They arrived in a small kitchen managed by servants. Senwosret took a sip of beer and ate a piece of cake. "Why split the army? Cambyses' army outnumbers us entirely by five-to-one."

Petubastis smiled and took a long swig from a jug. Then he considered Senwosret. "What makes you think their entire army will come through the town?"

CHAPTER 20

THEBES

SEKHET

Sekhet finished her morning prayers and ordered her slaves to clean the courtyard and the front. She was tired. It was time to relax. She went upstairs to an open balcony that overlooked the city. A gentle orange hue hung in the sky and evening brought cooler breeze.

Her favorite time.

She knew that a residence such as her own, that even came with a balcony, was a luxury only afforded to those close to the royals or high priests. She was proud of her husband; their ambition had got them a long way, giving them the chance to enjoy comforts even as others toiled. She looked left to the north, towards the magnificent temple of Amun. Priests said that these temples were thousands of years old. They gleamed in the evening sun. The great pillar hall, the tall walls, the Obelisks and statues of Pharaohs dead long ago, all brought a flood of emotions in her. They could not let a Persian rule this land!

But today was a special day; it marked the anniversary, a critical moment, when they had decided to turn their back on the Pharaoh Psamtik and bow to the Persian King. What had Amasis, Psamtik's father, ever done for them? And Psamtik himself was a failure. If they had not sought Cambyses' patronage, then they too would be marched off for execution after Pelusium. Instead, her husband received elevated positions and they were rewarded well.

What use was loyalty if you died begging for your life or if you were relegated to be a whore in brothels dotting Thebes?

Her husband was away. Far away. And she feared for him. But this was another opportunity—once more to leverage the position of power they were in to rise higher. That was Amun-Ra's plan for them. And Horus' too, she was sure. Aberis was a fool—he knew no tactic than to trample what was before him. He knew no subtlety and his mind was closed to possibilities beyond what came out of the King's mouth. Her husband would lead the noble by the nose to his disgrace, she smiled. The Greek nobleman, Eribaeus, who had eyed her hungrily every time he crossed her path, would be a good ally. She would push up her breasts and sway her waist whenever she met him, driving him wild. The pervert had even propositioned her twice, and she had cleverly flirted yet avoided any dalliance with him. She had told Jabari, and they had a good laugh. They would use this man.

But one thing bothered her.

It had crawled into the mind like a wasp and had grown every day. A wasp placed there by her husband.

Babak.

Why was that reedy, bug-eyed Persian in the detachment? Babak had risen in the ranks of Cambyses' advisors. Babak's wife was no less—she had a mind of her own. Sekhet had found out that the terrible woman had even converted herself to appease the Persian gods—such abasement and shame. Sekhet would never do such a thing. Her husband had bitterly complained that Babak had injected himself by insinuating that the Egyptian advisors could not be trusted, and yet the rat had not revealed *that his own wife was an Egyptian*! The gumption of the man! If there was anyone that could cause her and her husband's plans to fail, it would be the bastard Babak. There were rumors about why Babak joined the contingent. Something about his sickly child in their miserable little mud hut a mile down from her villa. She had also heard some news that their sons had died a few years ago during a rebel suppression led by Aberis. Her husband had accompanied Aberis, she was sure. Was there something to it all? She was worried and anxious. She took pleasure in *Roxana's* (wonder what the woman's real name was!) wretched life—not yet rich enough for a fine house like hers, but the temerity to consider themselves at the same station.

Now one way to keep Babak's growing influence in check was to take away the people he loved. And when better than when he was away? Jabari had given her some ideas before he left.

Her bright husband. One who might one day become the chief advisor to the King, or if the gods continued their blessings, even Pharaoh himself.

He had designs for Babak.

Just like she had for his wife.

CHAPTER 21

HOROSIS

WATER BEARERS

"The bastards! These sister-fucking, bald, dog-fuckers!" cursed the expedition leader. They had already been harassed incessantly for the past few hours by Egyptian bandits who quickly attacked sections of their detachment and then escaped—taking advantage of the column's rules: do not pursue and do not break rank. The plan, one most prudent for survival, was to protect the sheepskin and water-bag beasts at all costs. Aberis had decided to send one heavily armed detachment instead of two, without a separate backup force. Scouts went with the detachment to relay any problems and only then would a backup depart. The defensive posture meant that the attackers could inflict continuous small wounds and enmesh them in a minor war of attrition. So far, they had lost several hundred men to fast-moving boulders, arrows, burning haystacks, and spears, and they had killed as many, he reckoned. But it did not diminish the fact that their march had slowed down considerably—which means they would anger the noble in the main column which stayed far away from Horosis. They would likely be stuck here after the sunset, which would bode ill for security.

But what let loose the expletives from the man's mouth like arrows from an archery range was what he saw before him, at the mouth of the eastern end of the oasis. There, in front of them, rising like dark blobs, were the putrid carcasses of hundreds of cows, sheep, fowl, asses, and other animals. They lay belly-up, floating, and turning the clear water brownish-black. *Killed to poison the water*, thought the leader, for each floating beast had its entrails pulled out of its belly and left to dangle in the water. He knew never to fill water from ponds and lakes that had death in them. Physicians said that the souls of the dead corrupted the sweetness of water, and when consumed caused great sickness in the living. Besides, if he took poisoned water back to the troops causing mass contamination then there was no question he would be flayed, flogged, and buried. The problem was that to get closer to the clearer water on the far end of the oasis, they would have to trudge a narrow path by the trees, leaving them ripe for more ambushes.

But he knew he had no choice. He took a deep breath.

And then he ordered his contingent of five thousand men to form a four-column order marching in a defensive formation. They would march rapidly through the path, not stopping for any reason, until they reached a safer area.

He knew that by the time the day was over there would be much more misery.

Back in the main army, miles away from Horosis on a new path ordered by Aberis, the situation was getting dire. The constrained supply of water and rationed food caused fraying nerves and flaring tempers.

"We should have marched with the entire army!" Shouted Aberis. "The water contingent is getting attacked and here we are, wasting away in the sun! It was all your idea," he said, pointing at Jabari.

Jabari looked desperate. "That would only expose all our baggage train and other supplies, Your Excellency, and slow us down. It would give us no advantage over the tactics of the bandits! The path to the oasis is strife with ambush points!"

Aberis paced around like a caged lion. Babak remained quiet waiting for tempers to cool.

"And I was right to insist that there would be an ambush," Jabari whined.

"The scouts say that the water contingent will not return until early morning. Prepare another contingent of ten thousand, supply them with a day's ration of water, and have them escort the water bearers," ordered Aberis.

"I propose the Greeks go," said Babak. "They are better trained to handle the rapid hit and run attacks."

Eribaeus protested. "My men are amongst the fighting elite, why waste them on a water-carrying mission?"

"Would you rather have them all die of thirst then?" asked Aberis, glaring at the Greek.

Eribaeus cast a baleful look at Babak, who kept his eyes firmly on the noble. After much recriminations and finger-pointing about what they should have done, could have done, might have done, would have done and so on, Aberis put an end to the bickering by finalizing his orders. The Greeks would leave late at night, march rapidly to the oasis that was about twenty miles away—taking six to seven hours with rapid pace—and then bring the trapped water detachment. A few messengers on asses would go with them and rush back if there was any trouble—though Babak assessed that no one knew what they would do if the Greeks got into trouble as well. But the consensus was that whatever resistance existed in Horosis would not be able to withstand twelve to thirteen thousand men, if the initial detachment still existed. And so, the Greeks, with their fluttering plumes and colorful skirts, set off to save the water contingent.

When the water detachment leader finally saw the relief party arrive, he was beside himself with joy. Having lost over five hundred men through the ordeal of the previous day, he had almost prepared to secretly abandon the cause and run away with the men—hopefully vanish somewhere without ever being found. But no such shameful act was necessary as the pale bodies in their armored tight formations began to advance to their position. But the Greek captain told them a different story—aside from a few light skirmishes they had encountered little resistance. The leader told the Greeks to stay away from any water that was closer to the eastern-end and that their men should take their turns in line to fill their bellies. This caused further delay and frustration, but the men were all too grateful to saturate their throats with water and to rest when they either waited their turn or waited for the others to finish. The shades of the palm trees were like a gift from the divine, and laughter, absent in the past few days, returned to the groups.

"Where did the Egyptians go?" the Greek asked.

"Wherever they came from. Maybe that fortress?" the Persian captain said—pointing to the large structure to their northwest. It was an imposing fortress with a temple inside. Stories swirled of rebels and shamans within those walls.

"Perhaps His Excellency should turn the army this way and we lay waste to this oasis," said the Greek.

"All you think of is to lay waste—what if we need to return this way after we subdue the Ammonians?"

The Greek reconsidered his position. But he argued some more for the need to kill every living man, woman, and child in this town for what they had put the contingent through.

"We could, if we have the time and resources," said the Persian. But by now the sun was rising in the sky, and they had to rush. The camels and asses were all loaded. The personal sheepskin and clay pots were all filled—with each armed soldier carrying enough for several, and each laborer carrying more. When it was finally time to return, the Greeks created a defensive wall around the water detachment and escorted them out from the oasis until they again reached the open desert. The return was then uneventful, and they were met with great celebration.

Perhaps they would now finally be on the way with no more nuisance.

CHAPTER 22
HOROSIS
BABAK

"The fastest path to Farrasis is this way," Babak explained, as they all squatted on the ground, holding a worn papyrus map with crude etchings on it. *If the Bedouins make any more uncomfortable noises, I might have to kill them,* thought Babak.

Aberis' eyes moved between Babak and Ritapates. Jabari hovered nearby. The return of the water detachment was a welcome one, but in the process they had lost two full days, lost over six-hundred men in the attacks and from the march, and the master of logistics told them that their situation per person was not much better now than before—considering the march ahead.

Gods work in strange ways, Babak thought. He had already foreseen this.

"This is too close to the ridges," said Ritapates, squinting in the dimming light.

"That might be, but it gives us protection from the winds. Besides, the ridges are too steep for anyone to mount attacks," said Babak. He hoped that his confident voice would put arguments to rest.

"Have you been this way?" asked Jabari. And before Babak replied, Jabari turned to the Bedouins, "have you been this way?"

They shook their heads vigorously, indicating *no*, and they were uncomfortable.

"Well?" Aberis fixed his eyes on Babak.

"I have. It has been a long while," Babak lied. "And these Bedouins do not know every corner of this expanse," he said.

"What do you say, Jabari?" Aberis asked the Egyptian. Babak noticed the strain in his voice. No doubt the man was beginning to recognize the folly of taking a giant army through hostile deserts. It was like tying a buffalo's carcass to the leg and trying to outrun an angry bull.

Jabari made fretful sounds and furrowed his brows. *You have no good answers, for you have never set foot in these regions*, thought Babak. The unforgiving sands beneath his feet were different than the soft rugs and purple cushions of his corrupt temples.

"Following an unfamiliar path, even if it is one that Babak here says that he has once experienced and is shorter and faster, comes with its risks. But it is a path away from Horosis and the ridges protect the army. We risk more attacks if we attempt to stay on the original course," he said, clearly unhappy but having no choice in the matter. The Egyptian's eyes searched Babak's, seeking to find something nefarious.

Aberis shook his head and turned to the Bedouins. "Does the weather get better?"

They muttered something, and Jabari turned to the noble. "They say it only gets worse."

Aberis sighed. "We have no choice but to keep the pace. No wonder the wretched Ammonians were bold to defy us, they hide behind the protection of the desert!"

A fact that was amply evident right from the beginning, thought Babak. But he was secretly pleased that they had chosen to follow his direction, even if it now took the army off the normal paths through the aquifer route. Aberis prepared to issue new orders—continued rationing, early march, and instant execution for anyone breaking orders. Men filled their waterskins enough for many days. But it was imperative that they reach Farrasis, otherwise they would all be doomed.

"But, Your Excellency, I did not yet say that that is the path we should take," said Babak, spacing every word, and with his eyes firmly, connecting with each man's as they moved to the next.

"What?" Aberis asked. His eyes narrowed and jaws clenched.

"What are you doing?" hissed Jabari, close to Babak's ears. But he ignored them.

"We were attacked near Aostris. We were attacked at Horosis. Their forces were stronger and bolder. They most certainly know where we waited as we sent our water detachment. They know our path, and they will wait for us by the mouth of a vast valley here," he said, pointing to a region on the map, "before we near Farrasis. They might even attack us before that, when we move away from the ridges."

"But you just said—" began Jabari, his veins pulsed on his skull.

"Let him speak," said Aberis.

"We are like an elephant that walks in an open plain inviting hungry jackals. The attackers have the advantage of the terrain. Our size burdens us."

"That is obvious by now."

"What are you suggesting?" asked Eribaeus.

"That we move swiftly through the night, much farther west, where they would never guess we will be, and turn north through the open Sand Sea on a rapid march until we reach Farrasis. By the time they find out, it will be too late for them to organize, and if we reach the Oasis in time, we can withstand any onslaught."

The group stood quietly, each man staring at the other. Finally, Jabari cut through the uncomfortable silence. "You conspire to lead us to death!"

Babak knew he had to react quickly before the accusations flew uncontrolled. "And you call yourself an advisor as you lead us to a certain ambush!"

Jabari turned to Aberis. "There is a reason it is called the Sand Sea, Your Excellency. What we have experienced so far is nothing to what—"

"Have you been to the Sand Sea, Jabari?" Babak retorted. "Do you know what it feels like?"

"What, no—" Jabari responded, and realized that he had, in an instant, discredited himself. *Keep making a fool of yourself, you treasonous Egyptian.*

"Then perhaps you must bite your tongue before you accuse me of anything." Babak said, "I have walked through the Sand Sea, and while it poses a great challenge, what do we want? Do we want a hostile ground and a foxy enemy hounding us, or do you want a hostile ground, perhaps harder on us, but where no one can bother us as we march?"

"He makes a sound argument," Eribaeus said, looking at Aberis. The noble was deep in thought, knowing that the weight of the decision would lay on his shoulders. The man had made many tough decisions in the past—one that required wiping out villages, burning towns, breaking bridges, executing long lines of crying men, women, and children, storming forts, and threatening those who stood in his way. But Babak knew that none compared to facing an unyielding and unforgiving ground.

"Tell me more of the Sand Sea, for we did not anticipate crossing it so soon," Aberis said, finally. The original plan required entry to the Sand Sea after the last supply station at Farrasis.

"Yes, Your Excellency," Babak said, and he rudely elbowed Jabari out of the way. The Egyptian was livid, but he controlled his temper for the evening had not gone his way. Babak wondered what swirled inside that angry bald skull.

Babak then hunched in front of the papyrus map and pointed to a region that had nothing in it. The area he showed was vast and empty but lay south of the spot that indicated the location of the Ammonians.

"The Great Sand Sea was so named by men that walked it. When you see it, Your Excellency, you will recognize it as such. It is where the rocky undulations and hard ground ends and then begins an endless wave of dunes. They say that the Sand Sea extends far to the West, where no one has ever been, perhaps to the end of Libya. They say it extends to the edge of the earth to the south, and to the north it ends at the Temple of Ammon."

"The power of the Oracle—" began Jabari.

"Be quiet," said Aberis, admonishing Jabari. Babak smiled inwardly. Even in this dreariness, the joy of seeing Jabari humiliated could not be suppressed.

"It is said that the combined power of Jupiter and Amun keeps the sand at bay," continued Babak, quietly appraising Eribaeus. The Greek pulled his shoulders back hearing the name of his God.

"If I agree to this deviation, then how are we faring on the supplies?"

"Our condition with the supplies is dire, Your Excellency. We must traverse either path quickly. We will make it to Farrasis. We have already lost time, water, food, and men. It will take us five to six days. The Sand Sea offers an unfettered path—slow and steady. On the other hand, the path through the desert valley may be quicker, but makes it much easier for the enemy to launch bolder attacks and there is a higher chance of confronting surprising terrain."

Aberis paced around the tent. The noble stroked his greying beard and took a small sip of water, suddenly mindful of the rules he had himself set on the men. "Who is organizing these attacks? The Ammonians? This does not feel like the action of a few disgruntled local chieftains."

Ritapates, who was quiet all the while, finally spoke up. He had a high-pitched voice. "The Ammonians are certainly behind this, Your Excellency. There has been some news of a renegade Pharaoh who has established himself in these regions, but little is known of him. They say he was once a general under Amasis, some say he is Psamtik's brother or son, but all we have are rumors."

Aberis considered the response but asked nothing more of who the attackers might be. Instead, he turned to Babak again. "What will it be like? Leading the army on this Sand Sea?"

Babak straightened his back. He knew they all appraised him. They sought to see what was in his mind.

"What the eyes see all around is orange and yellow rather than green and blue. It is dry instead of wet. The waves are of sand, not water. In some places the dunes make way to arid flat land with black rock jutting from it.

The heat is unrelenting, and each breath burns at the height of the sun. There are no places to rest or find shade. The march will test the greatest of resolves," Babak said. *A frightening vision now would save his hide later when they experienced what it was like.*

"Well, then would it not make sense that we stay on a safer course?" said Aberis, tracing his finger on the original path that avoided the

Sand Sea.

"We have seen so far that the desert of western Egypt is not much more forgiving, Your Excellency. The path we choose, just because it has less sand, is no less treacherous. No matter which path we take—the next water and shelter is still the same distance away," Babak said. "What matters is whether we trick our adversaries by taking action they do not foresee, or we walk into a dangerous trap, thirsty, hungry, tired, and slaughtered with no strength to fight. And that is what it will be if we listen to Jabari."

Jabari's head yanked sharply at this sudden rebuke. "You son of a filthy dog, how dare you!"

Babak turned and shouted at him, "and yet it was you who hinted that I was the one planning something!"

"How do we know that you are not?" Jabari retorted.

"How do we know you are not?" Babak countered.

"Enough," yelled Aberis. "I need my advisors, not two squabbling idiots. It is my decision and it is I that decides the ways."

Much to the fuming Jabari's surprise, Aberis dismissed them and asked only that Eribaeus stay. A cool wind fluttered the tent flaps, and the two stepped out. Jabari and Babak parted ways and Babak began to trek to his tent, not too far from the noble's.

Thwack!

Powerful hands pushed Babak and he felt the air swoosh his face and the ground race at him. As he crashed on the ground a sharp rock cut his cheeks. Babak quickly pivoted and turned to face his attacker.

Jabari.

"You fucking whore mongering Persian bastard! You think you can discredit me in front of the noble," Jabari hissed. "Watch what I will do to you!"

"We were just–"

Jabari kicked him again on his thigh. "I know what you are doing! I know it. Watch your mouth, you dirty swine. I will slit your throat and let you bleed like a pig if you do this again!"

Before he could respond, Jabari viciously kicked him in the ribs, forcing Babak to double in pain. Jabari kicked him in the back again and Babak's lips smashed against the dusty rocky ground. Agony bloomed in his battered face. He grunted in pain and waited for more, but there was nothing but silence. Jabari had vanished.

He groaned as he regained his composure and got back to his feet. His body hurt, but he was thankful that no limb was broken. He lay alone, quietly, until his head cleared, and the pain dulled. By then, the guards had heard some commotion and arrived at the scene. Babak sent them away, saying that a soldier had mistaken him for a thief. He had to make up the story if asked—it would do no good going to Aberis with a complaint against Jabari as if they were quarreling children. The irate noble might have both flogged, which was not the desired outcome. He had to preserve himself for what was to come. They helped him to his feet, and he let out a gasp as his abdomen and waist screamed in pain. But he was able to walk. The cool air of the night helped.

It was now time to wait for Aberis' decision.

Walk with me to the unknown, thought Babak.

CHAPTER 23

THEBES

NEDJEM

Nedjem sat cleaning the meat and preparing to boil it with some spices. Their modest sun-burnt mudbrick house had a little living room, no courtyard to speak of, and just one small storage room. They had decorated the walls with little pictures of flowers, trees, and pretty pottery. Nedjem hoped they could have afforded something more, but so far, they had chosen to save their barters for another day. They had depleted much of their savings dealing with Amastri's illness and sending a scammer on a mission that he never returned from. But today she had a visitor—her neighbor, a portly grandmother with the biggest mouth in all of Thebes.

Hemmu.

Hemmu was as annoying as any neighbor could get. The old woman made the neighborhood's life her business, loudly commenting on every man, woman, and child around her, offering unsolicited advice and chastising them for their ways. Nedjem put up with her, for Hemmu had no agenda. She cackled, complained, and annoyed everyone, but then she also showed concern for Nedjem's daughter, made delicious cake and brought it to her, and endlessly selected the right boys for Amastri when she would be of age. She also made sure to suggest a few fine men, of Egyptian stock of course, perfect for beautiful Nedjem just in case that ugly Persian husband of hers died. She also made sure to share her observations of Persian men. *Noses are too big. Very crooked. Greedy pigs. Bugs grow in their disgusting beards. Really small penises and all of them have only one testicle, what about your husband's?* Nedjem was usually horrified and amused at the same time by the woman's chatter. She had scolded the hag many times, but none of that deterred a woman who had seen much in her life. "You know what I speak is true", Hemmu would cackle, and then resume uttering every offensive thing she could think of. "I am sure Esmurre masturbates thinking of you," was her last observation.

But today, Hemmu had something else to gossip about. "You certainly have someone interested in you, Nedjem! You might have had three children, but you make some men's cock's sing!"

"Oh, Hemmu!" Nedjem rolled her eyes. *What was it with this woman?*

"No, no. I am not joking this time. I saw this man, not very handsome, but will do, come by your house and walk around multiple times the last two days. I had also seen him follow you when you went to the market."

Nedjem was alarmed. "Did you ask him who he was?"

"I thought I should, at first. But then maybe I would scare him away," she said, looking at Nedjem shrewdly.

"How did he look?"

Hemmu scoffed. "Nothing extraordinary. He looks like—" and then Hemmu proceeded to describe another man who lived nearby. "Like that."

Nedjem knew no one who looked that way. But the old woman had a mischievous glint in her eye.

"You know something else, go on," said Nedjem, knowing that the busy body would not just let it go so easily.

"Well, I followed him yesterday."

This woman!

"And?"

"He seems to work at that haughty bitch's house."

"Which haughty bitch? There are many these days," said Nedjem. Many of the wives in Cambyses' court and Egyptian priestly and administrative class could be quite the queens.

"That one. The one who is the wife of that Egyptian priest who is busy licking Persian boots. The one who is away on this stupid expedition to burn our sacred temple in Ammon," she said, and made many signs to ward off evil.

"Which priest—"

Then it dawned on Nedjem. *Jabari!*

Jabari's wife, Sekhet!

Sekhet's servant?

"Are you sure?"

"Of course, I am. Don't question me! I saw him there this morning. I saw him with her. Anyway, I was only joking that he might like you Nedjem—but I don't like that man. He looks like one of my cousins who groped girls in the alleyways. No good."

What was Sekhet up to? After all, she had accosted Nedjem just a few days ago in the market. There had to be something! Babak had warned her of Jabari and his wife, so Nedjem could think of no good reason for this behavior except something ominous.

"Besides, he was here late last night. He left when I walked out of the house to piss."

Nedjem reached out and held Hemmu's leathery hands. "Thank you, mother. May Osiris bless you."

"Osiris has blessed me with an idiot husband who just won't die!" she cackled. Hemmu's husband was a habitual drunkard who was probably lying in a ditch somewhere.

"Don't say such things!" Nedjem admonished her. "Can you keep Amastri with you?"

"Of course. The poor child. I hope she gets better. She will make a fine wife for—"

"Yes, yes, I know. For your grandsons, for your uncle's grandsons, for your nephew's neighbor's sons, for—"

"You forget—"

"Shh. I want you to listen to me," Nedjem said. She explained her plan to Hemmu, who listened with a big toothless grin.

Nedjem waited quietly in the dark. She sat in one corner, barely breathing, waiting like a ghost in the stillness of the night, ready to prey on the hapless. Her heart thundered in her chest, but there was some relief too. She had placed her daughter under a neighbor's custody. *Watch her*, she had implored the neighbor, *it is not safe for her at home.*

Babak had always warned her to be wary and observe the world around her. With him gone, and with unscrupulous actors at work, Nedjem's safety was heavy on his mind.

All day today she had trailed the man Hemmu had talked about—she had found him in Jabari's house, and stayed far away as she watched his activities. He even had the audacity to circle her house in the noon, acting nonchalant, but attempting to peek through the small opening on the side. Her senses were heightened—she had to act for her safety and her daughter's. With Cambyses away and no real Egyptian administration, she knew there would be no justice if something happened to her.

There were few sounds from outside, except the howling of a few street dogs. And then the hissing and mewing of the feral cats that roamed with impunity.

She waited. She had purposely left a small oil lamp alight in one far corner. It would draw attention. She clutched the heavy bronze rod in her hand and took a deep breath.

And just then, she heard her door scraping gently, and it opened ever so slightly.

CHAPTER 24

THE GREAT SAND SEA

JABARI

Aberis had decided to lead his men across the Great Sand Sea. That was three days ago, and it felt like an eternity. Jabari squinted in the harsh morning sun. The sun beat down on them relentlessly, like a heated hammer in the hands of a relentless demon. His legs felt heavy, and each step to extricate his feet from the grainy sand hurt his thighs, shoulders, and feet. Around him, in any direction, were endless gently undulating dunes that looked like waves—just as Babak had described. They all had an orange-golden hue and were adorned by gentle ribbons made by the wind.

The wind.

The wind had a mind of its own. It raged when never expected, and then it died bringing deathly stillness, and then it raged again, blanketing the men in miserable coats of fine sand that covered every exposed patch of skin and entered every pore.

Men welcomed the night after a grueling day. But that happiness was always short lived. Ordered to travel at night, most men had light clothing and tents were in short supply. When they lost men, Aberis had ordered that more tents be left behind to speed up the march—less weight, more speed, he had said. The nights were cold, and once the heat of the day left the body, the chill caused men to huddle and complain. It was difficult to sleep, which then caused difficulties during the day march.

Not a thing, apart from this long, exhausted column, breathed life. Not a spot of green—no cactus, palm, dates, shrub—nothing. It was as if a great curse had descended on this land and sucked the life out of every being, leaving only a dry sandy husk of earth. Jabari, like many others, looked to the sky for birds. A bird indicated life and water nearby. What was important was to see if the bird was ascending or descending—for that was the surest sign that it was coming from food and water or going towards it. But there were no birds. There was simply nothing in the sky except the angry eye of god.

Jabari looked behind him—the column stretched five miles—like a thin vine laid dry on a pigmented floor. The men walked in clumps, rather than in a disciplined column. A shimmering haze borne of dust hung low in the air as far as the eye could see. Disturbing messages were already circulating—many units were already close to the end of their allotted rations. Some had gambled on the assumption that if entire units wet their lips before their allotment, then the water masters would be compelled to give them more rather than lose the unit to thirst. This greed that fed the thirsty mouths of these inconsiderate wretches put the others to risk—those that braved the heat and thirst, those that trudged even as their throats cried and their backs turned dry and itched until the skin broke, those that held on to their rations and

demanded no more than scheduled.

But what could a captain do?

Kill each man that cried for water?

Abandon the men that once fought by his side and saved his hide?

Such were the present difficulties.

Jabari cursed Babak. He had led them here. *I should have killed him*, Jabari thought, *and convinced the noble to stay on course*. The hoarse-voiced cunning bastard was ahead somewhere, no doubt whispering things to His Excellency's ears. In the next melee, if there was enough cover, Jabari would stab Babak or enlist someone who could. He could no longer allow this insolent man to drive the path forward and put seeds of doubt in Aberis' head.

They cannot know and should not know that I have been in touch with the Ammonians, thought Jabari, silently. Every doubt that Babak created would cause them to look harder at Jabari.

Babak.

Babak.

The man was an enigma. Jabari knew much about him—from his spies and Aberis'—but their relentless march made it difficult to know everything there could be. He knew that Babak came from somewhere south of Babylon, that great land from where Cambyses and his father Cyrus came. He knew that Babak was a military advisor, though he had rarely, if ever, held a sword or slain a man. He had seen Babak's wife, and she looked Egyptian rather than Persian. Babak had advised Cambyses's commanders on the way to Egypt, and then in Pelusium—he was shrewd and brilliant.

Why did Babak needle him so?

What was his intention?

PART III

CHAPTER 25

GREAT SAND SEA

SCOUTS

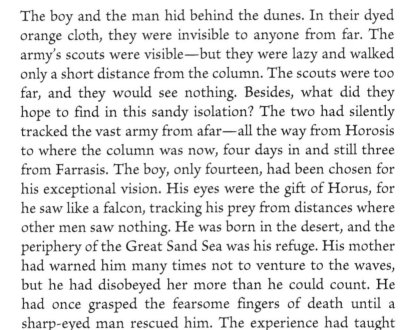

The boy and the man hid behind the dunes. In their dyed orange cloth, they were invisible to anyone from far. The army's scouts were visible—but they were lazy and walked only a short distance from the column. The scouts were too far, and they would see nothing. Besides, what did they hope to find in this sandy isolation? The two had silently tracked the vast army from afar—all the way from Horosis to where the column was now, four days in and still three from Farrasis. The boy, only fourteen, had been chosen for his exceptional vision. His eyes were the gift of Horus, for he saw like a falcon, tracking his prey from distances where other men saw nothing. He was born in the desert, and the periphery of the Great Sand Sea was his refuge. His mother had warned him many times not to venture to the waves, but he had disobeyed her more than he could count. He had once grasped the fearsome fingers of death until a sharp-eyed man rescued him. The experience had taught him to respect the land. And be better prepared.

He felt a breath down his neck. "They have slowed down considerably," the crackly-hoarse voice said.

"Will all be dead soon?" he asked.

"No. This is a large army. They were nearly fifty thousand when they started, and they still probably have considerable reserves. Aberis will not hesitate to execute or abandon many if it means to conserve water. They will make it to Farrasis even if it means a few more thousand lose their lives."

"How many more should die before the Pharaoh can take them on?" the boy asked. He received no answer except a gentle ruffle of his hair.

"Can you make out the locations of their baggage trains?" the man asked. "Yes," said the boy. He then pointed out to sections where the dust appeared to hang higher and the distant spots seemed to have greater density. "There," he said, "where you see more dust in the air and more whitish regions, that is where their baggage trains are."

The man patted the boy on the shoulder. "Your eyes see things mine are blind to, son."

They watched the slow procession far ahead for some more time. The man then spoke again. "Mentu, how much farther will they have to go before they meet the big bluffs?"

"At this pace, another day at least," the boy said. *The Big Bluffs, where the dunes met tall, rocky bluffs with many hollows. Where the army would find it prudent to rest and finally find some shelter from the sun. Where he would rest if it were him,* he thought. *And, where someone could wait.*

"Excellent," the man said. "We should return now."

"Yes, father," he said, proud and happy.

They both turned and ran down the large, sloping dune, to a waiting party with camels. Unlike the invading army, they were well supplied, their lips were wet with enough water, and their bellies full of cake and bread. The boy was ecstatic. He felt a tingling sensation in his stomach and groin—he knew he was rendering service in a way beyond his greatest wishes. In a single mission he had a chance to serve a Pharaoh and those he loved dearly.

I will be the boy who becomes a man as few others can, Mentu thought, smiling as he climbed the kneeling camel.

CHAPTER 26
THE WESTERN DESERT
PETUBASTIS

The man and the boy stood with their heads bowed respectfully.

"Senwosret," Pharaoh Petubastis called his general.

Senwosret, who stood nearby inspecting a lineup, sprinted towards them.

"Yes, Your Majesty," he said, and then turned to the two standing before the Pharaoh.

"The scouts have returned with news," Petubastis said. Senwosret nodded and summoned two of his trusted lieutenants and a master of the baggage train.

"Tell us," the Pharaoh ordered.

The man began. He told them the army's journey across Horosis to the eastern periphery of the Great Sand Sea and their slow trek along the plains. He told them how the army was now about four miles long, with significant spaces in between, and how the baggage train was split into six different sections. He also talked of the boy's remarkable vision and how they identified the various sections when they had the chance to be closer. The senior officers, including their general, were at the head of the column, given by the insignia and emblems. Persian units were in the front, followed by the Greeks, and then some other units that looked different—perhaps from the lands near Persia, he did not know. And then the rear was again reinforced with Persian units, and they were lagging. He also spoke of how men dropped like dry scabs along the way, and that they had no doubt lost at least a few thousand. The dead littered some sections, he said, and the column had moved on. They had so far shown no change in course. The man did not know if the Persian immortals—special units with highly trained soldiers—were with the army. He did not know who the immortals were.

All signs showed that they would be at the Great Bluffs in a day or more.

"And from where we are, Your Majesty," the boy said, unafraid to speak in the presence of his god, "the bluffs are only a few hours." The Pharaoh turned to the baggage master.

"And we are well supplied. The men have moist throats and are eager to show their worth, Your Majesty," said the man.

"Excellent," the Pharaoh said. He patted the boy's shoulder affectionately. The boy's dark eyes shined, and his wiry frame stood straight with pride. *With the help of such committed subjects and the power of Amun behind me, an army of fifty thousand is nothing*, thought Petubastis.

"You both will be rewarded handsomely," the Pharaoh said, and he nodded at the man next to the boy. "We will teach a lesson the Persians will never forget."

"Yes, Your Majesty," they both said in unison.

The Pharaoh called an attendant and asked him to bring something. Soon, the man returned with a gorgeous necklace—a red, blue, and gold patterned ornament with an image of Horus in the front.

"Here," The Pharaoh said, giving it to the boy. "A fitting gift for a boy with the eyes of god!"

Mentu was overwhelmed. He fell to his knees with respect and accepted the gift with raised hands. The man looked at Mentu affectionately.

"The stench of Persian flesh and Egyptian treachery should be vanquished," said the man. He was older than forty, but an eminent presence shined through him. There was resolve in his eyes. And pain. Pain that Petubastis did not know more about. But every story in the sunbaked homes had tears in it. Of children lost to sickness, of men lost to war, to slavery, to imprisonment, to unjust conflict. In just the last year, Petubastis knew, a great many Egyptians had lost their lives, and many to the treachery of their own.

Such a shame! He thought, brothers put to death by brothers.

"Senwosret," the Pharaoh turned to his general. "Prepare the men for the march. Send a message to Amunperre that we are moving, and that the Egyptian from the Persian court that he so favored is no longer in our favor."

"Yes, Your Majesty," said Senwosret. He then bowed and dashed off to issue orders. The Pharaoh took a deep breath and expanded his powerful chest. He had shorn his royal garments and today he stood with nothing but a kilt with a golden belt with a royal dagger. He inhaled the crisp desert air and smiled.

"Look around us," Petubastis said, sweeping an arc towards the magnificent vista around them. The sun made the ground maroon, and the dying light glinted off dark rocks jutting out of the ground. They were at the edges of the Western desert, before the steep bluffs descended into the Great Sand Sea. "This land. This land we will keep."

CHAPTER 27

THEBES

NEDJEM

Nedjem was sure she could hear breathing outside, or perhaps her heart was playing tricks. Then the flimsy door opened inward and a figure, heavily hooded, entered inside. Nedjem had to control her panic and anxiety, for she knew that an armed man could easily overpower her. She prayed to Amun and begged him to give her strength, and then she filled herself with resolve. Her husband was out there, alone, in the far unknown, amongst vicious and dangerous men, so she too could do her part with bravery.

The man's attention went to the little lamp. His eyes were still adjusting to the darkness. He turned slowly, appraising the room, looking for her. She had repositioned herself, now crouching, ready to leap like a lioness on its prey. And then, when the man angled turned slightly away from her side, she launched herself on him. He was fast as he recognized something coming at him, but not fast enough. Nedjem swung her heavy bronze rod and smashed it on his head.

The man staggered and fell.

But the strike was not powerful enough. The man grunted and turned, facing her. Now his covering had fallen off, and his dark, piggish eyes glinted in the light.

It was him! The man who scouted her home and worked at Sekhet's.

She tripped and fell on him. Strong acid rose in her throat, but she knew she could not pause. The man's hand shot up and gripped her armed hand even as he struggled from the first blow. She slapped him hard, but it did not remove his grip. She could not swing the other hand and he shook it vigorously, causing the heavy rod to fall on the ground with a thud. A sudden strength rushed into her heart. She pivoted, allowing him to continue gripping her arm, and then she kneed him in the groin with a mighty force.

The man bellowed and let her go. Nedjem rolled on the floor and recovered quickly. She grabbed the rod again. The man was still doubled up in agony when she smashed the rod again on his chest. She felt the ribs crack. His eyes opened wide in surprise and realization that he had badly miscalculated. He raised his hand but was too late to stop her from smashing his nose in, breaking it, and dislodging his teeth. She did not stop—she brought the rod down with all her strength on his forehead, bashing his skull in. The man began to shudder and shake, he released his bowels and blood spurted from his mouth.

Nedjem sat on the side of the room, shaking, sobbing, as the man's twitching slowly stopped and he lay dead. There was a commotion outside. Hemmu, her sons and husband rushed in and were horrified to see the scene before them. And not too long after, after hearing Hemmu's narration (with several pointless details), and Nedjem's explanation that the man intended to rape or murder her, they helped her dispose of his body and clean the floor. The neighbor's husband and sons hauled the body on a cart and dumped it into the river which was not too far away.

Nedjem finally calmed down by the time the great god Ra rose after rebirth. But a new resolve dawned on her as well—no one, not a king, not a noble, not a commander, not a priest, not a priest's wife—no one would harm them.

Not again.

She would teach Sekhet a lesson.

CHAPTER 28

THE GREAT SAND SEA

JABARI

It was just before noon that the hazy giant bluffs appeared at a distance. *Finally!* This was the location that he waited for eagerly, and so had many men. The last day had been brutal. A sandstorm had risen from the South, descending upon them like an angry god, burning their skins with fine sand and wind that whipped them without mercy for hours. The entire column had to lay where they were, desperately building weak and ineffective tents, many of which had flown away leaving weeping men. Several camels had made haste and had vanished in the blinding sand-filled air. It was as if the night was upon them, even though the storm had started late in the afternoon. It had raged on for hours until it finally died, leaving a great tragic scene in its wake.

Many of the feeble men had simply given up their desire for life and lay where they were. The physicians and messengers had told them to drink their own urine if they must, and many had attempted so. But then soon there was no fluid left, and many had pissed blood. There was news of some men killing the others and drinking their blood—though that act of savagery had brought them no respite, and those that committed it had died of sickness soon after. A great many beasts had died too—for they were shown even less mercy than the thirsty men. It was an irony imposed by the gods that the animal that carried water had died for the lack of it. Men stumbled upon bodies of their companions in search of their scattered belongings, and when the opportunity arose, for fallen waterskins. Compassion dried and vanished just like water in the arid desert. Many men grappled with each other to get water or bread, and they stared into the terrified eyes of the other as they stabbed them. Many surrounded the water carts and begged the guards. Some wept with no tears in their eyes, for the body produced no more, but their laments went unheeded. Some went even as far as suggesting that the officers cut food rations to the Indians, because, as news had traveled, the Indians could eat the dead soldiers. To this the Indians objected greatly, accusing the rumor mongers of greed and deceit. They insisted most vociferously that they ate no meat at all, human or otherwise. The captains could only control so much, and it had taken late into the day to bring order. Aberis, mad with anger and desperation, had ordered the stronger units to arrest and execute hundreds to set an example. When they had woken in the morning, a wandering traveler might say that theirs was a battlefield with so many dead and dying, but little would they know that the war was only within them and with a hostile land. Not one man in that field of death had died of an enemy's arrow, ax, or sword.

Jabari willed himself to take each step, and the column moved on, relentlessly and lethargically. The bluffs renewed hope—they would offer some shelter, rest, and heralded the nearness of the next water source. He had managed to pick up pace in the last few miles to be near the Immortals. The King of Kings had sent five hundred of the special force, just in case. These hardy men, the finest of warriors, had so far braved with little loss. It helped that they were provisioned with more water and bread, and they had the patronage of the noble. By staying closer to them,

Jabari knew that he would have protection in case of conflict. It was late afternoon when the head of the column finally arrived at the bluff line—the tall ridges rose high above, sandy and rocky, with various platforms and level ground on which the men and beasts could rest. Overhangs and outcrops were in great demand—and the hardier of men scrambled for the shade much to the glare and frustration of others, but no one objected. Soon, a kinship developed and spread, as men who spent a short amount of time in the shade made space for others. The smiles returned. It took an hour for the last units to drag their feet and arrive. Soon, the length of the bluff-line was dotted with whitish-yellow turbans, gray tents, and a great stench of humanity.

Messengers made their way relaying orders from the front—the men would be allowed to rest for several hours, some units would receive additional water, there would be instantaneous trial of several hundred troublemakers, all men would have to finish their supper and prepare for a night march under the shining moon, and that the next water destination was near—only a day or two away.

Jabari rested under an overhang, savoring the clay cup and drops of water. The temperature had dropped a little and the while the sun still beat on them from the west, the geography provided some shade along the bluff line, and the tents gave comfort. He was with a few soldiers who were talking about rain. One of them was an Indian who seemed quite conversant with Persian, and the rest were Persian soldiers, he learned soon, from the arid regions near Gedrosia.

"Rain. It's beautiful. Not like this place. Just think about it—water from the skies, flowing by your feet, more than enough to drink, swim," the young Indian said.

"That's hard to believe. It rains for months?"

"Yes. I live near three major rivers. And it rains every day, morning to night, for months. Everything turns green, and the ground is wet and muddy."

"I live near a river too, they say it is the biggest river in the world," said a soldier from the regions of Babylon.

The Indian scoffed. "The rivers where I live, the *Ganga* and the *Sindhu* are the biggest rivers on earth by far!"

"Are you going to compare your cocks next?" asked another cheekily. The topic returned to water.

"Does that much water pouring down not peel your skin?" asked one of them.

"Who inducted this village idiot to the army?" shouted another man, looking around dramatically, drawing laughter.

"Well, I've never seen rainfall for days at end! What do you do?"

"No," said the Indian, "it just gets cold and wet. You just protect yourself. You pray to lord *Ganadhipati* and hope that no sickness enters you."

"Is that the elephant god?" asked another man, and the Indian nodded.

"So much rain would be beautiful," said the other. "Wouldn't it be a miracle if the skies darkened right now and a cold shower descended upon us?"

"Wouldn't it be," said one more. "I'd like to drink something other than my piss."

That drew some more sad laughter. The description of rain and cold days was lovely, and conversation turned to delicious kebabs and spiced meat after days of eating clumps of hard bread. When he could no longer bear the food fantasies, Jabari decided he had to do something else— something important.

It was time to talk to Eribaeus.

CHAPTER 29

THE GREAT SAND SEA

PETUBASTIS

The Pharaoh and his men waited. They watched hidden, well behind the bluff-line, the men ready and raring to go. Senwosret had devised a most devious plan, one enough to strike terror and confusion in the invaders' hearts. The general was ahead, and hundreds of his men lay buried near the overhangs. *The invaders are so complacent*, the Pharaoh thought, *for they think they are alone with nothing but the desert as the enemy*. The gods had gifted them great hearts that had strength and wisdom.

Today would be a momentous day. One in which a great army was vanquished by glorious Egyptian renegades. Cambyses had used traitors and cheap tactics to subdue this land. But in a strange way, Cambyses had also opened the opportunity for Petubastis to be Pharaoh—for if it were not for Cambyses, then the weakling Psamtik would continue to rule this land.

Psamtik, Petubastis thought bitterly, *that useless half-brother who had weaseled his way into his distant father's mind*. And now Psamtik was in Babylon, fucking Persian maids and boys while his land faced subjugation. Petubastis would right this wrong. The Pharaoh had the sharp-eyed boy, Mentu, by his side. Mentu provided commentary on what he saw, for his eyes caught what most others missed.

"It appears they are all here, Your Majesty. No reports of any other units still following, and I notice nothing else."

"Can you see the Immortals?"

The boy hesitated. "I do not know how the Immortals—"

Petubastis laid a gentle hand on Mentu's shoulder. "Do not fear. Look for groups that seem more confident and better organized than the other. They should be closer to the front near their general."

Mentu squinted. "There," he said, pointing to a distant patch. The Pharaoh smiled—there was not much he could make out. Some of his men nodded seriously, as if they saw, but Petubastis knew it was only a façade.

"What do you see?" the Pharaoh asked one of the men, and he stammered with embarrassment. The Pharaoh laughed. "The boy has the eyes of Horus, let him speak."

"I see a structured pattern—like the weaves of a fine fabric. They also look cleaner than the rest of the sorry bunch. Their swords glint better. But they are few, Your Majesty. I see no such formation anywhere else."

"Very good. Based on what our spy has said, can you identify the units?"

Mentu described as best as he could, based on what he was told how the units looked like. The Persians were obvious. The Greeks were easy to recognize as well. But the rest—the Syrians, Medians, and so on, were a guess.

"What about the baggage train? Where do you see most water carriers, and can you make out treasure units?"

Petubastis knew that to disrupt water supplies would significantly demoralize the enemy and looting the precious belongings could create mutiny. Mentu was unable to tell much, but they had some ideas. The Pharaoh then asked Mentu to run to the hidden forward lines, find Senwosret, and relay what he knew.

Petubastis had also relayed some specific instructions to men on what to do in case they were captured. The insider from the army had given some splendid ideas on how to seed suspicion. This battle would be fought with hands, with swords, with the help of nature, and the deployment of insidious mind games.

The benevolent Ra would die soon and the priests back in Horosis would prepare for his rebirth, but until then, there was much to be done.

He turned to his senior officers. "Prepare the signals. We attack at my command."

CHAPTER 30
THE GREAT SAND SEA
ERIBAEUS

Eribaeus relaxed with Jabari. Getting away from the filth of thousands of soldiers was such a respite. The view from here was almost beautiful, once one looked past the ghastly tents and men. *It would be nice to entertain a beautiful woman under the calm skies and gentle sand beneath the feet,* he thought. He had many on his list, including Jabari's wife. Eribaeus wondered how the oily Egyptian had bagged such a stunning woman. Her firm breasts, full lips, swaying buttocks—he felt his loins stir. How he wished he could fuck her under the stars. But his restless mind wandered again. The Egyptian advisor was a strange man, but powerful, for he had connections with the Priests who held great sway over the people. The break gave them an opportunity to seek common ground, and Jabari had sought him out. It would be foolish not to listen

to what he had to say.

"You are a brave man to leave the pleasures of your olive gardens and orchards to march here in the treacherous sands," said Jabari, smiling at Eribaeus. The Egyptian's forehead crinkled. *The lips are turned up in an insincere manner,* thought Eribaeus.

"As you are. You could have been by the side of the King, or even with his holiness Wedjahor-Resne in Memphis."

Wedjahor-Resne, that shameless High Priest who had blessed Cambyses and turned against his own Pharaoh.

"If I may open my heart to you, nobleman," said Jabari, spreading his palms, and leaning forward conspiratorially.

"Of course," Eribaeus said. He pulled down his head cover and kerchief mask. He hated it, but it was necessary for this sandy journey. He moved closer to Jabari.

"What benefit will the King of Kings bestow upon you after this conquest?" asked Jabari, with a sly smile.

Eribaeus was taken aback by this blatant question. But it also hinted that Jabari might have interesting things to say—things that he might be able to leverage if needed.

"Jabari, if you wish for me to speak, then perhaps you should first reveal your motivation for this invasion. Surely this is not a mission for you to endure this hardship just to help Cambyses' army go raze a temple?"

Jabari laughed hollowly. "You are an astute man."

"We have not reached where we are by being subdued or stupid."

"Indeed. I will speak what is in my heart, and I trust you to do the same—our partnership will have an enduring future, just as how profitable it has been in the past."

Eribaeus nodded. He took Jabari's hand and firmly squeezed his palm, and then leaned forward to kiss the Egyptian's cheeks—a sign of affection and friendship. Jabari wiped his bald head and grinned.

"The King of Kings has earned his glory as the ruler of many Kingdoms. But in Persia he should be," Jabari said, and Eribaeus felt the Egyptian's eyes search his. He nodded.

"Egypt feels a greater kinship with the Greeks. Our ancestors traded with each other across the Great Green Sea. We shared wine and bread, pottery and papyrus. We never sent armies at each other. Do you think the Persians will stop at Egypt?"

It was a clever question. One that Eribaeus had thought about much. "Emperors do not stop expansion. Today, Egypt. Tomorrow, Greece," he said.

"Then does it not benefit us both to see a powerful Egypt and a powerful Greece, with us playing great roles?"

Eribaeus flicked his finger at an approaching messenger and forced him to return. "What do you have in mind?"

A sudden gust of wind kicked up some fine dust, irritating his eyes and causing him to cough.

Damn sand!

Jabari looked uncertain. Eribaeus squeezed the man's shoulder. "What we speak is between us. Do not think I hold great affection to Cambyses. I am not here just to earn some coin through my mercenaries, either. If there is a greater glory to be had, then I am willing to listen."

Jabari looked elated. He rocked back and forth and clasped his hands. He took a deep breath. "I have communicated with the priests of Ammon. They say that if we find a way to prevent Aberis from reaching his goal, then I will be appointed High Priest, and with your help we can send Cambyses back to Persia."

Eribaeus was dumbfounded. *The audacity.* "That is an audacious, risky gambit!"

Jabari's chest puffed up with pride. He narrowed his eyes and fixed them on Eribaeus. "That is not all," he said, his voice low, barely audible in the steady hum of the windswept sands. Eribaeus leaned forward.

"They will appoint me Pharaoh, and I will elevate you to greatness you never imagined!"

Is this Egyptian a raving mad man, or is he just brilliantly diabolical? Wondered Eribaeus. He thought Jabari had some plot to further enrich himself—perhaps be appointed as the Priest of Ammon and become a local lord, or even displace Wedjahor-Resne in Memphis. But Jabari dreamed big—big like Eribaeus. He dreamt of becoming King of Egypt!

"You are remarkable," Eribaeus said, grinning. Jabari broke into a toothy smile. But seriousness returned soon.

"It is an exceptional thought, and I see mutual benefit. But what makes you think that the words of Ammonians hold such power over the land? Can just my Greeks beat the remaining Persians?"

"What makes you think we have just your Greeks?" said Jabari.

CHAPTER 31

THEBES

SEKHET

Every day, just when the god Amun-Ra began his rebirth in the eastern skies, Sekhet went to the Great River for her morning prayers. She took the winding path from her house, away from the sewage tracks and dirt pits, along the palm and acacia plantations, and came to a relatively quiet section where the river bent towards the south. The serenity was a welcome change from the hustle and madness of Thebes. That morning, the chirping of the birds and the gentle sounds of the flowing river did not calm her mind. Her faithful servant had vanished without a trace. She had given him an important and risky task. They had conspired together, and she had paid him well—kill Roxana, spare her child, and make it look like a failed attempt at opportunistic molestation. He had scouted Roxana's house, understood her pattern, and chosen a time late in the night where he could carry out his mission.

Where had he vanished?

Had he been caught? She had tried but failed to find out if Roxana was alive. The house apparently was empty the last two days, and the neighbors said they had no idea.

Where did he go?

Did he decide not to carry out the act at the last minute?

Did he not care for his rewards?

Did he run away with her—though that made little sense?

Sekhet knew that he was desperate for grain and garment barters, and she had dangled much. The man had every incentive to carry out this murder.

She was frustrated and anxious.

The glinting waters looked inviting. It was quiet, with only a few worshippers here and there. The ripples reflected the rising sun, and it looked like the gods had sprinkled water with gold. She wore a comfortable garment that draped around her body and ended at her knees—appropriate for the ablution. Besides, she could dry quickly.

Sekhet took a deep breath and dipped her toes in the water. She hated this part—it was cold. But she braved it, like she always did, and walked further, raising some mud from the river floor. The coldness slowly gave way to warmth, and she felt comforted by the water. She stood submerged to her shoulders, and prayed to Amun-Ra, letting his rays fall on her back. Once completed, she closed her eyes and stood there, basking in the gentle morning sun.

Suddenly, she felt something tug at her feet.

What?!

For the briefest moment, a terror seized Sekhet's heart.

Crocodile!

But it did not feel like a crocodile's bite. It was something softer, like... a hand?

Sekhet tried to scream, but the strong pull caused her to lose her balance and she tumbled. She opened her mouth involuntarily and water rushed into her mouth.

She screamed underwater and thrashed about, but the hands were now on her shoulder, pushing her down. She began to choke. And then, just as suddenly, the hands left her body and she was free. She sprang upwards, bringing her head out of the water. She coughed and spluttered, and then took a deep breath.

But in her panic, she still had not seen the attacker. The hands wrapped around her again, pulling her back into the water.

No! Help!

Sekhet had no chance to scream, for she was submerged again, and her lungs exploded with pain. She thrashed about for a while until she was pulled up again. Sekhet gasped for air—whoever was attacking her slapped her hard and pulled her back towards the land, gripping her neck. Almost blinded by fear, Sekhet wobbled and collapsed on the riverbank. Muddy water spluttered from her mouth and the awful drowning sensation passed. Once her air passages were clear, she doubled on the sandy bank and vomited. But just as she was recovering, her attacker grabbed her wet hair and yanked it hard, almost ripping it off. Sekhet screamed, but there was barely a sound. She lifted her arms to swat the attacker's hands, but she was weak and paralyzed by terror. The attacker slammed her head to the soft wet ground, and Sekhet almost passed out.

When she came back to her senses, a cloudy, hazy figure came to view.

Roxana.

Bitch from the underworld!

Sekhet tried to scream again, but Roxana placed a firm palm on her mouth. She had a knife in her hand and a demonic fury in her eyes. Sekhet stopped struggling and began to wail. "Please let me go! By our sacred gods, please!"

Roxana stared at her intently, without saying a word. She waited for Sekhet to calm herself.

"You come at me again and I will cut off your head and feed it to the sacred crocodiles," she said. "I know where you live. I know who you are. And don't think I don't have supporters of my own. I know your husband is behind this, but I want you to prepare for a life without him."

Sekhet's eyes went wide, unsure what Roxana was implying. But her voice was stuck in her throat and she nodded fervently, hoping to get this woman off her.

"The man you sent?", she said, grinning diabolically, "He rests at the bottom of the river, or perhaps in the belly of a fat crocodile."

Sekhet struggled to contain her shock. She had no strength or will to protest or profess innocence.

Roxana smiled as she got up. "Don't. Ever again."

Then she suddenly swiped the sharp blade on Sekhet's cheek, slicing a small section. Sekhet screamed and began to howl.

Roxana stood up, her eyes were cold and unforgiving.

And then she left.

Sekhet was alone at the bank of the river. It took her heart a while to calm down until she could breathe normally. She held her cheek to stem the blood that now dripped on her wet arm. Sekhet broke down sobbing

uncontrollably. Her chest heaved and shoulders shook.

She would leave this dirty business to Jabari.

When would he be back?

CHAPTER 32

THE GREAT SAND SEA

ERIBAEUS

"What?" said Eribaeus.

Jabari rubbed his cheeks and continued to smile conspiratorially. "A large army of renegade Egyptians is building forces to support us. It is led by a reckless man who is an estranged half-brother of that idiot Psamtik. The High Priests of Ammon do not like him—once he does what we want, we will dispose of him and take control."

"And this man, what is his name? Why is it that we have not heard of him?"

"Of course, we have heard of him. Remember all those conversations about potential rebels in the west? It is this man—he has been quiet and secretive all this time. The attack in Aostris? It was his doing."

"Did you have something to do with it?"

"I—" Jabari began, and suddenly Babak appeared from nowhere. Jabari made a quick sign to Eribaeus to change the topic. "The water will last for a few more days and we should be able to supply the army for our conquest."

Babak made quick strides to the overhang, ignoring the guards. Eribaeus waved them off, and the wiry Persian made his way. He looked frantic. Babak was also dressed strangely—he had tied a bright blue silk scarf to his neck, worn two shiny red bracelets on his wrists, and draped an ugly orange cloth to his waist. *Looks like a court jester,* Eribaeus thought.

"What are you wearing, you—," Jabari started, but Babak cut him off.

"His Excellency was wondering where you two are," he said, his eyes darting between the men.

"Jabari and I were lamenting this miserable journey. He was regaling me with tales of his youth," Eribaeus said, winking at Jabari.

Jabari made a lewd gesture, grabbing his crotch.

Babak ignored Jabari. Eribaeus knew that these two did not get along. There would be more to discuss with Jabari, but this was not the time.

"Must we join you?" asked Eribaeus.

Babak nodded.

"What is the urgency?" Jabari asked.

Babak looked at them both with a stern look on his face. "I do not know. He seeks you. There are some reports of movements beyond the bluff lines."

Eribaeus was alarmed. His eyes connected with Jabari's only for a moment, and then shifted to Babak. But Babak had caught their eye contact. Eribaeus cursed, but this was not the time to question Jabari. The men hurried down the gentle slope, kicking up sand in their wake, and walked briskly to Aberis' tent. The noble sat inside. Anger radiated from him.

"Where were you?" he asked.

"By the bluff, Your Excellency," Eribaeus said. Jabari nodded.

"We have reports of some movement, but it is not confirmed," Aberis said. But his eyes were now fixed on Babak.

"Are we being led into an ambush?" Jabari said, his eyes turned to Babak as well. *The gumption of this man*, thought Eribaeus. *A consummate actor.*

Babak looked pained. "Your Excellency, it is not unusual for scouts or even common folk to track an army on the move in the most unusual places," he said, ignoring Jabari. "These movements, can they confirm military columns or armed rebels?"

Aberis shifted on his feet. "No. Possible sightings of individuals."

Babak spread his hands and cocked his head, as if to indicate, *what did I say?*

"But you said before that the isolation here would afford protection, and now you say there could be scouts," said Jabari, not letting it go, pointing an accusatory finger at Babak.

"What are you implying? I never said no one would observe a marching column—I only said this would prevent obvious paths of ambush and large-scale attacks."

"Sure, you did—" began Jabari.

Aberis cut him off. "Enough. I am getting impatient of the two of you quarreling. If there is a traitor amongst us, I will find out and the man will wish he had never been born. But for now, let us prepare."

Babak glared at Jabari. Eribaeus considered what he could do—tell Aberis about what Jabari said? Curry the noble's favor and end Jabari once for all? The bastard Egyptian no doubt had something to do with these mysterious scouts. He was unable to complete the conversation with Jabari, but it would be too risky to go with him again... he would have to wait. Eribaeus knew that the good that would come of Jabari's demise would only last as long as the morning mist.

But on the other hand, talking to Babak and exploring what the wily Persian conspired would be helpful.

Aberis broke his chain of thought. "Send orders to double the sentries all along and send scouts with armed guards behind the ridge."

As the men scrambled to convey orders, Eribaeus made sure to step shoulder to shoulder with Babak.

"Babak," he said, "There is something I wish to discuss with you."

CHAPTER 33

THE GREAT SAND SEA

PERSIAN SCOUTS

The scout and four soldiers walked carefully down the sandy escarpment, their robes billowing in the slowly strengthening wind. The fine sand had begun to obscure the vision as the wind swept across the dunes, south to north, hitting them in the face from the side as they walked west. They were now beyond the army's visibility, hidden behind the swells of the dunes. So far, they had not seen anything—no moving shapes, no glints of metal, no grunts, neighs, or any sounds of beasts in employ, no footprints, and no debris left behind by intruders. The orders were to explore until only silence greeted them.

The soldiers grumbled incessantly. "There is nothing here," one man said. "We were entitled to our rest and here we are, dragging ourselves in this god-forsaken land."

"Let us just sit here. Let us wait for some time, and then just return."

"If anyone speaks of this, we will be left to die," another soldier

said, looking unsure.

"Who will?" one of them said, and they all laughed. The scout looked uncomfortable, but he had walked enough as well. What gods had he angered to endure this pointless mission when the others rested? They then agreed to a consistent story—nothing but sand, no sign of life, and that they had ventured far beyond. In fact, even beyond what their unit commander suggested.

They then ambled towards a rocky bluff with an overhang. It was shadowy underneath—a welcome. The men then clambered up a small steep slope to get to their destination, and once there, they rested their backs to the brittle, sandy shelf. Each man let out a happy sigh.

"If I could be here with my neighbor's wife instead of you," one of them said.

"And she would leave you and come to me instead," the scout said, making signs that suggested a gigantic penis.

"Mine stretches from here to Babylon," the third said, and so they went on, until one of them declared his penis would reach the end of the world and return. And then they closed their eyes. They hoped for a little nap away from all the noise, stench, and suffocating togetherness of the army.

It was then that the scout felt the sand beneath his feet move.

"What—?"

Before they could react, figures sprang from the shadows, quickly overpowering the men. About ten heavily armed Egyptians beat and kicked them. They disarmed and dragged them in a heap.

It took a while for the scout to come to his senses. They had tied his hands to the back. Finally, one of the Egyptians approached.

"What is the army preparing to do?" one of them asked. The powerfully built Egyptian spoke halting Persian. Somehow, they knew he was a scout, perhaps by his attire.

The scout shook his head. "We were just taking a stroll!"

The man nodded. In an instant, an Egyptian yanked back the head of one of the soldiers and cut his exposed neck. The other men shouted in fear. The soldier flopped about, clutching his throat as blood spurted and wet

the ground.

"Tell. We let you live. What is the army preparing to do?"

He looked frightfully at the men, his eyes frantically darting from one man to the other. These were not ordinary villagers. These were unquestionably trained soldiers.

Who were they?

"They are preparing to march ahead—"

The man nodded again. And then another soldier was rolling on the ground, making horrible noises with the sound of air escaping his severed throat. The scout sat shocked. Blood rushed into his ears.

"What is the army preparing to do?"

The scout evaluated his options and prayed to his gods. They would surely forgive him for what had he done to deserve a lonely death in a foreign land, sent away from the protection of his army. After all, he was just a scout, not a soldier!

And so, the scout shared what he knew.

CHAPTER 34

THE GREAT SAND SEA

JABARI

It had been a while and nothing untoward had happened. The scouts were out; some had returned with no news, and the sentries along the bluff and intermittent dunes reported nothing untoward. The sun had slowly begun to set, and bands of red, orange and blue suffused the sky. Jabari wondered how long they would have to be in this alert position.

He longed for more rest. He, along with several other officers, was near one of the pitted overhangs. It provided good cover.

That was when a loud whistle pierced the air. Startled, Jabari and the others turned to the source. To their left, at a distance, there appeared a sudden mass of men. They had emerged like ghosts from the sand, almost naked and with their swords and axes held high, rushing at a leisurely group of Syrians. And then screams arose to their right, and there they were, another mass, attacking. In an instant, the entire bluff line and dunes came to life as sand kicked from thousands of feet. An astonished Jabari scrambled to his feet and his guards surrounded him. The Egyptian had never struck another man with a blade, for his weapons were his words and deeds, and where he brought death it was by another's sword than his own. He ran down with the others, seeking cover. "Take me to safety!"

But all around them was mayhem. There was no question that the attackers were well armed Egyptians. Jabari could see his countrymen from where he was, from a distance where there was no conflict. The military units were still reacting, even as waves of attackers came running down the dunes, rushing headlong into Aberis' men. The Immortals, who were camped near Jabari, organized themselves at an impressive speed—creating a defensive line with their spears and swords out. They met the incoming armed men with savage ferocity, cutting them down, chopping their heads, and moving with grace. Jabari marveled at the Immortals. But how the others fared was unclear—the tired and exhausted soldiers fell in large numbers even as they grouped and fought. Jabari saw, even though the air obscured by dust and flying garments and limbs, that the outnumbered invaders were massacring the army. At one point, Jabari thought he saw a chariot in the distance, drawn by horses. *Petubastis?* He wondered. But his guards had formed a perimeter around him.

But just when he thought he was safe, a gang of Egyptians, perhaps forty to fifty, turned his way. They rushed past the busy soldiers and headed straight towards Jabari. A great panic rose in his chest. *Wait, no,* he screamed silently, looking frantically around to see if he had enough support. But even as the men came closer, a group of Immortals in their flowing orange robes dashed at them from the side, engaging the attackers. The clash of swords and spears was loud, but the men were still getting closer, their eyes mad with hate.

But I am with you!

His loins felt weak. Piss trickled down his thigh and he turned and ran. He hoped that the guards would bear the brunt and he would be far away. But everywhere around him were fighting men, and the evening light with suffocating sand and dust made it hard for him to see anymore, even as he dashed towards whatever space appeared before him. Jabari stumbled and fell, bruising his palms on the ground. He coughed as he inhaled the dust. He jerked with horror as a turbaned head rolled towards him. He sprang back to his feet, praying desperately for an escape.

But when he tried running, he saw a blur of blue and red by his side, and the man tripped Jabari who went flailing to the ground. He fell on his back and shouted in pain. His eyes burned with sand in them. He wiped his eyes and tried to get up.

But the man punched him in the face.

Jabari yelped.

Who—?

Babak!

What!

This unholy motherfucker!

"What are you—" he started, and Babak's fist rammed into his nose. Jabari rolled in pain, holding his face as blood flowed from his broken nose and dripped on the sand.

How does this wiry little bastard pack such a punch!

He felt a powerful kick on his ribs. Jabari gasped and turned with his back to the ground. Babak straddled the Egyptian who shouted and screamed for help. But his voice was lost in the cacophony of the skirmish, and no man paid heed in the melee and dust. Babak was surrounded by the attacking Egyptians and yet they made no move on him.

"What do you want!" Jabari spluttered even as his blood splayed with his words.

"How much did you enjoy watching my sons die?" Babak said, slapping Jabari. His ears rang like temple bells. Jabari clutched his ear.

"By the grace of Amun, what are you—"

Thwack! Babak hit him on the side of his skull and Jabari wailed.

"I. Know. What. You. Spoke. With. Eribaeus."

No, no, no, no, no.

"I don't know what you—"

"Remember Eshanna? I know that it was your idea to Eribaeus and Aberis to kill the men for amusement. Teach them an unforgettable lesson, you said, apparently," Babak growled.

Jabari jerked back in horror. He remembered Eshanna but had no idea that Babak's sons were there.

Babak put his fingers around Jabari's throat. The Egyptian could now see Babak's wild, yellow eyes, as if like a mad lion peering down at its prey. His words failed him as the pressure on the throat increased. He gasped and grunted, trying to respond. He tried to swing at Babak but realized that someone else had him pinned down—and it was not Babak.

What is going on?

"I know you were in touch with Petubastis!" Babak hissed. Jabari's vision began to darken, and his ears began to pound. *Babak knows Petubastis?*

Then Babak leaned closer to Jabari's ear, and his hot breath stank in his face. "I also know you had nothing to do with this ambush," Babak said, and the mad Persian smiled.

As his mind began to cloud, Jabari tried to make sense of it all. It was then that Babak reached to his belt and pulled out his dagger. Jabari's eyes widened, and he kicked around frantically. But Babak plunged the dagger deep into Jabari's chest.

A red-hot searing pain rose in Jabari's middle, and blood spurted like a fountain. Jabari's life passed by his eyes, and his fleeting final thought was a stunned wonder—*Babak is working with Petubastis?*

PART IV

CHAPTER 35
THE GREAT SAND SEA

ABERIS

Aberis swung and stabbed and hacked at the enemy. Aided by the Immortals, the noble showed his fighting prowess as he joined the men. During a brief lull, the messengers had communicated that the attack came in waves, and that the troops in various sections of the column were engaged. It was clear that the marauders were not as great in number as his army, and they had concentrated their forces on the areas near the baggage trains. Few had tried to attack the head of the column, which caused Aberis to muster his forces and chase down the enemy further down. But the attack had wreaked havoc—as evidenced by the dead, the dying, the upturned carts, running asses and camels, chaotic fighting formations, and wailing runners.

The Egyptians, he noticed, were a mix of hardened warriors and peasants. Some fought with the grace of dancers, and others rushed headlong like mad fools onto thrust spears and swords. But the surprise, the hostile terrain, the exhaustion, all had caused great suffering to his large army. In another terrain, perhaps in the flatlands of Syria or even the ravines of Cappadocia, this attack would be destroyed. But as it is the nature of such events, the battle began to die at sunset. The remaining Egyptians ran back to the dunes with few in pursuit. Aberis' men had no strength to run across the sandy sea with no certainty that a greater trap did not lay in wait beyond what they saw. Eventually, whistles pierced the air signaling an end to hostilities, and the units began the grim task of accounting for the dead and loss to supplies. Tired, bloody, and with entrails of the bastards still stuck to his torso and thighs, Aberis walked the partial length of the column, exhorting his men to stay strong, offering words of encouragement, recommending rewards, signaling those that must be painlessly executed, and admonishing commanders that looked defeated.

He was also particularly anxious about his own treasure cart. Had that been attacked? Looted? He had dispatched his most loyal Immortal commander to ensure that his possessions were safe. He was relieved to find out that the secret was safe.

Once his rounds were complete, Aberis summoned many of his senior officers and advisors. The noble was livid and had worked up a fine rage as they assembled in his tent, now billowing under a strong wind that picked up sand and compounded their misery. The men huddled under an oil-lamp, the dull orange glow reflecting on the dirty, bloodied, sweaty, and sticky bodies.

Aberis. Eribaeus. Babak. Ritapates. And several commanders of various units.

"How could this happen? What were those motherless scouts and sentries doing! How did no one catch this?" he screamed, his imperial nose and deeply set eyes creating an intimidating visage.

The men remained silent. Aberis quickly turned to Babak. "You said there would be no attack! You said they could be just scouts!"

Babak bowed. "I did, Your Excellency. And I was wrong. This was deliberate and willful treachery."

Aberis was immobile. *Treachery perpetrated by whom?* "And how do we know you were not the one that led us to this?"

"How could I possibly engineer such an attack, Your Excellency, and why? What connection could I have with whoever these men were?"

"Well, we will find out, won't we?" Aberis said, ominously, as he turned to an officer near the entry.

Babak stood straight. "But I know who the traitor is, Your Excellency," he said.

Aberis' head whipped back. "What?"

Eribaeus shifted on his feet. Ritapates was immobile.

Aberis stared at Babak. This strange and wiry man— there was something about him. Aberis had struggled to recollect when he may have encountered Babak before and in what capacity, but the fleeting memories

escaped him.

"Well?"

"Who is not here, Your Excellency?"

Aberis turned to look at the faces.

And then he furrowed his brows, thinking.

It eventually dawned on him.

How can it be!

"Where is Jabari?" Aberis asked.

"Dead," Babak said. "He attacked me during the fight, and before that he was proposing to find a way to end your march—tell him, Eribaeus!"

Eribaeus head jerked like a scorpion had stung his cheek. Aberis turned to the Greek and gripped his throat like an iron vise.

What is the Greek trying to do! These sons of mongrels!

"I had nothing to do with this, Your Excellency!" Eribaeus squawked, fighting with Aberis' grip. "Nothing! Please let me speak."

Aberis let him go. But he ordered two officers to disarm the Greek and hold him. Eribaeus, cocky and confident just a moment ago, looked frightened like a boy. He looked around anxiously, searching the faces

of the men that now looked at him with suspicion.

"Your life depends on what you say," said Aberis, whispering as his temples throbbed.

Who do I believe?

Eribaeus nodded energetically. His pale face had turned bright red, and his curly brown hair fell on his eyes. "Jabari came to me with a proposal, Your Excellency. He said he had connections with the priests of Ammon and that he had established communications with a renegade Pharaoh of this region!"

Aberis sucked his breath.

Dogs! Cowards and treasonous piglets borne of common whores!

"And?"

"I had nothing to do with it, Your Excellency! I was as surprised to hear as you are now. I promptly relayed it to Babak," he said, his eyes searching Babak's face.

Babak stepped forward. "He did, Your Excellency. And before we could decide what to do with the information, the men Jabari sold us out to, attacked."

Aberis berated them, but he knew that not much could be done. If they were telling the truth, then there was no time to relay and prepare, for the attack was already underway.

Babak continued. "My intention to come this way was to avoid what we experienced. But this ugly man, a man who shared our tent and trust, would not let go of his ambition. He sought to become the new High Priest and influence the future of this Kingdom, Your Excellency, and you had no place in it."

Aberis continued to stare. "How do I know you both are not lying?"

Eribaeus, encouraged by the change in tone and Babak's intervention, spoke up. "He knew the priests, he knew the renegade Pharaoh, and he even suggested that the Persians will abandon the Greeks and therefore it would be in my best interest to align with him. But I paid no heed to it, Aberis, Your Excellency, for my loyalty is to you and the King of Kings!"

"Let him go," Aberis said, after contemplating. If Jabari was truly the culprit, and it seemed like he was—for who else had such a connection to other Egyptians—then an imminent threat was over. But one never knew how deep the rot was, or if the poison of treachery had spread.

Eribaeus, relieved, wanted to do no more in the tent. The unctuous Greek bowed to Aberis. "Your Excellency, there is much to be done, may we leave?"

Aberis considered what to do, and he was not done yet. "Not yet, Eribaeus. What fool would I be if I just relied on words?"

As they waited nervously, Aberis whispered to one of his guards who stepped out. In that shaking tent, the men stood quietly with not a word spoken, until the flaps rustled. Aberis asked that everyone step out of the tent.

And there, tied and beaten, lay several Egyptians— enemies.

Captives.

The unfortunates who survived.

"Let us find out if these wretched scoundrels know something," Aberis said, appraising Babak and Eribaeus. He then turned to one of his guards and ordered the logistics and supply masters to report to him.

"Let us begin, shall we?" he said, as a masked torturer stepped into the scene, holding the most unholy instruments to inflict horror upon the hapless men.

CHAPTER 36
THE GREAT SAND SEA

PETUBASTIS

Pharaoh Petubastis lay on his back, resting against the cool rock. His muscles ached, and his thigh throbbed from a broad gash inflicted by an enemy sickle. Physicians had patched it with poultice and herbs, but the pain pulsed through him. General Senwosret sat beside him—the man was invincible, thought Petubastis, for Senwosret had not a nick on him, and he continued to energetically dispense orders to the men. The news was not encouraging, and they were just completing the assessment of their raid. Petubastis groaned as he stood, and two aides came running to support him. The Pharaoh swatted them away and hobbled to his small makeshift tent—he had sworn not to rest in luxury while his men braved the sand and winds. Inside, he took a sip of water and wiped his blood-crusted chest and torso. He then rubbed his skull and sat on his reed stool.

It felt good.

After a while Senwosret joined him in the tent. The General was in a good mood, hiding whatever anxiety in his belly.

"Assessment?" asked the Pharaoh.

"We have lost half the army, Petubastis. And a third more injured not be able to fight anytime soon."

Petubastis sighed. "If only they had not caught sight of some of our men," he said.

"It would have made little difference, Your Majesty. Perhaps let us inflict a little more damage, but it would not prevent our losses. They have a much larger force, better trained, even if they are exhausted and caught by surprise."

The Pharaoh nodded. His men had fought bravely. Fanatically. But many were peasants, teachers, carpenters, tool-workers, and some were even priests. Many were only boys. And yet they had stayed by his side and fought bravely. Most of the casualties were these poorly trained soldiers—for most of his best fighters had made it back, after conducting lightning raids and running away. The enemy had no strength to pursue.

But for now, he would have to rest and recoup and rebuild the army. The question was, had he inflicted a mortal wound on the snake that slithered through the desert?

"How much did we hurt them?" he asked.

"The men estimate many thousands dead, more than us. You saw them, Your Majesty, they fought like men with no strength in them. They prevailed due to their numbers, not their skill or will. We also cut loose and killed many of their cart animals, broke a great many water pots, and spilled their grain in the sand. And here," Senwosret said, sweeping his hands, "that means a death sentence."

"Do you think they got our spies inside?" Petubastis asked.

"We do not know, Your Majesty. The men were aware of whom to spare, if they recognized them, but in the dust and madness of battle, who knows..." Senwosret's voice trailed away.

"We must regain our strength. But for now, let us wait a day, and let us strip the fallen of whatever belongings and metals that we can use as supply," the Pharaoh said.

"Yes, Your Majesty. Perhaps they will depart in a hurry, leaving us with a rich field to pick from."

"Were we able to find out where the treasure carts were?" he asked, hopefully.

Senwosret looked at his feet. "No, Your Majesty. It is guarded somewhere closer to where their noble is. And besides, we are certain that the Immortals are with him."

"We anticipated this outcome. We have achieved far more than we hoped, biting the Persian beast and letting it bleed to death slowly. Do you think our man knows what to do next?"

"We can only hope, Your Majesty," Senwosret said, and they smiled at each other.

CHAPTER 37

THE GREAT SAND SEA

BABAK

Babak stood stoically as the men before him screamed and begged for mercy. The torturer knew his trade; after each question to the victim, asking him to identify and explain who was helping them from the Persian side, and when unsatisfied with the answer, he would slice off a body part. And thus, he began with the ears, the nose, a piece of the lips, and then he gouged an eye, as the man writhed and shouted, and yet he gave no name and shared no secret.

And when the effort yielded no result, the torturer sliced the man's belly and let his entrails hang and let the writhing soul lie on the sand. He then moved to the next, and so it went on for four men, who were either brave, mad, or truly innocent.

But the fifth man had a story to tell. He had soiled himself. His eyes were wide open with fear. Drool dribbled from his broken lips. His face was bloody, a result of smashing fists.

"Who was helping you?" Aberis asked, grabbing the man's chin, and lifting his face.

The man flinched and stuttered. A translator stood close by.

"What is he saying?" Aberis asked the translator.

"He says two men," the man said.

Aberis smiled.

Babak's heart beat harder. His stomach was tight in knots, and he hoped that in the flickering flames of the lamps no one would notice his demeanor.

"Who, who two men?" Aberis shouted. His eyes had a manic glee, and they reflected the light. Aberis was fifty years of age, and yet the hard campaigns and brutality of his life had not diminished the fire within him. The chance to uncover a conspiracy and make the perpetrators pay gave him boundless joy. More than once, Babak had witnessed the noble crucify hundreds of men and women if he believed they crossed him. Cruelty was his hallmark, compared to some others in the court who exercised judgment in what they meted out to their perceived enemies.

"Priest. Priest."

"What?"

"Priest. Egyptian."

Aberis stepped back, confused. He turned to the others.

"What Egyptian Priest?"

"Jabari. Your Excellency," Babak said. "He performed ceremonies in Sais and Memphis before joining the King of King's campaign."

Aberis clenched his fist. Babak could not make out the expression in the dark shadows and the play of light.

"Yes, yes, I know. You don't have to lecture me. That pig-fucker," he swore under his breath. "I wish he were still alive."

Aberis took a deep breath and looked around. Only a bluish tinge remained on the horizon, and all around them was deathly stillness except the wails of the dying and the tortured.

"You gave me one. What about the other?"

The man looked up with his one good eye, the other swollen and shut. His lips were bloodied and broken, but words still came from them. He said something, but Aberis could not hear. Blood rushed into Babak's ears and his heart thundered.

"What are you saying. Speak loudly!" Aberis shouted.

Babak stepped back into the shadows, but the man's good eye followed him.

To Babak's frustration, an attendant brought another flame closer, illuminating the men standing in the circle— Aberis, Babak, Eribaeus, Ritapates, and a few other senior officers. The man looked at Babak and nodded gently. Babak's breath felt like molten iron, burning his lungs as he waited for the man to speak.

The man exerted himself. "The Pale One," he said. "The Pale…"

"The Pale One?" Aberis repeated the translator. "What does he mean?"

Babak noticed the look of horror in Eribaeus' face—but the Greek did not react, lest he draws suspicion to himself.

Babak leaned towards Aberis. "Your Excellency," he whispered.

Aberis whipped his head back in irritation. "What is it?"

"They refer to the Greeks as Pale Ones."

Eribaeus was straining to hear what Babak said.

Aberis recoiled as if in shock. "Everyone! Leave us," he ordered. "Only Babak and I stay here."

Eribaeus could no longer control himself. "Your Excellency, I—" he began.

"Step back!" Aberis shouted, his voice sharp and urgent. Eribaeus retreated along with the others. Babak and Aberis now hunched near the man.

"Tell us and we will end this quickly for you," Babak said, as he squeezed the man's shoulder. Aberis seemed irritated by this gesture but made no comment.

"Go on," Aberis commanded, impatiently.

"They say he is a nobleman. Mercenary. Hates the King," the man said.

Aberis cast a baleful glance at Eribaeus, who now sulked in a corner. He turned to Babak. "That bastard."

"I always suspected him, but had no proof of his mischief, Your Excellency. The wretched were amongst us," Babak said, his face scrunched with dramatic anger. "This man has been true to his word."

Aberis was lost in thought. And then he turned to the man again. "Have you seen this man? What else do you know?"

The man sputtered and struggled. Babak rose and fetched a cup of water and let him drink. They waited for him to recover. By then, the screams of the others had died down, and their bodies had stopped twitching.

"He would help capture you if possible. I know nothing else, Your Excellency. I am a lowly lieutenant," he said, and his shoulders shuddered.

"We know what we needed to know," Aberis said, and spat on the ground. He turned his back to confer with a commander from the Immortals.

Babak bent close to condemned man's ears. "Pray," he whispered. "Pray now. Amun will bless you in the afterlife."

The man nodded and bowed. And before Aberis could ask something new, or change his subject, Babak swiftly retrieved his dagger and stabbed the man, holding his neck and pushing the head to his shoulder—as if in an embrace. A gentle sigh escaped the man's lips as he collapsed and died.

Aberis reacted, but it was too late. "Why did you kill him?" He shouted.

"We made a promise to him, Your Excellency, forgive me for acting hastily."

Aberis glared at Babak. "Next time ask me before you decide to execute one of my prisoners," he admonished Babak, but the tone said Aberis no longer cared.

He turned to the men and announced loudly. "Kill the rest of them. Let the men rest for a few hours and then we move."

Eribaeus, curious, tried to come closer again but was sent away. He left, fuming.

Aberis turned to Babak. "Walk with me. Tell Ritapates to join us. We need to decide how to deal with that snake."

It was a delicate affair. Jabari was disposable, but Eribaeus was not. He commanded an entire battalion of mercenaries, and he wielded great influence.

"I want to flay that shit-eating bug and leave him to dry in the desert," Aberis muttered. "To think that cunning maggot has been with me all these years."

"His men follow him without question, Your Excellency. If you kill him, we will have unrest in our hands. The Greeks are hardy men, you need them. The *Shahanshah* favors them as well."

Aberis nodded. He wiped his shoulders and continued to walk with no destination in mind. "Life would be simpler if men had loyalty to a cause and stayed on the course like how the sun rises and sets every day, don't you think, Babak?"

"Indeed, Your Excellency," Babak said.

"We have to decide how to deal with him. Let him sweat. We will watch him. And when the time is right, I will end him."

They had strayed farther from the tents, walking on a sandy, undulating ground. It was cool to the feet, shifting, sliding, grainy, but pleasant. It felt like walking in thick honey, except the consistency was coarse and prickly. Aberis was lost in thought. He finally turned to Babak.

"Once we get back, we have the grim task of assessing our losses and planning our next march," he said.

"Yes, Your Excellency."

Aberis suddenly slapped Babak on his shoulders, causing him to flinch. "I remember you at Pelusium, but surely our paths crossed before?"

Babak was alarmed. The hairs on his neck rose. *I cannot say I did not meet him,* Babak realized. What man would not remember meeting a distinguished noble? "I was in your campaigns in the Levant—"

"Before that. Before. When did you first join the King of King's force?" Aberis stared intently at Babak. His imperial face was like a hawk's, and even in this hard march, Aberis maintained a distinguished look. The sides of his eyes crinkled, and his mouth curled up in a knowing smile.

Babak's heart thudded—not because the noble asked when.

Not because he had to struggle to recollect.

But because the day was so clear, burned in his eyes, scarred in his heart, and dug deep in his belly. That day, three years ago, when the people of Eshanna filed out of the citadel walls, ready to face Aberis' men.

CHAPTER 38
ESHANNA, THREE YEARS AGO
BABAK

So, there they stood, all two-thousand unarmed men, women, and children. In the hot sun and humid air, they faced rows of armed soldiers. Babak had twice tried to get closer to the noble, who sat on a horse near his front line, wearing his full military regalia. The guards had pushed him back. The pathetic bunch, in dirty, tattered clothes, with barely an able-bodied young man amongst them, waited for what might come next. Some children cried, and their anxious mothers tried to pacify them, worrying about the wrath of soldiers.

Babak knew they were being punished.

They had been under this sun for the last hour, and they had been met with silence and only glares of the army. No one could move or rest. A few elders and some women had fainted, but they were left on the ground. Some relieved themselves where they stood. Babak's face felt hot and sticky, and he could feel Roxana's trembling fingers in his palm. Amastri clung to her mother.

Their sons were among a group of men and boys tied and made to line up along the banks of the marsh. Babak had managed to catch a glimpse of them as they were trotted out. Some of the men were beaten as they walked.

They are peasants and boys!

But Babak had resisted the urge to run or shout out their names. He had seen this before—and any act of emotion would be met with swift brutality, often leading to the death of every member of the family. Babak had whispered to his crying wife's ears. "Be strong and be quiet. Or we will all die. And that might be the best outcome."

Finally, an announcer ambled to the midpoint between the standing townspeople and the soldiers. He placed a small wooden platform on the ground and stood atop.

"People of Eshanna," he said. His voice was loud and clear, and it carried well into the crowd. "His Excellency Aberis has made this long journey on behalf of the King of Kings, he who is blessed by Ahuramazda."

Aberis made a dismissive gesture by twirling his wrists, and continued to tug on his lustrous, coiffured beard. *Must give him great pleasure to terrorize helpless villagers*, thought Babak.

The man continued. "You have rebelled against the King. There are consequences."

Babak heart skipped a beat. Rebellion was a dangerous word.

Some people in the group began to wail, and some began shouting that they were innocent. The announcer raised his hand and shouted at them to be quiet.

"Where is Angash?"

The crowd was silent. People looked at each other, unsure what to say, and many craned their necks to see where their chief was. Babak waited to see what would happen.

"Angash?" The announcer spoke louder. "Come forward and kneel!"

But no one came forward. Aberis was clearly irritated—he expected a pliant man to come running.

Finally, Babak raised his hands and stepped forward, leaving his wife and daughter behind. "I represent Eshanna," he said, speaking slowly and gently.

The announcer looked at him quizzically. "Are you Angash?"

"No. Angash left the town abruptly. He left us to face you."

The announcer walked to Aberis and they spoke. Eventually the noble ordered something, but he did not get down from his horse.

"Who are you?" The announcer asked.

"My name is Agakhi," Babak said. "Some call me Bab—"

The man barely registered what Babak said. "What is your role? How are you related to Angash?"

"I am the town administrator and Angash was the lord. In his absence, I will negotiate with the noble."

The man's swarthy face broke into a broad grin. He trotted back to Aberis, and Babak saw that another man had joined Aberis by his side.

A Greek man.

They all conferred and laughed. Eventually the announcer came to Babak and bowed. "You may proceed. His Excellency wishes to speak."

Babak felt thousands of eyes on him as he walked. He approached Aberis and the Greek man. He knelt. Then he removed his turban but kept his eyes firmly on the ground, waiting for an order.

"You say you are the town administrator. Can anyone corroborate?" The firm voice was the noble's. Babak did not look at him. He nodded.

"If we find out you are lying, it will be a very slow death, do you understand?"

"Yes, Your Excellency."

"You know why we are here."

"Yes, Your Excellency."

"And why do you think we will negotiate?"

"The King of Kings and Your Excellency are merciful—"

Aberis cut him off. It was almost as if the noble had no interest in anything he had to say or offer. Babak saw the horse's feet turn and Aberis had moved away, leaving him alone with the Greek.

"Be glad he did not chop off your head, you donkey," the Greek said, enunciating the language well.

What were foreign mercenaries doing here?

Babak said nothing in return.

"Eribaeus, come back," the noble called, and the Greek turned his horse and trotted away.

The negotiator, a tall, uniformed man who did not give his name, now stood in front of Babak. "Get up," he said. "We will negotiate terms and I will relay them to the noble for approval."

"Yes, sir," Babak said, rising to his feet. His thighs and back hurt from having stood for so long and now kneeling. *My age is showing*, he thought.

Babak stepped back as the negotiator clasped his hands. "What did you say your name was?"

"Agakhi."

"You are appointed to negotiate on behalf of the elders?"

"In the town chief's absence. Yes."

"Your role?

I already told you, idiot.

Babak was secretly pleased that the Court had even bothered to negotiate. Before Cyrus' time it usually meant burning the village and carting off people as slaves or servants. Such tactics had reduced, for they created great resentment and impacted tax and grain collection. So, the new approach was to punish the people, just enough so, and keep them working in gratitude for the mercy bestowed upon them by the rulers.

"Administrator. I manage tax records, collection, complaints—"

The negotiator cut him off. "Fine. What are your terms?"

"We begged the King for a reduction in taxes this year due to poor harvest. Besides, a sickness swept over the town and killed many farmers, reducing our production. If we send the allocated quantity, then we will starve."

"But you killed the collector."

"It was an acci—"

"A collector sent by the Court. That is rebellion."

Rebellion. That term. Again. Such a message, if allowed to take root, was deadly.

"No, sir. It was a few hotheads, desperate and frustrated. The town kneels to the King and the people have no desire to be anything than loyal citizens."

"You never handed them over," he said, accusatorily. Babak squinted to look behind him—Aberis and the Eribaeus sat next to each other on the horses. An Egyptian was next to them.

What is an Egyptian doing here?

"They ran. Those fools knew the consequences of such impudence."

"And you did not see it fit to have them arrested in the first place. You let them go."

Babak bristled. "It was not in my authority, sir, the chief under whose watch it happened was dismissed."

The negotiator was doing no negotiations. It was an interrogation—but to what end, Babak was not sure.

What did they want?

"Well, here are the terms," he said, with dramatic flair. From an ornamental bag in his waist he pulled out a clay-slate with fine writings on it. "The King demands this."

Babak bowed.

"You will receive reprieve this year, but you will make up for grain next year."

Babak was surprised.

"You will identify, and if you cannot, we will choose ten people from the town and execute them as an example."

He inhaled sharply—not out of terror, but by surprise. Only ten? That was a departure from the past. Perhaps Cambyses would continue Cyrus' policies.

The negotiator's eyes scanned his tablet. "One more thing," he said. "The town will pledge never to question the Court's assessments, on pain of extermination."

Babak nodded vigorously. He looked at the mass of his townspeople. He knew they waited anxiously for what was about to happen.

"We accept," he said, trying hard not to show his relief. "We deeply thank the Great—"

The negotiator lifted his hand, as if to silence Babak. His dark eyes bore into his, and the gold ring on his finger glinted off the afternoon sun. "There is one more thing."

Babak's heart stopped.

"Yes?"

"The noble had to recruit Greek mercenaries to come here from far away. They must be paid."

Babak said nothing. *Pay them with what?*

"What could a poor town pay them with, sir? May I beg the chance to discuss terms with the noble?"

The negotiator stared down Babak. He was taller, bigger, and the cap on his head was intimidating. "A sparrow does not negotiate with an eagle, Agakhi."

"Please, this town—"

"Go back and wait for your orders!" he screamed, his hot breath in full blast on Babak's face. Babak scrambled back to the waiting group and rushed to his wife and daughter. He pulled them to the front but let them stand behind him. There was much distance between him and the troops, and he could only make out the figures of Aberis, Eribaeus, and a few others talking to each other, laughing, and gesturing to the negotiator. Eventually the negotiator left and vanished behind the soldiers, and a half-naked Greek commander, wearing one of their skirts, stepped forward. He walked menacingly to Babak. A Spartan mask covered his face, and he held a long spear in his hand.

"You," he said, pointing to Babak, who stepped forward.

"Tell them. No run. No shout. No protest," he said, in broken Persian. His eyes shone with glee. Babak turned to the people and gestured for a few to come forward and carry the message to the rest.

Thwack!

His ears and cheek stung from a sharp slap. Babak turned and the Greek screamed at him. "Hurry!"

Burning shame and anger exploded in Babak, but he kept his composure.

Not here. Not now.

Babak quickly issued instructions. They would have to bear the burden. The King had forgiven this year. They had to pay for the mercenaries (but he did not say what). There would be a punishment (but he left out the executions). And no one should protest, run, or scream—or it would get worse. As the message spread there was some murmur, a few smiles even, and several shouts of glory to the King and some got on their knees to pray. There were audible sighs and cry of relief.

Oh, you poor people, thought Babak. He felt guilty for having left a few details out, but it was necessary to preserve everyone's lives. But his sons? He could see his elder son in the group that was kneeling near the marsh. The younger was not visible. Some of the older men had fallen to the side. Why were they not being released?

And then there was a whistle. The Greek grabbed Babak by the arms and said, "Come. Watch."

Instinctually, Babak grabbed his wife's hand, but the Greek hit his hand. "Only you."

Babak ran along with the Greek, who stopped near the first line of soldiers. They waited. And then there was another whistle. Three rows of soldiers jogged towards the frightened mass of people. They systematically surrounded the huddling mass, with each soldier situating himself a few feet from the other and ensuring that an impenetrable ring around the frightened and whimpering people. Babak could hear them, but they were brave, and were not yet panicking.

Then another group jogged towards the citadel gates. Babak knew why. The town would be ransacked for their belongings—all their life's savings would be gone. If they were lucky the houses would not be set to fire. This is how the Royal Court treated its own people, obedient for decades, in service of its ambitions, for just one infraction. The soldiers vanished behind the gates as the people watched in despair. Some wept, but others suppressed their anguish. As the mercenaries ransacked the town, the soldiers began to separate the men and women, and resistance was met with beatings. Babak watched in horror, but the Greek next to him only grunted, "For safety." Soon, the townspeople were in two large pools—men and boys, and women and children. All corralled in two large sections surrounded by soldiers.

And then they waited.

The sun continued to glide across the humid sky. The air became sticky and buzzed with bugs and insects from the marsh. More people fainted, more relieved themselves where they stood, children wailed and cried, and mothers begged the soldiers for some relief.

There was none.

Then smoke rose from beyond the walls of the citadel. First in one place, and then in another, and then another. Soon, the tips of flames were visible beyond the walls, and Babak saw several soldiers shout in glee, laughing, clapping. The Greek next to Aberis was smiling, but the noble himself looked bored. Soon, the men who had entered began pouring out, hooting, carrying sacks of loot, and some dragging people who had tried to hide. Babak hoped that some of the gold and silver he had hidden under the floor would remain undetected, giving his family a chance to survive. He and his boys would have to break their backs to rebuild what they had lost in an instant.

The soldiers carried their loot to the center and heaped it. It was a pile, but surely disappointing given the size of the town. What glory did the noble seek by robbing farmers, weavers, metalsmiths, barbers, fruit sellers, and cleaners?

Aberis and Eribaeus then inspected what the soldiers got. They looked unhappy; the Greek was shaking his head and becoming increasingly angry as he gestured at the huddled people. Aberis was arguing, but Babak could make none of it. Eventually they seemed to calm down, and then their smile returned.

"Who is your lord?" Babak asked the Greek next to him. "He must be powerful to have the noble's ear."

The Greek looked back, and grinned. "Eribaeus. He is a nobleman and commands our units. You Persians need us to teach you how to fight."

Babak silently lamented at the noble's use of wretched foreigners to destroy his own. Such was the fecklessness of politics. Then Aberis and Eribaeus conferred with two captains—one Persian and one Greek. And then suddenly two full units began to jog to the huddled mass—and Babak watched in a panic the people were all pushed together again into a dense mass, pushed on all sides by soldiers. They stood on uncomfortable, grassy, thorny ground.

Then there were murmurs.

And then the screams and shouts began.

Soldiers were reaching out and pulling out random people—old men, young men, boys, women, girls—there was no pattern to it.

"What are they doing?" Babak asked the Greek next to him.

"Watch," he said, and grinned.

Soon, a hundred hapless, shivering bunch was driven towards the already kneeling group of about fifty men and boys. They were then ordered to stand-up. The Greek pushed Babak and made him walk to this group.

This is it! The end! Why?

He tried pleading with the Greek to no effect. And when he neared the group, someone clubbed him on the back causing him to collapse and scream in pain.

There was some silence.

And then he heard Aberis' gravelly voice. "This is what happens to the insolent. The empire wipes them like the bugs they are," his voice was cold and firm.

Babak did not turn.

"Now, watch. Remember this day. Let your town never forget under whose mercy they live, and let you remember your masters."

Babak nodded. He realized that Aberis was still on his horse, right behind him, so close that he could feel the animal's breath.

"Why don't you enjoy this, townsman, for this will make you feared!" That voice was the Greek's—the man called Eribaeus. His accent was thick, and he chuckled at the end of it.

My sons. My sons are there!

Babak turned slowly, still bowed. He knelt and placed his head to the ground. "O' glorious nobles, blessed by Ahuramazda, beloved of the King, my sons are there, by the grace of the benevolent god and king, I beg you! They are children and they have done no wrong."

There was silence. Then the Greek spoke. "Your sons are where?"

"In that group," Babak said, pointing to the frightened men and women who now stood near the edge where the reedy marsh began.

"Even better! Those little urchins will not grow up to be arrogant and useless like the men of this town!" said Eribaeus, and Aberis laughed. "Let this day be the iron brand on your heart, townsman."

Babak suppressed his tears, but a pure incandescent rage grew in him, spreading like a flame under a dry grass-roof, filling every organ, every nook and crevice. It soared to his head, and it engulfed his belly. He shook and shuddered but knew that to show any emotion would mean certain death to him, and his wife and daughter, for they would not stop. The dark brownish ground absorbed his tears and spittle.

"Get up, you bastard, negotiating, indeed!" shouted Aberis, and a soldier kicked Babak in the ribs. He stood and was forced to face the group. Now that he had revealed that his sons were there, these cruel men would no doubt force him to watch what was about to transpire. At the sound of a whistle a line of archers, a mix of Greeks and Persians jogged towards the bewildered mass. Some of the condemned began to shift on their feet and others began to shout. But they had nowhere to run, surrounded by soldiers with long spears and backing up to a watery, reed and dead wood-filled marsh. The archers took a position at a distance and stood silently, waiting for the next order. And then, the mass of the townspeople was driven closer, to be spectators of what would be meted out to their brothers, sons, fathers, mothers, daughters. They were now not too far away, still held back by three rows of soldiers and enforcers with clubs.

After a few beatings and announcements, the population finally became silent and watched in terror as Aberis stepped down from the horse. Babak was finally able to see the noble as he walked ahead, his flowing robes trailing behind him as he stepped on a stool placed in front of the archers.

"Listen to my words, people of Eshanna. The King has granted you mercy. I have granted you life. But a lesson must be taught, and such disobedience merits punishment. May no man or woman forget this day, and may you thank Ahuramazda for your return to rebuild your homes today."

The few sobs and prayers were swiftly shut down by others. Aberis continued. "These people," he said, pointing to those standing by the marsh, "they have attempted to raise their hands on us, and they have attempted to run from us. And some of them have been chosen by the finger of god. And they have a choice. May you witness this today, people of Eshanna, and may you remember!"

With that, Aberis stepped down and walked back, and his hard eyes never once even looked at the people or Babak in pity. Then, it was Eribaeus who stepped to the stool. He addressed the condemned group near the marsh.

"You. Today you will decide your fate, just as you decided the King's collector's," he began, amplifying his soft voice. "At the whistle, you will run to the marshes. At the count of ten, the archers will let loose their arrows. If you survive the marshes until night and escape the arrows, you will live."

Once his message sunk in, a great cry of anguish rose in the air. The relatives made noise, but they all knew that to make a move would only lead to greater suffering. Some soldiers laughed and others looked on quietly. Babak's temple pounded in tension and stress.

My sons!

The condemned had registered the message. By then, several of the older men and women had already been exhausted and were lying down and paid no heed to the words. The younger looked back at the marshes, calculating their odds. Some others simply stood and wept, their shoulders heaving. But as a group they showed great bravery—there was absent any hysterics, and no one begged for mercy. Babak finally got a glimpse of his younger son, only ten, holding the hand of his brother. Babak's heart broke at the sight. Hot tears streamed down his cheeks and acid rose up to his throat. The boys stood stoically. Babak placed a hand on his heart and prayed Ahuramazda to grant them eternal happiness.

And then loud whistles rented the air, and the announcer began.

"Ten!"

Babak again tried to run, but this time another man gripped him by his arm and pulled him back. It was a tall, well-built Greek soldier. He leaned and hissed in Babak's ear. "Do not get your family killed, Persian. Do not run."

Babak looked at him. There was kindness in those eyes. "Do not run. Let those who remain behind live. I know my lord. Please stay where you are," the man said.

Babak nodded slowly as the Greek relaxed his grip. "Pray for them," he said, and then stepped back.

"Come back, Danofis!" Babak heard Eribaeus call. And Danofis vanished from the scene. His words were the only acts of kindness all morning.

Some of them near the marshes turned and began to scout for a place to run. Of those fallen, some struggled to rise to the feet, and a few others collapsed again.

"Nine."

A few men held some women's hands, trying to lead them. They stumbled and turned, trying to run towards the marsh. One old man stood up and began to curse.

"Eight."

Babak's boys held their hands and carefully made their way to the left side, to a dryer path that led deeper into the marsh where the water began. It was a short path, and they were with a few adults.

"Seven."

The cursing old man now rushed at the soldiers, screaming for their death and the noble's. As he gesticulated wildly and limped forward, a laughing Greek soldier stepped forward and stabbed him with a spear. The elder collapsed, his thin, bony body thudded on the ground and he was still. Babak's boys were beginning to jog, still not too far away.

"Six."

Suddenly four young men turned and ran towards the soldiers. They were swift, and one managed to grab a spear and tried to wrestle it, but he was quickly hacked away by two swords-wielding soldiers. The others were quickly hacked or impaled. The soldiers were clearly enjoying watching the panicked people trying to go deeper into the marsh, trying to go outside the range of the arrows. But it was a cruel path. The water rose quickly, and they were all barefoot. Sharp dead wood rose from the ground. Many had stumbled already, and some were screaming in pain or terror, as they were pierced from below or began to sink in the dark muddy waters.

"Five."

Some had vanished behind short reeds, where many others, having seen the fate of their fellows, still scrambled to find safety. A few simply turned and came back to face the archers—but they knelt and sat simply. Giving up.

"Four."

Babak's boys were further away. It was harder for him to see them, but there they were still holding hands, walking resolutely, their bodies half submerged. But they were not moving anymore.

Move. Move. Run. Hide! Do something!

"Three."

The boys were still not moving. Babak strained to see why, even as he ignored the cries and laments and taunts all around. There were some men in front of the boys, blocking their way.

"Two."

Those remaining on the banks—some stood unsure, others knelt, a few others continued to scramble looking for places to run or hide, but there were few and none offered enough protection. The boys suddenly turned. They were clearly visible. He could not make out their expressions, but they stood tall and proud. And they then began to walk back towards the archers.

"No! No!" Babak began to shout, and a few Greeks behind mocked him, repeating his words.

"Be quiet, or it will be the rest of your family next if they are still alive," warned the negotiator who was next to him. Babak's lips quivered and he suppressed his sorrow.

"One."

By then the sounds had almost died. Those who found station stayed there, those who were walking continued to do so without a word, and those flailing in the waters continued. Some had already drowned. But most simply stood, staring into nothingness, waiting.

And then the soldiers let loose the arrows. The bolts whizzed high in the air, arcing gracefully before beginning their murderous descent on the hapless. The first arrows struck those waiting in the front, piercing through the flesh, and in some instances knocking the victims off their feet.

Men and women began to run in no sensible pattern—tripping, falling. The next set flew in the air, and Babak strained to see his sons. And there they were, still walking slowly, coming towards him.

No, no, no.

Then the arrows swooped down, striking the boys in their chests, thighs, smashing into them with brute violence. They collapsed without a sound, and in the rising dust and mayhem Babak could no longer make out their figures as more fell nearby. The roar of blood in Babak's ears hid the sounds of anguish and mockery. He tried to run but was hit again, causing him to fall on the ground and writhe in agony.

And so, it went on.

Arrows after arrows.

Whoops of laughter as the bolts stuck elusive targets, or finished off those still rolling on the ground, spilling their blood onto the mud that was once home.

Eventually, the powers tired of their amusement and ordered cleanup. Soldiers swept the area and stabbed those still alive, as Babak watched in mute shock—his mind no longer comprehending the events around him. Soon, it was all over. He was sure no one was alive—there was no choice. It was just a show for the men that had traveled so far and had nothing much to loot.

It was morbid entertainment.

Once the wailing and weeping subsided, an announcer once again re-iterated terms, demanded absolute compliance, and just like that, it all ended. Aberis and Eribaeus turned their horses and ordered the men to march. Babak watched Aberis, Eribaeus and the Egyptian go, laughing and conversing amongst themselves. The

Egyptian was imitating the old man who tried to rush the soldiers.

As soon as the soldiers were a safe distance away, the huddling mass exploded and they ran to seek their loved ones, loudly lamenting and shouting their names. Babak ran to his sons—and it was not hard for him to find them. There they lay, peacefully, like cherubs blessed by Ahuramazda, but with arrows sticking into their chests and torsos. Blood oozed from the mouth, nose, and ears. Their eyes were unseeing—there was no light in them, and there was none of the brightness they once had when they saw their father. Babak hugged them and he wept and wept and wept, until he felt his wife's body on him, on them, screaming.

It was then that Babak knew that he would do anything to bring justice to his sons. To his despondent wife. And to calm a monstrous rage that he knew would burn within him until he died.

CHAPTER 39
THE GREAT SAND SEA
BABAK

Babak took a deep breath. "If I remember right, it was during the Eshanna revolt," he said.

Aberis slowed his pace. They had ascended a gentle dune that looked out into inky darkness and had decided to return to the comfort of the flickering lights of the camps. Guards walked behind them, holding lamps, but the night smothered the light as quickly as it rose from the wick.

"What role did you play in the revolt?" he asked.

"I was the one who assisted the King of King's early scouts and the town chief on when to lay siege to the town and identify rebels," Babak lied.

"I see," Aberis said, slowly. "I remember a little about that—a town by the marshes, I think?"

"Yes, Your Excellency."

"I think your town chief ran away, or maybe he died; I don't remember. We would have ended him, anyway."

"Of course, Your Excellency,"

"Sometimes you must teach people a lesson," he said. Babak wondered how much Aberis remembered of that day. A man who lies in blood for long forgets what it smells like.

An attack on a helpless village that only sought reasonable taxes. Scores dead in the hands of mercenaries who came from foreign lands.

Took my young sons' lives for amusement.

"Eribaeus, that scoundrel, what made him turn?" Aberis asked, rhetorically. When Babak offered no response, Aberis continued. "Where is your wife? Is she back in Thebes?"

Babak knew that Aberis had a habit of asking questions for which he often knew answers. That was how the noble caught people in a lie, leading to their ill-health of loss-of-life.

"She is, Your Excellency."

"And I hear you have a sick child?"

"Yes, Your Excellency. She withers away from an affliction that they say is peculiar to Egypt."

"The King of Kings appears to remember you. Did you not seek the Royal Physician's guidance?"

"They suggested some herbs, Your Excellency, but the sickness persists," he said.

Babak's mind drifted back to the days when his little girl ran around with glee.

When she complained about her bigger brothers.

When she threw tantrums because her mother would not let her wear perfume.

When she looked fearfully at her father and waited for his smile to run into arms.

And he no longer knew if his only surviving child was still alive. He gently turned his face to the direction beyond the tents; there, many days away, were the two he cared for the most, and he knew they waited for him to return, accomplishing what he set out to.

"I have been told you had sons."

Babak's forearms tingled. "They died in a campaign fighting the Massagetae."

"They were soldiers?"

"No, Your Excellency. Cooks and road menders. They had not reached the age."

"Ah. Our lives are hard. I lament the loss of young men," he said.

Babak cast an incredulous look at the noble, knowing that Aberis could not see the fury in his eyes and heart.

"I as well, Your Excellency."

"Well. Your wife lives. And perhaps your daughter will too," he said, almost carelessly, and then shifted his attention even before Babak could utter a word. Aberis barked an order at one of the guards. "Tell the logistics and supply masters to be at my tent when I arrive."

He then quietly moved close, next to Babak.

Babak felt a powerful grip on his neck; it was firm, but not dangerously tight. It propelled him forward. Aberis' face was close to his ears, and Babak caught his breath.

"If your wife is alone and your daughter is dying, then why did you force yourself into this campaign?" Aberis hissed in his ear.

Babak considered his responses. He knew this question would arise at some point. Whether Aberis waited all this while to ask, or whether he had learned something new about Babak, he did not know.

"Herbs. Your Excellency."

"What herbs?"

"They say that the priests hold a secret potion with the power to cure my daughter's affliction."

Aberis' fingers loosened their grip on his neck.

"Why could you not send a messenger to get it?"

"We tried. He never came back. Perhaps he ran away with the money, or he revealed that I was a Persian in service of the *Shahanshah* and they refused."

It was only the sound of Aberis' breathing, the crunchy sound of soles on the sand, and the soft whizz of the shaking flames.

Babak closed his eyes briefly.

Is this it?

And then Aberis removed his hand from Babak's neck.

"They hate the *Shahanshah* with the passion of a thousand suns," he said. "And now you know why this campaign is dear to his heart."

Babak managed to squeak out an assent. He felt his heart lighten in an instant, and great stress vanished from his belly. "I am at the King's grace and your service. And now you know that I need this for my child's life."

Aberis grunted. By then they had reached his tent, and guards waited along with the supply masters. They entered Aberis' tent and he ordered that they be seated on a worn-out mat that offered scant relief from the rough ground. Once seated, Aberis ordered the sad man to say what he found.

He bowed and began. "I beg your mercy to deliver this news, Your Excellency."

That means bad news, thought Babak. Aberis only grunted in irritation and flicked his wrists for the man to continue.

"We have concluded a count. Ten-thousand four-hundred and sixty of our brave men are no more—dead, ran away, or unaccounted for since our journey from Horosis."

Over ten thousand! Babak was astonished at the scale of destruction. He was certain they had lost two to three thousand in the week's journey—many had simply fallen off, like flies, and died by the side of the road. After the thirst and exhaustion, large sections were afflicted by severe cramps, dysentery, and vomiting. As he had seen many times in the past, when some were touched by the brush of sickness, that sickness sought others nearby. So, they had to be isolated and abandoned, and in severe cases swiftly executed. Men had even walked with filth running down their legs and vomit on their necks and chests. Some ran away, he was aware of that, but where would they go? A few hundred deserters had been captured and executed. But then Aberis had decided to let the runners run. They would die anyway, and now this attack by Petubastis had led to mass casualty. The severity of the ambush, combined with the weakened, disorganized state of Aberis' army had all contributed to this travesty.

What would an experienced general do?

What would the King of Kings do?

Babak thought that Aberis quietly rued the decision not to press for an experienced military commander to accompany him, but he could not let the men know.

Aberis looked aghast. The noble's eyes had sunken deeply, and his face was etched in worry. No doubt he saw his ambition crumble like a sandcastle under the onslaught of desert winds. Aberis took a sip of warm wine, only reserved for him, and grunted.

"Go on. What of the food and water?"

Ten thousand dead, and not a word of sympathy.

The man explained losses in animals and damage to the baggage trains.

"What does that mean to our supplies?" Aberis asked, sharply.

The man stuttered and tried to respond. He looked pitifully at the men around, perhaps worrying that his head would be rolling on the ground soon for bringing such news to the already angry noble.

"The losses in men somewhat compensates for the losses in supplies. But we now have seven days of water at the current consumption rate, assuming we lose a few hundred men every day."

Aberis was deep in thought. He swayed where he sat, kneaded his hands, and scratched his cheeks. "Food?"

"Eight days."

He then turned to Babak and Ritapates. "How many more days to Ammon?"

Ritapates spoke first. It was almost as if he had to make his voice heard before Babak spoke. "The maps suggest twelve days from here, Your Excellency, with a stop at the oasis of Farrasis."

Aberis' face relaxed. "Well, then we can supply the troops with water," he said, hesitatingly. But then he turned to Babak. "What do you think?"

Babak shook his head. "It seems *Ritapata* has learned little from our travails in this journey."

Ritapates was visibly annoyed. "What makes you—"

"Let him say what he wishes to," Aberis ordered. "What is it? I think I know what you will say but let it come from your mouth."

"Who here believes our army would fare better if we had followed the inner route from Horosis to Farrasis?"

No one answered.

"You know the answer. By the grace of Ahuramazda and Your Excellency's brilliance we have avoided a far larger massacre. Had we walked the known route, the enemy, aided by that traitor Jabari, would have harassed and butchered us in areas that were most favorable to them. We took the westerly route to the flat sandy lands, which made it difficult for them to track and attack at will. Did we also not face them in Horosis?"

Most men nodded. Ritapates pouted, knowing he had nothing to say and realizing where Babak's argument headed.

"Who here thinks that this insidious enemy is so stupid that he will let us go unchallenged through this hostile land, into the next oasis, so we can fill our bellies with water and march like uncaring children at a festival?"

A couple of commanders guffawed, drawing Aberis' irate look.

"Any commander here knows—"

"Yes, yes, we know, Babak. Don't lecture us," said Aberis, but there was no malice in his voice. "If this renegade Egyptian has enough support in the wild and enough fools to lay down their lives for his cause, there is no doubt that he will continue a battle of attrition. He will shake us like a storm shakes a great tree, causing its leaves and branches to fall and its roots weaken until crashes. In this wasteland he has the desert to his advantage, and our path to victory cannot be through ground he controls."

"But, Your Excellency," started Ritapates.

"Quiet!" Aberis admonished him. "Do you have a compelling alternative?"

Ritapates bowed and apologized until Aberis was satisfied. The noble continued. "Babak may be right. This Egyptian rebel surely waits for us near Farrasis. He has no doubt poisoned its water as he did in Horosis. And then we will lose more men in meaningless fights and for want of water. And you are too stupid to see this!"

Ritapates looked ashamed and not a word came out of him. Aberis continued. "What we must know is what path gets us to Ammon the fastest. Babak, tell us what you think while the guards fetch the Bedouin."

Babak asked an attendant to spread the worn map in front of them, and all the men came around, some kneeling, some squatting, and some sitting. Eribaeus had not been allowed into the tent, though he could be heard outside, shouting for Aberis' attention.

"Tell him I will see him later," said Aberis, irritated. Babak knew that Aberis would not yet act on Eribaeus. They returned their attention to the map under the flickering lamps.

"We are somewhere here, Your Excellency," said Babak, showing them at a location northwest of Horosis. "And here is Farrasis." He let the men ponder the place—Farrasis was days to the northeast, and then they would have to turn west again towards Ammon.

"And here is Ammon, directly to our northwest. And if we refuse to put our heads through the Egyptian's trap, we will reach Ammon, unhindered, and complete our mission."

"How long will it take?"

"Nine days by rapid march. Ten or eleven, with a weakened army, for we must expect casualties and a slower pace in the final days. This is a brutal march."

"And you are certain this will take us to Ammon? Can the Bedouin guide us?"

The Bedouin who stood at the entrance nodded vigorously to the questions, until Aberis muttered, "These mindless idiots will say yes to anything."

"It will. The map says so. I have known from my last visit," Babak said. But he knew something the others did not. The maps were not entirely accurate. The true location of Ammon, as he had been informed, was further to the east of where the map showed.

"Any water or shade on the way?" Ritapates asked. He had shifted from voicing opinions to asking questions.

"None," Babak said, with certainty in his voice. "Expect a true Sea of the Sands. We will travel unhindered, but the only life will be us, and the only water is what we carry."

"Ammonian scum, hiding in the sands," cursed Aberis. The noble took a napkin and wiped his face.

They pondered on the discussion. Finally, Aberis spoke. "What stops the renegade from bringing his forces to Ammon?"

"Nothing. But the travel to Ammon is arduous. He has lost men too, and if they are forced on a rapid march to reach the temple before us then they will be in no condition to face our armies," said Babak. "Besides, we will be far better prepared to fight them."

"How do we know they have not amassed an army of our size?" asked Ritapates. Babak clucked as if Ritapates had said something stupid, causing him to visibly get agitated.

"If they had an army of our size, then they would have confronted us where they were best positioned—Horosis. Instead, they have resorted to small scale attacks when they think they can escape. They do not have a large army, and we must bring them to the battlefield on our terms—not theirs."

Aberis nodded. "All great Generals say this: move as your enemy least expects and confront where you most want."

He loves to quote great warriors, as if it makes him one, thought Babak. *This powerful but simplistic fool understands little of warfare.*

"You speak the words of any commander's heart," said Babak, pre-empting any commander's objection to the plan. The three who stood in the tent frowned and then wisely chose to shut their mouths. After all, they could have countered—what if the enemy had chosen to fight a battle of attrition until they were ready for a large-scale offensive? What if a large army was already at Ammon ready to ambush? Those were questions they could have asked but did not.

"I have heard that the Great Sand Sea is featureless as we move further west. How do we trust these Bedouin?" Aberis asked. It was a legitimate question, and one that certainly played in the minds of others in the room.

"I know an Egyptian cook in the baggage train who knows this region well, and he was in Jabari's grace. We bring him as an addition to the Bedouin. I trust that he knows more than wanderers," Babak said. "But I leave it to your wisdom whether you wish to employ his services. It would be easy to induce him to be truthful, with promise rewards when the destination is reached."

The others fidgeted, and finally Ritapates spoke. "Why is it that so few know this area? What lays beyond it?"

Aberis scoffed as if it was another stupid question. "Look around you, why do you think so few know? Why would anyone in their sound mind come here?"

Ritapates was silenced and he continued to examine the greatness of his own feet.

Aberis looked at the men around him. "Well? Does anyone else have a more presentable idea?"

No one spoke.

"Bring the man, Babak" he said.

As they waited, Babak rode a camel to fetch this Egyptian cook. The cook was not too far from the noble's tent, and they made their return swiftly, which pleased Aberis. The cook was a slender, short man, and his face betrayed his age. He wore nothing but a loincloth, and as was customary for the Egyptians, he had little hair on his being except what grew since their departure from Thebes.

"Tell them," Babak said.

The man bowed to those before him, and he spoke haltingly in their language. "My forefathers came from Ammon. I have lived in Farrasis and Aostris. And I have many times traversed through the Sand Sea."

"How did you know Jabari?" Aberis asked.

"Not by relation, Your Excellency. He sought me out after he heard of my life during a night camp," the man said, seeking Jabari in the tent.

"He is dead. Did he make any promises to you?" Aberis asked, his voice deceptively soft.

The man hesitated—his eyes seeking comfort among the hard men around him. "He wanted to know if there were alternative routes by which one could take a smaller army faster to Ammon."

Aberis looked around incredulously. The commanders shook their heads dutifully.

"That bastard! Did he say when, where? Fear not, cook, no harm will come to you if you tell us the truth," Aberis said, holding a small pouch of silver coins and dangling it in front of the man whose eyes opened wide.

"No, Your Excellency, only that he would seek me when the opportunity arose. I had no idea what he meant, and I would dare not ask questions to the priest and advisor to Your Excellency and King of Kings!" the man said, with great humility.

Aberis did not question the cook. Instead, he turned to the question of the route. "You say you know this region well. Can you, along with the Bedouins, lead this army through this nothingness. If we encounter no difficulties, I will triple your rewards and you shall have a house and plot of land in the town of your choosing."

The man bowed repeatedly. "I know the paths well, Your Excellency."

"What lies further west?" Ritapates asked.

"After thirty days by the Sand Sea one reaches a vast range of mountains, beyond which, many days of walk still, one reaches the Sea they say—but I have not been so far."

"What god lays to waste such large tracts of land?" muttered Aberis. "Are there ravines, cliffs, places ripe for an ambush on the way?"

The cook smiled broadly. His eyes shined with mirth. Babak admired the man's poise and confidence. "No, Your Excellency. The wise ones named this the Great Sand Sea for it holds true to its name. There is nothing—not a strand of life nor a place for succor. Other than an occasional ridge made entirely of sand and small spots of rock that one may encounter after a day of marching. It is true that sand replaces the likeness of water."

Babak quietly examined their faces. They all contemplated the coming days. He felt a sense of pity for some but extinguished the thoughts from his mind.

"We must decide quickly," Babak said, his voice loud and rang clear in the tent. "Our position is precarious. I have presented you with the choices, but you are men far more conversed in campaigns and battles. But we must decide, or there will be no battle and no glory, for the sand will drown us all."

Ritapates signed loudly. The decision weighed heavily on Aberis, and his shoulders slumped.

Ambitions have prices, Babak thought. And he knew Aberis nursed great ambitions for himself.

Finally, one commander spoke up. "So, what do we do, Excellency?"

Aberis inhaled and sat staring at the map. And then he finally spoke. "We cross the Sand Sea and go directly to Ammon."

The men stood silently, listening to the slowly increasing wind outside, howling, protesting, lifting sand and slinging it against the tent. They were about to embark on a journey into the great unknown.

And then Babak spoke again. "I have another idea, Your Excellency, one that might merit consideration even if it goes against your valiant heart."

CHAPTER 40

AMMON

AMUNPERRE

The ancient voice, cracking and deep, came through the opening in the wall. The Oracle never showed itself, and they said that the being was at once both man and woman, and spoke the truth of what it saw, and sometimes foretold things to come. "The army moves. It snakes through the sand. It treads where it should not."

"Yes, Your Holiness," said Amunperre. He was standing by the opening along with two other priests, a local Egyptian nobleman, and a Greek merchant who had much influence in the region by way of trade and connections to his land.

"They have left Horosis, and by now they will have faced the sharp blades of the rebel. But it will not stop them."

Amunperre was surprised by the Oracle's knowledge. He always wondered how the Oracle knew, and if it truly had a connection to god or if it simply employed spies as he did. But those were forbidden questions. "A King is a King, Amunperre. What pain does Cambyses bring to you?"

"He is no Egyptian. He sent an army to burn us to the ground."

"Why must he be Egyptian? Will not a just king, no matter where his birth, be good to the people?"

"We have spoken of this before, Holiness. He is no just king. That he sent an entire army towards us shows his unsteady mind and vindictive behavior."

"But is that not what a king does? To quell rebellions. To bring peace?"

Amunperre wondered why the Oracle was now questioning what they had debated many times before. "That may be so, Holiness. It is not the act of putting down a rebellion, but it is what he wishes to do once he is legitimized by this temple and by all priests of Egypt."

"And what is it that he wishes to do? After all, he prayed to Apis, he has been blessed by Wedjahor, and he has shown no disrespect to our gods."

Amunperre knew this to be true. Those opposed to Cambyses had spent much time spreading rumors about the Persian King—that he was of unsound mind, that he attempted to stab the Apis bull, that he tried to molest a temple priestess, that in a drunken rage he had knocked off the idols of Amun. None of those were true. From what he knew, Cambyses had respected local traditions and had sought legitimacy as best as an invader could. He had even spared Psamtik, and his administrators had so far not interfered in traditions. But for all the Oracle's power to see the future, it had not seen the obvious.

The sandstorms appear to cloud your visibility, thought Amunperre. "He wishes to decrease the power and influence of the temples, Your Holiness. He has spoken of tax reforms, reducing allocations to our temples, diminishing the influence of the priests that have guarded this land for thousands of years. This insidious king shows piety outwards while he conspires to weaken us from within."

The Oracle was silent. And then it spoke. "I wished to test you, Amunperre. Your concerns are true. After all, he sends an army to defile this town and destroy this holy abode."

"Your holiness. We first resisted Cambyses for we held dear the new Pharaoh after the death of Amasis. And now we must resist for his ascension will mean our end."

"You worry about the loss of your power, Amunperre," the Oracle chuckled. Amunperre turned to the others beside him and dismissed them. It was now for him to have a candid conversation.

"We now speak privately, Oracle," he said.

"Good. What of Petubastis?" said the voice.

"If he inflicts a bigger wound on the invading army and survives, he will recoup and stay on the cause."

"What of that Egyptian priest who accompanied the army? Where does his loyalty lie?"

"It lies with himself. He still marches with the army. Whether he will be with us, or turn against us, is unknown.

"What do you see, Holiness?"

"I see a dark shadow behind him. Do not place your trust in him."

Amunperre was pleased to hear that the Oracle assessed Jabari much as he had—the snake had ambitions far greater than what he expressed. Jabari had been in touch with him months before the invasion to Ammon began— and had sent his own messenger ahead of the invasion, laying out the terms. Two-faced bastard.

"Will Petubastis stay with us?" he asked.

"He is impatient. His heart does not think wisely. But it is prudent for us to nurture him. My vision is clouded in this regard."

Amunperre knew that the Oracle did not stay too long for conversations. He was pleased with what he heard, and happy that the Oracle saw the situation the same way.

There was one last question.

"How will we fight if Cambyses' army reaches here?"

Amunperre heard only the wheezing breath from the opening. And then the Oracle finally spoke.

"The curse of Ammon casts a shadow. The South stirs restlessly," it said cryptically, and there was no response when Amunperre asked for it to explain.

CHAPTER 41
THE GREAT SAND SEA

ABERIS

Aberis was intrigued. *Here we go again with this man.* "Yes?"

"We must converse in private, Your Excellency."

Ritapates protested but Aberis sent him away, saying the path was set and that men must prepare to march at the earliest dawn, and whatever Ritapates wanted to protest could wait for the long march ahead. He dismissed everyone except his bodyguards.

"I wonder if I rely on you too much," he said, turning back to Babak.

"Has my counsel been wrong so far?" Babak asked.

"I still wonder about your motives. You say it is about your daughter."

"She is all I have among my children."

"It is just a girl! There can be more, get yourself a new wife," he said flippantly.

Aberis thought he saw a fleeting emotion pass Babak's face. Instead, the man chuckled drily. "Perhaps."

"What is it? What is your new bold idea?"

Aberis found it difficult to trust this man, but he had no choice. So far, Babak appeared to give sound advice, even if in that annoyingly patronizing fashion. Who did he think he was!

"I beg you to hear me, Your Excellency. It is your decision and command we all obey, but it is my duty, as your advisor and the *Shahanshah's*, to bring to your consideration various means, no matter how preposterous."

What now?

Aberis stared at him. "It appears that your idea is truly preposterous. Go ahead."

Babak bowed and then squared his shoulders. "Our journey is in peril. There is no doubt, as your astute mind has already realized, that our army will be significantly weakened by the time we reach Ammon."

"Yes, I gathered as much, and so have the others."

"And there is no telling what Petubastis intends to do, and it is very likely we will face them again."

"Yes, and we already discussed all this."

"What do we know about the powerful priests of Ammon? Or for that matter, any Egyptian temple guardian?"

I wish I could flog him for his tone.

Aberis looked at Babak quizzically. "Do not ask me questions, tell me what you plan."

"The Priests of Ammon were not swayed by the King's words or deeds. But they certainly did not see his resolve and commitment by sending an army at them."

"Yes, that is not hard to fathom."

Babak took a deep breath. He leaned forward slightly and clasped his hands. "Would it not then make a great case for us to entice them again? Perhaps provide them a reason, even if temporary, to disassociate with Petubastis and welcome us in Ammon? Petubastis fears the influence of the priests just as much as anyone else."

Aberis seemed intrigued. He leaned back and scratched his chin. The grains and sweat irritated the skin and caused constant itches on his shoulder, back, thighs, and other regions. Many patches of his body had turned raw and red.

"What do you suggest?" he asked.

"Let us send a separate, small and nimble expedition to Ammon. Away from scouts' eyes, too fast for any army to pursue. We meet the High Priest and the Oracle and bribe them. We promise that the King bears no ill will, that the army in pursuit was only a signal, but that there shall be no impediment to their reign."

Aberis considered Babak's proposal. It was clever, even if bold to put forward. "But the *Shahanshah* has promised none of that."

"Only as a ruse, Your Excellency. And once we secure their cooperation, any resistance will be minimized. Once we have Ammon, we will do what the King asked."

Aberis considered this. "You are a clever man. Better than what I imagined you were. Devious as well."

"It is worth your consideration. It will minimize our risk and ensure success. No one shall know. If nothing else, we can delay the Ammonian support to Petubastis and buy some time."

"How confident are you that they will receive our offering and side with us?"

"I offer only a chance, Your Excellency. There is no certainty. But it is better than marching through this terrain and facing the full force of nature and man."

Aberis picked a dried date and began to chew. "And what bribe will appease them?" he said, finally.

"It must be substantial," Babak said. And then he described the Egyptian greed and desire for gold and silver, and that it would have to be significant to be attractive. Certainly at least worth the carrying capacity of three to four asses or camels. A good collection of silver and gold ingots, necklaces, rings, Persian silk, diadems, lapis-lazuli bracelets—all these, Babak explained, attracted the priests.

"Where would one get all that," Aberis wondered. Of course, he had no intention of revealing his secret cart in the baggage train. One that would cause even the greediest man to salivate. The cart had an exceptional bounty—hundreds of pure gold chains studded with gems, ingots, thousands of gold and silver coins, fifty ruby and blue crystal statuettes, one hundred exquisite Syrian bracelets, an astonishingly beautiful gold and lapis-lazuli adorned set of Amun, Horus, and Isis idols, an enamel-studded chariot idol from the Levant, silver idols of Ahuramazda and eastern gods, beautiful, engraved gold leaves with the story of Gilgamesh, several votive plaques, blue-glass drinking vessels, bronze and silver amulets, a hundred of the finest silk garments, a thousand gold rings, several polished black stone idols of exotic Indian gods, thirty gold bull idols, several ancient papyri, and many more precious items. He had all this hauled, and there was no intention of giving it away just yet. He would hold on to it.

"It must come out of our baggage trains, Your Excellency. And may I dare say, yours, Ritapates', Eribaeus', mine..."

What?

Aberis looked aghast. "That is your idea? That we push ourselves to poverty so we can appease priests that hate us? Will that even matter?"

"What options do we have? We cannot ask our commanders to part with their belongings for that will foment unrest. But us? What we lose will dwarf what we gain by bringing *Shahanshah* his victory. Besides, what we can do is take portions of ours but take all of Eribaeus'."

Aberis thought of the proposition again. He knew that this was a decisive point in his life. He had served with loyalty in Cyrus' court, ingratiating himself to the King of Kings in many humiliating ways. And then he had bowed to Cambyses. He had traveled far and wide, in the dusty barrenness of Gandhara, the desolation of Gedrosia, humid marshes of Babylonia, and many other places, in service of the King. As his confidant. He had played games that many might find distasteful. And now, he was at the cusp of victory leading men on his own! This would bring glory to him, legitimacy to the King, and then greatness to himself.

But this journey.

It would all hinge on his decisions.

He had more wealth back in Susa. What he would lose here would not amount to much, and he would recoup it all and more. Besides, he would not part with all of his incredible holdings—he would only let go of a small part. But Eribaeus? That treasonous dog-fucker would have to pay.

He had to decide and leave nothing to chance.

"Yes, Eribaeus will pay. Who goes with the bribe?"

"Who do you trust to be capable of traveling the distance and convincing the priests?"

Aberis was stumped. This posed a genuine problem. Jabari was dead. Eribaeus was a back-stabbing scoundrel. *Ritapata* was a dimwit. His commanders from the Immortals were capable commanders but inarticulate negotiators. They could win the war with swords, but the art of using the right words against slimy and calculating adversaries eluded them. He had no other political advisors in this army. Besides, sending valuables with poorer men was akin to asking tomb robbers to guard new tombs.

Unless of course... Babak.

Aberis eyed the man from Eshanna. He stood confidently, as if he knew that he was the choice. It passed Aberis thought fleetingly that perhaps Babak had engineered everything so far to come to this end, but he dismissed that. Aberis regarded himself as anything but stupid. Babak looked to be in passable health. He was thin, wiry, he had a way with words, and he knew enough Egyptian to make a case. When all this was over, he might even employ Babak in his Governor's court.

"It occurs to me that you might be the best choice."

Babak looked surprised. "I am honored to represent you, Your Excellency. Do you not have anyone else with passable Egyptian and political experience to make this mission? I would rather be by your side. Ritapates is not quite the tactician we all thought him to be."

"There is no one. You have provided some sound counsel. You say you know the paths. Go."

Babak knelt before Aberis. "As you wish, Your Excellency. If that is your will, it is my desire. I will bring glory to you and the King of Kings, and make those Egyptian blowhards see reason."

"Do you know how you will conduct this journey?"

Babak affirmed he could. He explained, using the map, how they would turn east, away from the Sand Sea, onto a path he explained was better for small groups even if longer, and then angle west towards Ammon. He would travel much faster and hope to reach the Oracle at least two to three days before the army—enough time to negotiate an agreement and send messages to Petubastis to stay away. He would take another Egyptian, a friend of the cook's, who knew the region, even if he was less traveled. And then a few guards.

Aberis agreed to it all. Now it was time to muster the bribe—which meant confronting Eribaeus. Ritapates could be easily browbeaten. He then summoned Eribaeus.

The Greek was apoplectic at the insinuation that he conspired with Jabari. He threw accusations at Babak and Ritapates, and then heaped abuses at the dead Jabari. But Aberis stood firm.

"If you do not comply, then you will leave me with no choice but to have Danofis arrest you and tell your mercenaries that you seek to subvert the King of King's cause. I am letting you live, Eribaeus, but it will be a long time before you regain our trust," he said, putting an end to the argument.

He would ensure that the King finish this man once the dust settled, but for now they needed a way to complete the mission at hand. Finally, Eribaeus made peace with his situation. He begrudgingly agreed to relinquish all his possessions—several gold bracelets, gold rings and chains, four exceptional silver statuettes of his gods, numerous quartz, ruby, and lapis-lazuli jewelry, a finely made gold-inlaid sword from some dead noble, a crown, and two handsome pouches of silver and gold ingots, several large bags of exotic spices and perfumes. He protested and cursed all through the night as they gathered his belongings and loaded them onto the travel beasts. Aberis watched with some sadness as some of his prized possessions were gathered—though he chose only to let a fraction of his belongings go, and even that was considerable in nature. He also decided to part with an ancient papyri that some said told the story of an army that fought a Pharaoh and died during the escape to Egypt's western deserts and held great secrets of god-gifted weapons. Aberis thought it could be a good addition to the priests' library—they liked such artifacts.

Babak himself had very modest savings—for he had left much of it, which was very little, back home with his wife. Ritapates complained, but Aberis was surprised that the advisor had much to spare, and he was asked to surrender three-fourths of his possessions. From him they got fine garments made of luxurious silk, and several gold ingots, rings, and chains. Finally, they all agreed, except for the complaining Eribaeus, that this was a bountiful bribe that would sway even the greediest priest. They would send assurances, including a fake letter from the Shahanshah, promising autonomy and increased influence even beyond Egypt. Suddenly, Aberis began to feel elated about this plan—they might get what they need with little resistance if this shrewd man accomplished what they had devised.

The Ammonians would be deceived and destroyed.

As they prepared to leave, still in darkness and only the slightest hint of light rising in the east, Babak came to Aberis.

"I had another idea, Your Excellency."

CHAPTER 42

THE WESTERN DESERT

ERIBAEUS

Eribaeus cursed and complained to no end. What grave injustice was this, he lamented, to be sent away with this wretched Persian for a side mission that had no value? The cunning bastard had ulterior motives and was behind all the misery, he insisted, but to no avail. Not only had Babak put a target on his back, but this slimy pig had also caused him to lose all his belongings and forced Eribaeus to accompany him to Ammon. Away from the comforts of the army, from his tent, from his water and bread and wine.

But why? What caused this to come? Who was behind this travesty? Eribaeus was confused. Somehow, he had been implicated in the plot against the army. Jabari was dead, apparently attacking Babak—but why did Jabari attack Babak? Jabari had confided in him. No doubt the Egyptian had questionable motives, and he had died before Eribaeus could complete another conversation. Little of it made sense—and he was perplexed. Apparently, a captured Egyptian had fingered him—but how? Why? Had Jabari spilled his name to Petubastis as a co-conspirator? Eribaeus had questions but none of the answers, except that Babak appeared to be behind it all.

But why?

Eribaeus dug deep into his memory. Where had he met this man first? When? But he came up empty. His earliest memory was somewhere before Pelusium. So, even as the loading completed, he demanded, and finally got, two guards of his own choice.

Just in case.

But he was also constrained by the situation that Babak and the Egyptian were the only ones who knew the path and knew the language. He had learned Persian, but not enough Egyptian except perhaps to say "Quiet" to wailing prisoners. Besides, why was Babak wearing garish garments—colorful and easy to attract attention? The fool had no sense. He had even asked why he was wearing such ugly clothing unfit for a man of his stature, and Babak had only smiled. When this was over, he would find a way to flay and crucify this dirty bastard.

As he inspected the belongings for his journey, Eribaeus cursed some more.

CHAPTER 43
THE GREAT SAND SEA

BABAK

As the sun made his way above the horizon, slowly coating the land and the army with soft honey-colored hues, Babak rushed to Danofis' tent. Soldiers still milled about, preparing for the march ahead. Danofis had just woken up, still groggy, and stretching his muscles, tending to the sore spots.

He saw Babak approach and raised his eyebrows. "Babak?"

Babak grabbed Danofis by his elbow and ushered him out of the tent to a location where they could speak without intrusive ears. It was cool and the crisp air was invigorating–all that would change in an hour and the land would become a cauldron. "Well, are you in a hurry, you old Persian bastard," laughed Danofis.

"Listen to me carefully Danofis. Have I ever wronged you?"

Danofis was confused. "What? Never. What is this about?"

"And you have never wronged me. You are a kind man blessed by the gods."

Danofis took a step back and expanded his chest. His face betrayed his alarm. "Babak. Your words say much but with no explanation. What is on your mind?"

"You know that your lord Eribaeus is accompanying me to Ammon."

"Yes. I have heard. We were all surprised. I have been unable to converse with him since yesterday."

"His Excellency Aberis has forbidden contact with him at this critical hour, so do not try. But you must listen to me."

"Listen to what?" Danofis asked, his face hardening. He advanced towards Babak and stood close. He turned and looked at his men now looking at them quizzically. "What is this about?"

"When you have the first chance in the night, flee, leave the army–"

"What?"

"Listen to me, you arrogant Greek idiot! This is an errand that offends all our gods, and you have seen what Aberis and Eribaeus are willing to do for their own benefit. Speak to no one, but Ahuramazda has appeared in my dreams admonishing us for this mission. A great tragedy will befall those that persist on this journey. Leave when you can, take the path back to Farrasis and when apprehended declare yourself a deserter and you will be spared."

Danofis looked completely dumbstruck. "Desert my men, are you out of your–"

Babak leaned forward and hissed. "Take those few you love, those who you know have deep regret with this mission and have no deliberate cruelty in their mind. Take them and live. I know things you do not, Danofis, please leave and god willing I will see you again," Babak said, with finality in his voice. He conveyed his words with as much urgency as he could muster. He then held a wordless Danofis by his shoulders and shook him. "May Zeus and

Ahuramazda be with you. But listen to me just this one time you plume-headed fool. And spread the word, let as many that wish to leave, leave now!"

"Why do you say this, who—" Danofis struggled with his words.

Babak stepped forward and hugged Danofis fiercely. He whispered urgently into Danofis' ear. "I am the man whose family you saved from death through your warning long ago in Eshanna. The town where our lords' men rained arrows on helpless townspeople forced to run into the marshes. I lost two of my sons."

Danofis recoiled with shock. He looked at Babak with wide eyes, his handsome features breaking into a strange mixture of surprise and fear. "Babak—"

But Babak only barely heard him as he turned left. He looked back to see Danofis still looking at him with the most flustered expression.

CHAPTER 44

THE GREAT SAND SEA

BABAK

The lightest of orangish-yellow lined the sandy horizon. Babak looked back at the army. There it was, stretching to miles, with tents dotted everywhere, men engaged in morning rituals, trenches of sewer polluting the pristine landscape, and sounds of preparation for the march ahead. He then turned to his contingent—one ass reserved for Eribaeus to pacify him, four for the valuables, six guards—four Immortals and two of Eribaeus' Greeks, three water and food mules, a cook, a guide, and two attendants. It would be quite the journey, and Babak hoped that it would yield what he desired. During the gathering of the bribe, Babak had learned of Aberis' vast treasure that accompanied the noble. He was frustrated that he could not extract more out of the man.

They bid farewell to Aberis and other men. They received well wishes and made a final inspection of all that they had. Babak knew that the Immortals would have received instructions from Aberis to kill him and anyone else that might attempt to subvert the mission—the men only followed the orders of Aberis and the King, and they would have to be dealt with.

Eribaeus still sulked. They had had little by way of conversation but Babak had only once told the noble to wait until they were underway before he could share more on why it came to be thus. Babak had convinced Aberis that sending Eribaeus away would minimize risk for Aberis back at the army, while keeping the Greek's men mollified that their noble was away on an important mission.

Eribaeus had finally acquiesced and prepared for departure. He was stiff in his departure to Aberis who only gave him a deathly stare and sternly warned him not to attempt anything foolish. He even told the immortals to keep an eye on the Greek, both for good measure and to heap more humiliation on the red-faced noble.

Babak quietly enjoyed the scene. He had plans for Eribaeus–perhaps even leveraging him as a bargaining chip.

Babak hoped that as they became a spec in the vast dunes, his attire, which so helped during the attack, would help distant eyes recognize him again.

And then they finally set forth on their journey. After a few hundred steps traveling northeast, the army, with its remaining thirty-thousand men, animals, hopes, dreams, ambitions, secrets, desires, anger, and love, slowly vanished from their sight as they climbed and descended a gentle dune.

CHAPTER 45
THE WESTERN DESERT
BABAK

It had been four days now. The relentless sun blazed in the sky. They had arced away from the Sand Sea and now skirted the edge of it again, with the dunes on one side and jagged rock and cliffs on the other. Everyone, including Babak, had underestimated this journey. The previous day they had lost two immortals, hardy men who no longer had the energy to walk, and a water mule, whose remaining burden now had to be spread amongst other weakened beasts.

They had become lethargic with their energy sapped by the heat and the strain of walking in hindering sand. Only once in their three days had they seen another living thing—a crow that flew to the east, in their opposite direction. Did it come from a place with water and people? Or was it going to one? They did not know. Eribaeus had bitterly complained for a day and a half until he quietened, with his parched throat having not much to say anymore. Babak had finally had a good night's sleep, even in the misery of this travel, the previous day. His mind was clear now, even if his body fought every step.

Where are they?

They were once again in a steep incline, descending towards the dunes. Eribaeus managed to squeak out a few words. "How much farther?"

"A few more days, noble. We are less than halfway."

He looked distraught. "We will die here, you half-wit."

"We have enough water, food, and we are not slowed down by a giant army. You have seen the world, noble, have you not been in such a journey before?"

Eribaeus grunted and wheezed. He looked sickly—the rose in his cheeks had vanished, instead replaced by an unhealthy pallor. "Never this way. What other land is like this?"

Babak squinted in the bright sun and inhaled the hot, dry air. His throat burned, but it was critical that they maintain discipline. The guards and others had behaved honorably—they dutifully carried out their orders, walked without complaining (at least in Babak's earshot), and when their companions fell, they performed dignified last rites before continuing.

So, they soldiered on. Taking each miserable step on the still hard ground, rocky, sandy, strewn with strangely shaped pebbles and white and black rock. Babak said nothing more, and Eribaeus went back to alternating moods of sulking and complaining. But it was three more hours that they walked in silence until Babak finally noticed a glint atop of a small bluff to their right.

A Greek guard noticed it too. He said something in his language to Eribaeus who looked up as well, but there was nothing to be seen. But they all agreed to heighten their awareness should they encounter someone or something.

"What witless dog would roam these lands?" asked Eribaeus rhetorically, or perhaps to convince himself. Babak kept walking without offering commentary. If there was any intent behind that glint, it would soon become clear. And then they continued to walk gingerly down the incline, taking care not to slip and fall, for an injury could mean certain death. The bluff loomed large now, and the hard ground sloped sharply to the left, opening to the Sand Sea. There were many notches and cracks along the bluff, Babak noticed.

Cracks easy for someone to hide and wait.

They finally reached slightly even land that looked like it would last another a mile, but the path narrowed considerably with little room to maneuver. They had to change to a single-file walking order, with the Egyptian guide in the front, Babak and Eribaeus following, then guards around the beasts, followed by the attendants and cook.

The group was now nervous.

They hastened along, knowing that this path afforded a mischief-maker much opportunity.

CHAPTER 46

THE GREAT SAND SEA

ERIBAEUS

He was deep in thought. Even if his body protested in anguish, Eribaeus' mind kept its fidelity. The bluff to the right had somewhat shielded them from the sun—the first time in three days.

It let him think.

What would he do when he reached Ammon? The idea was to bribe them and have them disown Petubastis, thereby demoralizing the rebel's deeply pious soldiers, and allow Aberis' army to do what it set it out to do. The deception was a bright idea, but was it in his best interests? Eribaeus wondered. Or should he find a way to kill Babak before they reached Ammon, and then join forces with the Ammonians against Aberis and eventually Cambyses? Jabari may have been right—an alliance between the Egyptians and Greeks was better for their long term rather than the Persians who were growing too powerful.

Egypt now. Greece next?

He slipped and regained his balance, cursing the ground. But even as his head was down, he noticed a sudden movement, and the rustling of gravel.

What in the—

Two figures emerged, almost magically, from the side of the bluff walls in front of them. Egyptian in their demeanor, they screamed loudly, making gestures for everyone to halt. Eribaeus panicked and shouted, "Ambush! Ambush!"

But it was too late. They had nowhere to run, and there were men not only in the front, but behind too. Two in the front, and three behind, but they had the advantage of the ground in this narrow pathway. Besides, they were armed with long spears, which made it much easier for them to thrust and stab those in the file. The swords of the guards were useless, and they had no place to flank the ambushers. As Eribaeus looked frantically, Babak said calmly. "Everyone, halt. Let us speak to them first."

"Who are they? Who are they?" He whispered urgently. The Persian did not respond. Instead, he placed a hand on Eribaeus' shoulder and then he began to walk towards the men in the front. The guards had taken a battle stance, but he knew it was a meaningless gesture. Any conflict here would lead to all their deaths.

They were supposed to be walking in desolate terrain! That was what Babak said!

Babak!

The Egyptians in the back had advanced slowly, causing the group to compress and stand in a dense huddle. The beasts stirred restlessly. The guards struggled to keep them in control, which in turn distracted them from conflict.

Babak and the Egyptian guide walked confidently to the two in the front. It was an odd sight—they appeared to treat him with no hostility. Instead, they stood there, waiting. One even looked like a boy.

They spoke briefly with many animated gestures. Eribaeus could understand Egyptian in fragments, but he could not hear what was being said. Eventually, Babak walked back, looking dejected.

"What is it?" asked Eribaeus, anxiously.

"They come from Ammon. They wish to know our business. Obviously, there was hostility once they noticed that I am Persian and you are Greek."

"How did they know we are here?"

"They said they watch this passageway. The news of the invasion has reached them."

"So? What do they want?"

"I convinced them that we have important messages to the temple, and that they risk their holiness and their Pharaoh if they do not give us

passage."

"And?"

"They will allow us if we disarm."

Eribaeus was alarmed. How many times had he pulled this ruse and then ended those that complied? Was this going to be the same?

"Tell them we will not disarm," he said, his voice hoarse.

Babak shook his head. "Do we have a choice?"

Eribaeus pressed on. "What of the Immortals? They can gut these men like fish!"

"Men cannot fly," Babak said, whispering. "Look around. We are in a single file, with very little space to maneuver. How do you think they will reach the men on either side with their spears pointed at us?"

Eribaeus considered the situation. It was hopeless. He looked at the smooth walls of the bluff and the steep embankment to the side. He cursed under his breath.

"Do you think you can convince them that we must be armed to prevent any untoward attacks on us? And that we will not lift our hand against them?"

"I can try," Babak said. The Persian then adjusted his garish blue scarf and trotted back to the man and the boy. He stood there, arguing, and Eribaeus could only make out fragments of the conversation. "No harm...

defense... be reasonable... beg you...let them go..."

Eribaeus noticed Babak playing the full game of humility. The Persian debased himself before this man and boy, bowing repeatedly and at one point even kneeling and groveling. It was a show, but one that was needed at this most critical hour. Eventually, the two seemed to relent. Their postures relaxed a little, and the harsh staccato of words softened. They entered a discussion that lasted several minutes as Eribaeus and the others waited anxiously. One of the mules had begun to bray incessantly, causing a handler to beat it to submission. Eribaeus' throat and feet ached, standing and waiting.

Babak finally returned. "They have made their best proposition. They say we must comply or fight to a resolution."

"I saw your theatrics. What did you achieve?"

"They will let us keep our weapons. The guards and attendants—all of them—must turn and walk away. They will give directions to the nearest town. The beasts can come with us. Just you and me, and the guide. Or we

fight."

What?

"That is preposterous," Eribaeus yelled. "What kind of negotiation is this?"

He looked at the two men and shouted some more—his voice was hoarse and tired. This stupidity. Such stupidity! Eribaeus turned to Babak. "You come with me. I will speak to them. Translate my Persian to their Egyptian as accurately as you can!"

Babak tried to dissuade him to no avail. They both then walked slowly, Babak behind him. Eribaeus faced the older man—his eyes flashed at the sight of the approaching Greek.

"Your proposal is just—"

At lightning speed, the man twirled his spear and smashed the flat end to Eribaeus' belly. The Greek yelped and fell to his knees. He then felt a sharp jab on his back and collapsed to the ground—tasting the dust. Babak shouted something, and then his wiry hands helped Eribaeus back to his feet.

"They say no negotiations. You have to decide."

Eribaeus groaned and nursed his stomach. "What do you say?"

"Let the others go. Why condemn them for no reason? Following these men to Ammon may be our fastest and most secure way. We will keep our weapons, just in case. And they have agreed to keep distance and walk along with us."

"Either plan makes no sense. We are vulnerable either way!"

"Then what do you suggest?"

Eribaeus was scared. What choice did they have? In fact, there was no choice at all. But he could be the sheep, or he could be the wolf—and he was no sheep. It was a boy and five men. What were they in the face of the Immortals?

Eribaeus turned to the men.

They were looking at him and Babak, unsure what to do.

"Noble, let us not—" Babak began.

But Eribaeus had made up his mind.

"We fight!" he screamed. And then he pulled his sword out.

CHAPTER 47

THE GREAT SAND SEA

BABAK

What is this idiot doing?

"No, Eribaeus, no!"

But before he could react, Eribaeus had pulled his sword out and was looking behind, yelling at the Immortals. The two guards, unsure of what to do, finally decided to take different courses. One of them sprang towards the men behind, lunging and missing the ledge narrowly. His move was impressive but suicidal. One of the Egyptians swiftly leaped forward and thrust the spear at an upward angle, catching the oncoming attacker. The guard tried to break his momentum but was too late—in a split second the spear had impaled the stupid man.

The attendants and the guide immediately sunk to their knees and then prostrated on the ground—signing that they would have no part in this. Babak was frantically shouting at everyone to stop.

Eribaeus began to panic—he then shouted for one of his Greek guards to attack the front. The remaining Immortals took defensive stances but stayed where they were. But one Greek guard, perhaps desiring of greatness, shouted war cries and rushed the boy and the man in the front. He made swift strides, his muscular legs effortlessly covering hard ground as he held his sword low. He was hunched like a cat, and for a moment it looked like he would evade the spear pointed at him and strike the boy and the man in one fell swoop. But the boy was no minnow. Just as a horrified Eribaeus watched, the boy fell to his knees like a gazelle, and a knife glinted in his hand. The Greek's sword missed his head, and at the same time, his arm shot up, stabbing the Greek in the thigh. The Greek stumbled, yelping and screaming helplessly. But in a flash, the other man was upon him, and speared him in the back. And just like that, before the blink of an eye, he was dead, his glory ground to the dust.

Now, there was a standoff. Two men were dead, the rest stood terrified. Eribaeus looked scared—his face was drained of blood, and even in this heat it looked pale and deathly. His eyes darted among the men and Babak's.

"Tell them we will comply!"

Babak raised his hand and walked slowly towards them. They appeared to let him approach, and then he spoke to them. He glanced back to look at Eribaeus, eyeing them anxiously. Finally, he returned.

"The terms have changed."

Eribaeus looked crestfallen. He nodded dolefully.

"We lose our weapons as well. They will allow our Egyptian guide to accompany us. The rest must throw their weapons to the side, and crawl on their knees and hands one by one until they are cleared to leave."

Eribaeus nodded.

Babak then interpreted the instructions: the men would leave, follow a trail mark that was visible from this vantage point, and in three days they would reach a small town where they would get food and water. They could then go as they please but were advised to stay away from military duty and integrate into civilian life for now. Each man accepted his order without protest, clearly relieved that they were being let go instead of being gutted here in the middle of nowhere. One by one they discarded their weapons to the side, got on their knees, and crawled to the back of the line. Once they cleared the three men at the back, they ran. Each man was allowed enough ration to survive their journey. Once they all cleared their way, it was just the Egyptians from the ambush party, and then Eribaeus, Babak, and their guide.

The group then began to descend. No words were spoken for the next hour, and by then they had returned to the sandy sea again, where to their west the featureless desert stretched to the vast beyond. As their feet sank in the warm sand, Babak made his way next to Eribaeus.

"That was foolish of you. You got two men killed for no reason."

Eribaeus scoffed. "What cowards would not at least attempt?"

"You gambled with their life. Not yours. Why did you not charge then?"

Eribaeus looked at Babak angrily. His hazel eyes darkened in contempt. "How dare you question my actions? Watch your words, Persian, your King favors me in his court."

Babak smiled. "I do not see our King behind you."

"You insolent dog, I have nothing to tell you. Let us reach Ammon and complete our mission."

Babak smiled. "You really do not remember me, do you, Eribaeus?"

CHAPTER 48

THE GREAT SAND SEA

A SOLDIER

He had developed a frightening headache and his vision blurred. It pulsated with such intensity he had never known. He was beginning to see flying camels, floating dead women, children with fangs, and horses with bodies of snakes. There was no end to this frightening sand, he knew. His stomach ached in hunger, and he was not alone, of that he certain. Every step felt like an exercise. He had no more water. He needed some moisture, *any moisture!* He had a large group of men coalesced around him, with similar needs and desperation. *How did many others preserve their ration,* he wondered.

He had been told, in hushed tones, that as a privileged Persian he had received more rations than others. He was sure they were lies–perhaps the Immortals received more or there were others, but he did not feel like he was better supplied. *Liars!*

His stomach grumbled again, and his abdomen began to cramp. A sharp pain rose in his belly and it felt like the juices of the stomach were burning his innards. The miserable sand hurt his throat as if someone had run nails inside. His tongue stuck to the roof and he could barely talk anymore. he placed a hand on a man beside him. A faithful companion, a friend. "We have to eat," he gasped. "We have to."

"No one. Not one man in this contingent has rations," the friend said. "And we won't get anything until dusk."

"Someone must have something? We should steal," he said, as lights pulsed in his skull.

"Maybe the unit leader. But he is surrounded by his guards."

"The guards would be hungry too, I've seen it in their eyes."

They nodded to each other. A quiet understanding. With every ounce of strength in their bodies they trudged towards the center of their unit, where the hefty unit leader walked with his men. There was no energy or light in their eyes. A deathly silence surrounded them, except the sound of shuffling feet in the grainy sand. Some of the men knew him. Knew his intentions. He tugged on the armband of a soldier walking behind the others. "Does he have food and water?"

The man shook his head. He whispered conspiratorially, "We are all hungry. He probably hides some in his pouch."

"How much do you all like him?"

The man eye's narrowed slightly, but a realization dawned on him. "No one likes him. He beat two to death yesterday for begging for a piece of bread."

He turned to his men.

The thirty or so, his gang, converged into a dense unit, closing in on the unit leader. The leader's guards realized the danger too late, but by then the man and his gang fell upon them like hungry hyenas. The leader tried to react and call others, but it was too late–they were alone in this segment of the thinly spread column. The ground here was uneven with gently rising and falling dunes, which means many could not even see them. He stabbed one of the guards who attempted to speak. *There is no more time!* The guards quickly gave up and the man and his underlings surrounded the lone leader. No one was killed. He knew he needed the guards by his side.

"What do you want? What are you doing?" he asked. His cap was torn in the melee, and his ample chest and belly heaved with exertion. The man had lost weight but still retained much of his flesh. *Greedy fat pig hiding food from us.*

"Bread. Water. Meat. You're hiding it from us," he said, squinting in the hellish brightness of the afternoon sun. His head pounded and he felt his veins contract and expand in his temple.

"What? Are you out of your mind? Get back to your lines and march!"

"No. Food. Now," he said. He couldn't talk anymore. The burning in his belly had intensified. He could feel the sharp jabs of hunger in his mid, in his chest. he moved closer to the leader, pleading with his eyes. "Please."

The leader reached to a club by his belt. The same belt, the man knew, he had used to club two hapless men to death. The leader then swiftly swung the club and struck him on the shoulder. He screamed. This was not working!

He nodded to his men.

They rushed the leader who reached too late to his sword. A thrust from behind and a swing for his neck was enough. The leader fell to the ground, his legs splayed comically.

The man knelt by the fallen leader and swiftly detached his supply belt as the others looked on. The water bladder was mostly empty, and there was nothing but a little clump of hard, dried bread. He cursed. How could anyone eat the prickly bread with their utterly dried throats? But the hunger... the hunger! He took a bite of the bitter clump and raised his hand for anyone else to take the rest–several men lunged forward and there was pushing and shoving for that little piece. *Pathetic.* They had all been reduced to beggars!

They realized that there was nothing else. They had killed him for almost nothing. By then he noticed that there were some Syrian onlookers. The Syrian contingent was right behind, and he knew that those units suffered grievously due to shortage of rations. The news was that they were even more poorly supplied than they were. "You are not the only one poorly supplied," he said, addressing the Syrian captain who looked at him.

"Many of my men are dying of thirst and hunger," the captain said. "I thought that the rumors that we were poorly supplied were unfounded."

The man laughed, even as a ball of pain welled behind his eyes. "You must be a very stupid man. You are no Persian. Of course, they screwed you like a common whore. But you are not alone. We are with you as well, my friend!"

So, they all contemplated their situation as a hot breeze blew. His hands began to shake. Several men sat down, close to giving up. The hunger burned in him and his throat needed moisture. Anything! It was as if a red-hot knife was being slid in and out of his ears. He looked at his men, most with incredible desperation in their faces. He looked back at the fallen man—with his ample belly, thick thighs, still oozing blood from his neck. He pulled out his knife and placed it on the soft flesh below the dead man's shoulders.

"Bring a pot," he said, to someone behind him.

CHAPTER 49

THE GREAT SAND SEA

ABERIS

How much further?

Aberis squinted in the sun that hung low on the sky. The land around had no feature—nothing but a vast sea of sand with undulating dunes that felt like the waves of the sea. There were no landmarks anywhere—not a rock, not a bluff, not a tree, not a bush. If one were blindfolded and turned around and then their blindfold removed, they would not know their direction from before. The sun acted as a poor marker of direction—for it moved through the day, and its orientation was slightly different each time. Aberis knew this much: even if they were slightly off, then over a few days of the journey they would be in a completely different

territory than before.

They had moved with much energy and alacrity for the first few days after Babak had departed on his separate secretive mission, but again, the unrelenting terrain had once more gotten the better of his men. The dead were littering the path. Aberis wondered what someone who has never been here thought of such death—were they such delicate flowers? Did they know that men died even in just a few hours or in a day in such weather? He had told his aides not to bring him stories from the units—they were depressing. His back hurt.

His waist hurt.

His left knee was swollen.

His face itched constantly.

His throat was permanently parched.

These ailments made it difficult to make good decisions.

Ritapates was in the front. The man he trusted, but one that was just not up to this march. He had begun to act strange the last two days—he had become lethargic, had to be goaded to walk, would not sit on the mules, and had become needlessly belligerent with the guards. And now he was raining down expletives at his guards for some perceived slight. He needed to be told to conduct himself with greater dignity.

"*Ritapata.*"

Ritapates turned. He looked irritated. "What?"

The tone!

"Your conduct is unbecoming of an advisor to the court."

Ritapates stopped as if someone had slapped him. He had a vacant look in his eyes and his face scrunched up with anger. He was shorter than Aberis and his gray beard and unkempt mustache made him look like a grumpy grandfather even though he was only a year older than Aberis. He strode to Aberis and stood in front of the noble.

"Or what?"

Aberis was taken aback.

"*Ritapata,* watch your—"

"What will you do, incompetent talentless bastard!" screamed Ritapates. His eyes were ablaze, and spittle flew from his mouth. "You are leading us to our deaths. You will kill us all!"

Aberis was stunned.

No one. No one had ever spoken to him this way. Not even the King of Kings himself. But Ritapates?

Had he gone mad in the heat?

Aberis was tired—now this.

"*Ritapata*, know who you are speaking to!"

Ritapates pushed out his chest and came close to Aberis, looking up at him. "Who? A third rate noble! That's who! You should have listened to me. You should have!"

Aberis' Immortals quickly surrounded the men. He signaled them to hold off.

"You are one sentence away from your head rolling in the sand!"

Ritapates stopped suddenly. He sat down, put his palms against his head and began to wail. He sounded like a wounded dog. "I will die. What will my wife and six children do? Why did you agree to burn a god's temple?"

"Get up, *Ritapata*. You are unwell. We hold no blame— we do what our King commands us to," he said. He was running out of patience. The sun was beating down on him as well, not just this idiot. But this man had served him for decades.

"We hold blame. You hold blame. You wanted it all— the glory, the governorship. That's why you agreed to come here," Ritapates said, still sobbing and his shoulders heaving as he squatted on the ground, surrounded by guards.

"Get up, you fool," Aberis said, and turned to one of him men. "Take him back, put him on a mule and tie him up. He has lost his mind."

Everyone was losing their minds here.

Ritapates would not go. He now lay curled up on the ground, muttering nonsense and lamenting loudly, refusing to cooperate with the guard who was perplexed, unsure what to do.

"Take him, what are you looking at," Aberis ordered.

The guard reached down and began to drag Ritapates, whose gown ripped on the ground and fell away, exposing his nakedness. Ritapates began to shout. "You fucking greedy coward. You never believed me! You will kill everyone if it means you can get what you want. Tell the guards that you have no idea what you are doing. We should have had a real general—"

"Stop," said Aberis to the guard, who dropped Ritapates. "Give me your sword."

The guard hesitated, but gave his blade to Aberis who advanced menacingly at the prone Ritapates.

"One more word and–"

Ritapates looked insane. His thinning hair was all spread, his eyes were open wide in a manic manner, and he foamed in his mouth. As he neared, Ritapates abruptly flung sand into his face. Aberis staggered back from surprise. Ritapates tried getting up.

It was enough.

Aberis held up his sword, holding the handle with both hands like an executioner. Ritapates looked up, uncaring, resigned to his fate. Aberis swung the sword down and struck Ritapates' exposed neck. But instead of cleanly cutting off the head, the exhaustion in Aberis' hand resulted in just cleaving Ritapates' neck. Blood spurted, drenching Aberis' robes. Ritapates fell, twisted grotesquely, his half-severed neck still attached to the torso. He began to struggle in his death throes.

Aberis was revolted.

"Cut it off! Cut it off!" he screamed at a guard, who then struck Ritapates twice until the head was severed from the body.

Aberis sat on the ground, shocked. Every limb in his body protested. He felt sorrow rise in his belly—Ritapates was the closest to family he had, and now the desert had claimed him. It took a while for him to gather his faculties. He ordered a respectful burial for the man and prayed for him. Ritapates was not too bright, but he had stayed by Aberis' side, and tried the best he could.

Aberis now had no one he could truly trust.

When would this nightmare end?

"How much further?" He pressed on the guide. The man seemed supremely confident, but Aberis was not. They had stayed on a course for days now, disregarding all suffering.

"As I had told before, Excellency, we need four more days."

"Four more days of this! We will all die!" He cursed, but now he knew the army had committed too deep—they could not return anywhere, they had no one to rely on, and their only course was to follow this guide.

There was some commotion behind him. "Your Excellency, please come with us. Trouble in the Syrian lines."

Aberis was irritated. "Tell the captains to deal with it. Why am I required to intervene in little disputes!"

He was already tired to his bones. He needed to rest.

The messenger looked uncomfortable. "Mutiny, sir. The entire contingent is refusing to move, blocking the ones behind, and threatening to fight."

Aberis felt lightheaded. These fools! Every stupid action delayed the army. They could let them stay where they are and move on, but that would only encourage more insubordination and defection. What would he do? Go alone and fight the Ammonians with his knife?

"Ask the Immortals to come with me and have three Persian battalions move and surround them."

They then hurried back—it was almost a mile and the leading contingents had to be told to wait. As he passed them, Aberis felt their eyes upon him.

Did they hate him for he was no general?

Did they respect him?

What would a general do differently?

They moved through the haze of the heat and struggled through the sandy ground.

He hated it.

Hated every foot of this place.

The animals, except for the camels, of which less than half of what they started with, had remained, were rendered quite useless. They struggled just like the men. Aberis had tried to ride one of the asses and had given up after the stubborn beast refused to walk, and twice dropped him on the ground. It took more than half an hour, but they finally arrived at the scene of trouble. The Syrian contingent stood, fully armed, with the captain and his lieutenants all positioned defensively. The three Persian battalions had just arrived, creating an encirclement around the Syrians. The rest of the army was now detached on both sides and watched as the scene unfolded.

"Who is in charge?" Aberis yelled, his throat already parched. He had flagrantly violated all rationing rules, unable to withstand the thirst, and he was dipping into the reserves. But he was their commander, and there was no one here to question him.

The Syrian captain, dressed in flowing light gray robes and coarse double-patterned deep brown cow-hide belt, stepped forward. "There are rumors that we are being led to our death."

"What?" Aberis was livid. "Who started these rumors?"

"Some men say that this Sand Sea extends forever until it reaches the land of the dead. And that dark forces are leading us that way. We should turn back."

He looked serious. His weather-beaten face, craggy, unshaven, dirty, conveyed his voice with great seriousness. Such rumors were dangerous.

"You hear wrong. The guide is confident. It is a few more days. You are stopping our progress and endangering the entire army!"

"We are barely moving! Our feet sink in this dreadful sand in places. I am forced to control our hungry and thirsty men and watch them die." he asked. There was desperation in his face.

"Not just you. This is an invasion! What did you expect? When have Syrians who have fought in far lands suddenly turned into town maids?"

The man did not respond to the insult. "We also hear rumors that we are severely short on rations. And we know that you have supplied us poorly compared to your Persians and Greeks."

Aberis bristled at the accusation that he knew to be true. But he could not, of course, admit in full view. "Every man, including me," he said, indignantly, mustering all the anger he could, "has been provisioned equally. I am struggling with you. Every drop that the Persian drinks is matched by every drop the Syrian drinks. These rumors are unfounded!"

A burst of warm wind blew sand onto their faces and Aberis' open mouth caught a fine scoop of sand. He spat and cleaned his tongue. Uncomfortable silence spread among them as they waited for the wind to settle. It was a surreal scene—the barely visible men, all standing in line prepared to fight, their robes billowing in the wind and sand, as

they baked in this terrible sun.

When the wind died and the air cleared, the Syrian spoke again.

"Do you know what the men are resorting to?" he asked rhetorically. *The gumption of this man speaking to me, his lord, like this!* And before Aberis could reply, he nodded to someone behind him. As they watched, two soldiers carried a large bronze cooking pot.

What are they—?

"See here!" the Captain shouted. Aberis leaned forward and the realization of what it was dawned on him even before he saw what was in it. The smell hit him first and he retched to the side.

The ribs were still there.

The Syrian began to shout. "Yes! Excellency. Some are killing other men and eating them because we are being deprived of rations! How much longer must we drink our piss and eat a brother's chest?"

Aberis' eyes began to tear with the odor and the thought of what was in the pot. Controlling these men was their problem, *not his!*

"You ought to control your men from such disgraceful acts. Is it someone else's problem that you are so weak?"

"This pot is from the Persian contingent," he said, smiling.

"It does not matter, you scoundrel! Get back and let us move."

The Captains shook his head. "We demand that we turn back. If you do not allow us, Excellency, we will fight and die here. But we will not take a step forward."

"You will all die if you try to return. We cannot give you rations for your journey. How will you trek another four days without any water? And then what assurances do you have that you will come upon any water? And do you even know where to go!"

The man grinned sadly. "If you do not give us our daily rations, we will fight now. While we might die, so will many of you, and this will create a rebellion in the ranks."

Aberis was confounded. "The heat is making you mad! Think of the riches and glory once we reach Ammon. The coin for your pouches, the women for your bed, the slaves for your home."

"We will die here, Your Excellency. The Scythians were right, this invasion is cursed. We are attacking their gods, and what good does it do to us? This will be our end. We want none of what you say we want. We wish to return," he said, and there was finality in his voice. The last time, Aberis had quelled such unrest easily and made an example of the rabble-rousers—but he was unsure it would work this time. The entire unit was up in arms.

"I cannot let you return," Aberis said, and nodded at the commander by his side. In an instant, at the signals of whistles, the surrounding battalions arranged themselves into battle lines and crouched.

Spears out. Swords drawn. Archers on one end.

But the Syrians were no minnows. They were already positioned—they had their archers and spearmen ready.

They were ready to die.

That was when Aberis noticed something. To a man, they had discarded their waterskins—all their belts had deflated water bladders—they had finished the ration for the day. They really had no intention of going further, and they had no recourse except to get their rations if they decided to return.

They would die fighting or leave with the water and food they demanded.

And Aberis, the fool that he was, was right there in the frontlines! If they let the arrows loose, he would become a porcupine in the sand. So, he made an excuse of conferring with his men and removed himself from the front. Once at a safe distance behind the attack lines, he made the final determination.

He pulled his order whistle and blew it loud and clear.

The archers, who were only a short running distance from the Syrians, arched their backs and extended their bows to the sky.

The Syrian archers did likewise.

A hail of arrows shot on a low arc in either direction, creating a strange whistling sound in the dry air, and slammed into hundreds of men on either side. The dull, soft thuds of bronze arrows piercing light leather corsets and flimsy bronze chest plates terrified Aberis.

And then thousands of men shouted and launched at each other. The Syrians fought valiantly and with fury— they had nothing to lose but life itself, and that they no longer seemed to value. They stabbed and killed as many they could, even as they fell by the tens, ganged on by an encircling ring three times their size. The rising dust obscured the battle within, and then Aberis heard the disturbing news.

The rowdy, riotous Scythians had joined the melee, taking advantage of the dust. These men, stubborn as mules, had not learned their lessons. They were master archers and soon the Persians began to fall like flies under the terrifying assault of well-aimed arrows that pierced through leather like it was animal fat. Aberis began to panic and called the Greeks. The Greeks, better supplied and disciplined, much like the Persians, seemed to get confused who they were fighting and began to kill everyone around them—including the Persian troops that were going after the Scythians. Captains rushed to Aberis, imploring him to call off the attack, for every fighting man was now trying to kill another, so long as he looked different. It mattered not who they were fighting for or against.

Better sense prevailed and the harrowed captains were able to convince Aberis to call off the attacks, which needed more of the Persian and Greek contingents to jump into the fray. Aberis had to twice duck beneath protection shields to escape arrows, and once ran around with his protection guard as a few escaped Syrians chased him like mad dogs. Finally, when it was all settled, thousands more lay dead in the desert. Almost all the Syrians were gone, and those captured were quickly put to death. Most Scythians were dead, and those that remained swore loyalty and said they had nothing to do with this and had stayed away. Aberis, realizing his precarious position, spared them but put them on supply and cleaning duties and cut their ration to just one water fill per day and one meal. That would kill them, he knew. Those gravely wounded would be given a merciful death, and those that were not had to fend for themselves.

As they surveyed the carnage, Aberis asked for quick assessments—they had now lost more than a third of the army due to the dangers of the desert, the attacks, and infighting. And yet here they were, in the middle of an unforgiving and inhospitable plain, and there was no way but forward. Aberis asked that the army be quickly mobilized so that he could to address them. It took a while to group the stretched column that was now nearly five miles in length. Once they were compressed, the units set up relays to convey the speech. The captains stood in the front near the makeshift podium to listen to what he had to say.

Aberis fanned his face and took another sip, hiding behind his bodyguards. He stood up the podium on a small, gentle dune that put him on higher ground for everyone to see. For the occasion he had donned a noble's purple-and-orange cap and a regal robe.

"Great army! I will speak briefly, for the hour demands that we remember our duty and be on the way. We have been tested like no man has ever been. You have been brave and resolute in your march to destroy the Ammonians who have taken the help of their rebel gods and godless men to shake your resolve!"

He paused for effect. Receiving no accolades from the dusty and dim eyes, Aberis soldiered on. "The *Shahanshah* has asked us to carry out this duty. The guide tells us it is only two more days," he lied, "and then it is cold water to your lips, salted meat, warm bodies to your bed! Do not despair."

There were sporadic shouts, but the men knew that insubordination would only lead to death unless the Persians and the Greeks, the majority, mutinied. Aberis was confident that they would not. There was too much pride in those troops, and they were promised more than the others. Not all were equal—Aberis knew that at every stage of his life.

"We will now begin our final march. And as we speak, there is another contingent meeting the Ammonians, asking them to surrender so that no more blood may be spilled."

There were some murmurs of what this might be, including some cheers and hurrahs from men hoping that they would get all they wanted—rape and plunder—without putting themselves to risk.

"Captains will decide what to do with the fallen soldiers' belongings, and we ask you to rest for an hour before we march again. I have ordered that all soldiers be given an extra cup of water and an extra meal for the night!"

That brought some cheering, even though Aberis knew that every additional cup and every additional piece of bread handed out now would jeopardize their journey. The captains had advised him that if they did not address morale now, there would not be much of a journey later.

As he stepped down from the podium, Aberis wondered how Eribaeus was doing and hoped that the next leg of the journey would be swift and decisive.

CHAPTER 50
THE GREAT SAND SEA
ERIBAEUS

Eribaeus' eyes widened. Babak had asked him, with a cruel, knowing smile, if he had ever heard of him.

Who was this man?

"What do you mean?" he asked.

"It was a simple question, noble. Do you not know who I am?"

"You are the insolent advisor—"

"No. What is your recollection of our first meeting?"

Eribaeus had no idea what Babak was alluding to. How could he remember every turban-wearing barbarian he met in his many campaigns? Who did this bastard even think he was?

"I meet many people, and I have been on more campaigns that you have fucked your whore wife. Why would I remember every beak-nosed bastard I meet?" he said contemptuously. His anger was rising rapidly—he was in this miserable position because of this man. How dare he ask these questions as if he was interrogating him. Him. Eribaeus. The one graced by the *Shahanshah!* The lord of ten-thousand mercenaries. One with great respect back home. And now dealing with questions from an unknown, lowly Persian officer or advisor or whatever he was.

"Remember Eshanna?"

"Eshanna?" Eribaeus strained to remember, but in this dry heat, the haze of memory began to clear. "The citadel by the marshes?"

"Ah, the images are coming back to you."

"What about it? It was some town which we had to subdue—fight the rebels, teach them a lesson."

"Did you fight any rebels?"

"Of course, we—" He stopped. It was coming back to him. That was the town where someone, a king's official or somebody, had been murdered. Aberis had sought his help to subdue the rebellious town, but before they arrived there, the town's chief had ensured that the able-bodied, fighting men had gone far away for something else.

Now he remembered.

The town was defenseless, and they had burned and looted as much as they could. And then, it was hazy in his memory, but they taught them a lesson by executing some. What was so strange about that?

"Yes, I remember somewhat. We encountered some resistance and—"

Whack!

Babak delivered a stinging slap, causing Eribaeus to swoon.

"You bastard!" an enraged Eribaeus lunged at the wiry Persian. But suddenly strong hands gripped him from behind and restrained him—the Egyptians had for whatever reason decided to hold him back. Babak stepped back and stared at Eribaeus. His eyes were dark and cold, but his lips upturned in a knowing smile.

"Is that what you remember?"

"What are you trying—"

Whack!

Eribaeus' spittle flew from his cracked lips, and he shouted in surprise and anger.

"Stop, stop—"

Whack!

"I remember! I remember now! Stop it!"

"Tell me what you remember," Babak asked. Casually stepping forward. His face only inches away. The grip on his hands was strong, preventing him from turning.

Eribaeus gathered his wits and breathed slowly.

"There were no rebels. No. They were sent away somewhere, I think. Please. I do not remember."

Babak stepped back. Eribaeus was relieved. At least not another slap.

"Very good. What happened after that?"

Eribaeus squinted. The pressure on his shoulder increased, and he snapped at the man behind. "Are you trying to break my shoulders, you backward bald-headed pig!"

Thud! Babak punched him in the gut.

Eribaeus collapsed, still hanging by his shoulders as the man behind did not let go. His stomach exploded in pain, but now his shoulder sockets felt like they would pop. He stood again, with his feet wobbling and feeling dizzy.

Then Babak made a sign to the Egyptian, and the boy stuffed a rag into his mouth. Eribaeus could not scream. With wild eyes he followed them. They tied his hands and feet and dumped him on the side. Then they dug a hole in the ground—it took some effort, but with five men at work it did not take too long. They had created a small makeshift tent and worked under it, while he baked under the sun.

What are they doing? No!

And soon, the pit was ready.

Two men came and began to drag him. He struggled and screamed—but nothing came out of the filthy rag. They dropped him feet first, and there he was, in a hole, in the desert, buried to his neck. Even as he tried to shout and plead, they filled the open spaces with sand so that it was just his face outside.

Then Babak squatted in front of him. He removed the rag and Eribaeus gagged.

"Go on," ordered Babak. It was burning hot. And he was now stuck in this nightmarish drama.

"We rounded up some villagers. I think. The town chief had run away, and they tried to negotiate," he gasped and wheezed.

"I see. Then?"

"I don't remember—don't hit me! Wait. We rounded up the people, and as is customary, we had to teach them a lesson."

"But you had already burned their homes and looted their belongings."

"Yes, yes. But you know this, Babak. Any rebellion cannot be left untamed! If we did nothing, the King would flay both Aberis and me. Please let me go. Do not do this!"

"The agreement was for you to pick ten people and execute them."

"Ah, that's right. That's what we did! You are right. Listen, we will reward you with—"

Whack!

Eribaeus began to weep. It took him a while to recover. He reached deep into the recesses of his memory. He would have to be contrite. Remorseful. Truthful. Perhaps then they would let him go. Clearly, this had something to do with Babak and something that happened on that day in Eshanna.

"It is coming to me now. We picked a few more just to teach them a lesson."

"The town chief. He ran away. Do you remember who else took his place?"

Eribaeus now stared at Babak.

And then—

Through the haze of pain and terror.

Through the dry and hot air.

His memory flooded back to him.

Of course! The man who represented the town. The man who begged for the life of his sons—or daughters.

Oh no!

"It was you? I did not know!"

"You decided that it would be amusing to round up innocent, surrendered villagers and have them rush to the marshes. Do you remember?"

"Maybe. Of course. Yes, yes. We should not have. We just wanted to give them a chance to run—"

Babak reached forward and boxed Eribaeus' right ears. Then he pulled it forward. A blade glinted in his hand.

"No, Babak!" Eribaeus screamed.

And then a blinding pain flashed in his ear as Babak sliced his ear off. He then threw it to the sand.

Eribaeus vomited. He felt the acid in his throat, and then the warm blood flowing on the side of his cheek. His throat burned, his lips were parched, and he was suddenly incredibly thirsty.

"It will get worse if you do not continue. What choice did you give them?"

Eribaeus sobbed. "I don't remember. I think we let them run but we had soldiers chase them…?"

Babak appraised him quietly. Then he spoke. "No. You had people picked randomly. You laughed at their pleas. Then you had soldiers shoot arrows at villagers running barefoot into the marshes."

Eribaeus kept his head low and sobbed.

"And then when I begged you to stop, and that my sons were there, you laughed. They died in a hail of arrows. They were only ten and twelve," he said, and blinked his eyes rapidly.

"You must forgive me. I did not know what I was doing. I know I was wrong! Babak!"

If only I could escape from this reedy, vicious goat-fucker, I would make an example of him and his entire dynasty!

Then Babak spoke. "When you stay in the darkness for so long, you forget what light feels like," he said, and then he stood and quietly walked away.

Eribaeus coughed and pleaded for water, but none was forthcoming. Soon, his tongue stuck in the impossibly dry throat. His great mop of golden hair felt like rocks on his head. His body felt like it was gripped and squeezed by a hot iron vase and agony pulsated through his limbs as his muscles began to cramp. He wheezed and gasped. Babak sat with the men, under a tent, and they had their meals.

No one paid attention to Eribaeus.

So, he stayed that way for the next two hours. His eyes began to droop, and his entire body felt like it was on fire. His tears had dried, and he was beginning to see gardens, flowing water, even his family that he had not seen for so long. His head began to sway.

Finally, Babak came back.

He had a jug.

Eribaeus barely registered the scene in front of him. But then Babak gently, but firmly held his head and placed the jug of water to his lips. Eribaeus drank greedily, relishing every sip of the life-saving liquid, almost choking.

He finished most of it.

He then breathed deeply, feeling some life return to him.

And then he looked up in gratitude. "Thank you."

Babak nodded but said nothing. Eribaeus slowly came to his senses, even as his body hurt. Maybe he could find a way out of this.

"The idea that such a lesson should be taught was not just mine... Aberis and Jabari were involved in it too."

"I know," Babak said. His dark eyes pierced Eribaeus'. The Persian's gaunt face, now accentuated by the strain of these days, and the fine sand clinging to it, made him look like a demon from the underworld.

Babak offered a piece of bread and some meat, and Eribaeus greedily ate it. Babak offered him more water.

"May gods bless you for the kindness, Babak! Maybe we could work out an arrangement. Maybe we—"

The blade in Babak's hand flashed, and Eribaeus felt a sharp pain in his neck. Shocked, he looked down. Blood spurted from the deep gash and drenched the yellow sand, turning it dark brown.

As darkness enveloped Eribaeus even in this afternoon sun, he heard a distant voice. "May you find peace in the afterlife, Eribaeus."

CHAPTER 51
THE GREAT SAND SEA
BABAK

Babak watched as life ebbed out of Eribaeus and blood pooled around his buried neck. He walked back to the makeshift tent. Then he spread his arms wide, and the boy and the man grinned broadly and came to him. They hugged him and he kissed their cheeks in affection.

"Mentu, dear boy," Babak said, "You have become a greater man than most men!"

Mentu beamed with pride. Babak turned to the other man and grabbed his shoulders affectionately. "And you grow a beard like a Persian, Abanare!"

The man laughed. "It is camouflage!"

"Indeed. I had scant hopes that you would find me."

"Mentu has the eyes of Horus. Besides, with your garish dress, you looked like a whore in a Memphis market. How could we miss you?"

Babak grinned. "You know why I had dressed this way," he said, looking down on his dirty and shiny blue scarf, red bracelets, and his bright orange waistcloth.

This was the signal to Petubastis' men to recognize and not harm him.

It had worked brilliantly.

The men then dug a pit near an overhang and transferred most of the treasure into it. The helpers were promised some of the valuables, more than enough for them to last years, assuming they did not trade it away for whores and beer. Mentu and Abanare would keep some for the discussion with the priests.

"What next, *Abbu?*" asked Abanare, using the affectionate term for Babak.

"I have a plan," Babak said.

PART V

CHAPTER 52
THE GREAT SAND SEA
ABERIS

As the sun began to set in the western skies, the dense column began to move again with purpose. The message this time was very clear: *move quickly or we all die*. Aberis had done something he should have a long ago—he had gathered former priests, sages, and holy men of all kinds from the various contingents, and threatened them with torture if they did not tell their units that the only salvation was to move forward and that they saw victory. They then went back to their men and did their part, quelling some of the unrest.

With flickering torches, they followed a path they were told was in the direction of Ammon. When Aberis looked back, it was as if a million fireflies marched in the deathly stillness of a dark night. When they finally stopped, they knew not what hour it was or how much to dawn, but they were exhausted. The horns sounded for everyone to pause and rest, take their bread, and do an assessment of the missing. Aberis felt proud of himself—he had commanded the day, put an end to the mutiny, and now they were marching with purpose.

The Ammonians would never forget the day when the army reached them. Those evil men and their gods had tried everything possible, but Aberis would show them what it meant to stand up against the King of Kings and his admirable nobles. As he put his head on the comfortable pillow in his comfortable tent, he imagined himself in a glorious Governor's court, dispensing judgment as men and women stood around him admiringly.

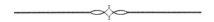

It was evening.

He was sitting on a boat.

It was swaying, like the gentle movement of a cradle.

He peeked to the side, and there was no water. It was just sand, and the dunes moved like waves—pushing, receding, rising. He tried to scream but no sound came out. A dune rose like a giant wave of water and sprayed him with sand. Then the shaking intensified, rocking the boat with violence. Aberis screamed again, and a few grunts managed to escape. His arms shot out to hold the side of the boat, and he—

"Excellency! Your Excellency!"

An aide was shaking him. Aberis sat up, disoriented, shouting. Men were around him. It was dawn, a gentle light filled the room. His face was sweaty and sticky, and it was already becoming warm. "What—What is it?"

"We have a problem," the man said anxiously.

"What now?" Aberis groaned. His thighs ached from the running the previous afternoon. The soles of his feet were on fire.

"The guide, Excellency. We cannot find him."

Aberis was alarmed. His heart thudded against his ribs. "What do you mean you cannot find him? He could be sleeping somewhere, drunk on beer, or in the latrine ditches."

"No. We have checked. He is nowhere. Some men are saying he ran away in the night."

Aberis felt his face flush and his belly tightened with fear. He ordered another full search, causing nearly a hundred messengers to reach into every part of the column and asking soldiers and the baggage train to check every tent and behind every nearby dune. They then fanned outward, scrambling to nearby taller dunes and looking out.

Nothing.

After hours, as the sun rose again in the sky, drenching them with heat that felt like being smothered by a heated thick blanket, Aberis realized that the guide was truly gone.

The bastard!

That son of a diseased whore!

Why?

Babak had said the guide was a good—

Babak.

His mind began to work, connecting the dots.

And then he felt like his heart was about to give out.

Babak!

Aberis stumbled into his tent and collapsed.

Who had inserted himself into the campaign?

Babak.

Who kept the main body of the army away from Horosis?

Babak.

Who survived the attack in the dunes and killed Jabari?

Babak.

Who killed the Egyptian captive before he could say more?

Babak.

Who pointed to Jabari and Eribaeus as conspirators with not a shred of

evidence?

Babak.

Who took the valuables—No!

Babak!

And who left them in the hands of this guide?

That bastard. Oh, that bastard. Why?

They had lost hours once again, and now they had no guide. Aberis knew that it would be a miracle if they could find their way to Ammon, but there was no way he could take this entire army. Some units would just have to starve or die of thirst—there was no other way. His lips quivered with frustration and exhaustion.

Why? Ahuramazda, why did you send me to suffer here?

His men stood around, looking anxious and worried. "What next, Excellency? Do we have a different guide? Can we go by the stars?"

Aberis nodded. There was something the guide said about following two bright stars in the sky. He would have to have the army simply follow the direction in the morning and hope that they stay on a straight line. *It would not be too hard,* he thought, *for there was nothing here that impeded their path.*

"Yes. We will follow the stars the guide suggested. And one more thing," he said specifically to the commanders of the Persian and Greek units. "Cut off all rations to the remaining Medians and Scythians, half to Indians. If there is a rebellion, slaughter them. We march tonight, no stoppages."

CHAPTER 53

ΛMMON

AMUNPERRE

These cheeky scoundrels, thought Amunperre. The two stood before him, their eyes twinkling and demeanor confident. He had seen them before when they had arrived at Horosis and met with Petubastis.

"Why should I believe you?"

The boy, Mentu was his name, reached into a large pouch slung around his scrawny shoulders. And from it he produced an exquisite gold statuette of Amun, adorned with rubies and lapis-lazuli. Amunperre's eyes opened wide at the artifact. "This is only a sample. He has a lot more."

"Beautiful. Very beautiful. What is it that you wish to convey and what do you seek?" He asked. These two arrived only a few hours ago, seeking an urgent audience with the High Priest. They had important news for him and offers to make.

"The Persian needs medicines for his daughter. He also says he has killed Jabari, the snake, and the Greek nobleman."

"Proof?"

The older man, Abanare, reached into his bag. And from it he removed Eribaeus' head, now desiccated. Amunperre recoiled but acknowledged the find. "How do I know this is who you say he is?"

"We were with him, Your Holiness. We also have his ring," Abanare said, and produced a fine gold ring with Greek lettering, spelling Eribaeus—Amunperre was a learned man, and he knew those letters. He had heard of a man named as such who had accompanied Cambyses.

"And you say this man, this Persian, has misdirected an entire army in the Great Sand Sea? This is the same man who has been assisting Petubastis?"

Abanare grinned. "He has. He says they walk further west, and that the guide with him would have abandoned them."

Amunperre nodded approvingly. The guide had arrived just the last evening, speaking the tale of a Persian who had saved his life at Pelusium and had then asked for the debt to be paid. But he would speak no more until either the Persian or a boy and a man arrived—they were the messengers.

"This Persian. What is his ambition—does he wish to dethrone Cambyses?"

Abanare shook his head vigorously. "He seeks no part of an invasion that defiles and destroys our temples. But he seeks no glory—he wishes to have this medicine for his daughter, and then he says he will vanish to the south."

Amunperre was not convinced. "That is it? He wants medicine?"

Mentu spoke this time. "And, if your Holiness pleases, some coin so they can escape and settle somewhere."

The High Priest laughed. The ask was a low price to pay for what they were going to avoid—at least for now. If the army to Ammon never reached or suffered significant losses, then Cambyses may be forced to accede to the priests' demands of autonomy and preservation of their ways and means. "He will be rewarded generously. But first we must get news of the destruction of the army."

The man shook his head. "No, Your Holiness. There is no way to get that. All you will need to do is wait. You perhaps certainly know by now that the army is nowhere on the traditional routes. And you know that such a deviation creates great peril."

Amunperre acknowledged it. The army would be lost, but these men also held the promise of great riches that he could benefit from, just in case.

"I will convey a message to the Oracle. Now, this medicine, what does his daughter ail from?"

The man reached to his bag and pulled out a papyrus. Amunperre held it close to his aging eye. There, in the language of the commoners, was a detailed description of what troubled the girl. *A familiar disease, with a familiar cure,* he thought. He also understood the Persian's approach of sending the Egyptians—for why would he listen to a man that advised Cambyses? But the man seemed genuine and had helped them much. He still suspected the reasons, but those were no longer his concern.

"We have the cure, and it is known to work with ease. But you must hurry—the disease takes life once it progresses. I will give you instructions."

CHAPTER 54

THE GREAT SAND SEA

ABERIS

It had been three days since the revolt in the Syrian ranks. Aberis had driven his army as hard as any general could—giving no significant pause, allowing no dissent, and ruthlessly destroying any resistance or doubt. There had to be a town with water somewhere, he was sure, and all it would take is a few days to find. And now, three days later, the tired scouts had only come with bad news—nothing. Not a sign of life. Not a crow overhead, not a snake on the ground, not a bush or a tree, and no man crossed their path. Aberis was frightened now—did this Sand Sea truly extend to the end of the earth? Were they headed to nothingness?

The last count was harrowing. By now they had lost most of the Syrians, Medians, and Indians. A great number in the baggage train had died along the way. Stories of horror the men endured had changed from a trickle to flood—fistfights, murders for water, men killing others to eat their flesh or drink their blood for moisture, night raids on baggage trains that now had to protected by the Immortals and large sections of Persian troops.

And there was no town or water to be found.

Which way to go?

Where to turn?

He had several Egyptians in the baggage train interrogated—surely some knew the paths? The Bedouins themselves were utterly incompetent—they had never been this far. And then two had died. The men looked to him for answers, and he had none, though he pretended to know the way. He had invoked the gods, forced the accompanying priests to spread falsehoods that safety was near, promoted men in their ranks and promised great riches and rewards to the influential commanders. But all that would only go so far in this savage land. And now, as he stood in the morning, the southern wind had picked up speed. It came hot and strong, singing a low ominous tune, pushing them aside and bringing with it a continuous spray of sand. Aberis despaired, when would the gods smile upon him? He hastily ordered the column to halt until the storm passed. Sometimes these lasted for hours, and in their peak intensity made it impossible to see anything outside. They pitched their tents and huddled, miserable, and Aberis lay on a tattered sheet and curled up in a fetal position. He had not slept well in days. His eyes burned and his face felt perpetually hot and sticky.

He lay that way for an hour even as the wind whipped the tents, and he heard shouts outside but ignored them. He knew that when such events occurred, sometimes tents flew away, exposing the men to the unrelenting harshness. Many ran away, disoriented, and got lost. His ears burned. His throat felt like sand had been rubbed on them—and yet he had no strength to reach out to his waterskin.

Aberis began to feel drowsy as the wind whistled and whined outside. At this time, they would usually slow the column for the mid-day meals.

His eyes began to droop.

CHAPTER 55

THE GREAT SAND SEA

PETUBASTIS

They had waited for hours for the army to come to this place. And just as their augurs had predicted, a slow and steady sand storm had developed through the morning and strengthened as the hours went by. It now blew with enough force for Aberis' army to halt. Visibility reduced rapidly—but by then they had a reasonable idea of what was where. At the head of the column was Aberis' tent, clearly marked, larger than the others, with a clump of bodyguard tents around it. The column itself was clumped—with denser clusters in places with large gaps in between. It was also clear to them that the baggage trains were far better protected than they were before—which meant that the men were also far more exposed in many other sections. But the army they now saw was much smaller than what it was. Petubastis had done what others had advised him not to.

He was to rest and recoup after the last attack. After initially agreeing, he had decided otherwise. And in this endeavor, he was supported by the Persian, who, with the support of Petubastis' trackers, had finally killed the Greek noble and then joined Petubastis. The Pharaoh was taken aback by the Persian. This wiry little man with intense black eyes and a hawk-like nose was astute in his observations and had helped Petubastis with the next steps. He was the reason why they had such success so far. He was also unafraid of the Pharaoh and had little reverence. Petubastis knew that the Persians did not see their kings as a god. Perhaps he would, in time. After all, they were barbarians, even if conquering barbarians. But his lack of worship translated to him speaking his mind, a refreshing change.

"The army must not raise its head, and I want Aberis," he had said. He had not explained what drove him to such vengeance. Mentu and Abanare had not returned from Ammon, and the Persian—Babak was his name—said that he had to send them back to Thebes. Petubastis asked no more questions, instead, they had then plotted how to catch up with the army again to inflict another damage.

They did not have the numbers any more to take on even a weakened army. Petubastis was injured. His trusted general, Senwosret, was now in Farrasis, building a backup defense line to hold the entryway to the oasis, just in case the invaders turned that way.

Babak had quickly stepped into the role of the advisor to check the Pharaoh against his impulses. The attack would have to be surgical this time, he had argued, none of the foolish bravery of charging his men to a wounded force. Remember, great Pharaoh, Babak had said, a bleeding lion is far more dangerous than one with a full stomach. He had convinced Petubastis with other arguments.

They were too far from supply lines.

The Persian Immortals were not vanquished.

The Greeks and Persian troops would have been taken better care of, even if others had died on the way. And they were better trained.

They would more watchful than ever before after their experience.

And if the attack was to happen, which Petubastis was insistent that it would, then it would be critical to be executed in a way that the invaders would not know which direction to turn. Following them would undoubtedly put the invaders back in the path of the towns.

Petubastis and Babak finally agreed on a different strategy.

This one would be far more surgical.

Their augurs had promised the right conditions, but they would have to wait and watch.

And finally, those words had come true. The small storm was here, and it would last a day at least.

Petubastis mind drifted back to the current, looking at the army that was now within striking distance. In this weather, not a soldier or scout was out, and no doubt they were all huddling and waiting for the winds to calm.

They slowly crawled towards their targets. Petubastis and his men towards an exposed section with a smaller baggage train, one Babak had said was reserved for senior officers and nobles. And then Babak, with two of his best men, were going towards what the Persian wanted.

And now, they would cut off the head of the snake and watch it slither and die.

CHAPTER 56

THE GREAT SAND SEA

ABERIS

Aberis was drifting off, sliding in and out of strange dreams of hands reaching out from the sand and disfigured old women with wings flying over the desert.

Suddenly, there was a commotion. Was someone shouting? Who in their minds would go out to do something in this—

The flap to his tent flung open and three figures rushed in.

"Hey, who—"

The men were heavily masked. They all wore their garments tightly wrapped around their bodies, like mummies. Aberis wondered if he were dreaming, or if these were evil spirits sent from beneath the ground. He tried to get up, but one of them slammed his fist to his face, breaking one of his teeth. Aberis screamed for his guards but none came in. He kicked and fought, but he was outnumbered, and they were strong. They swiftly bound him and thrust a rag into his mouth. He gasped, struggling to breathe, and then they dragged him out of the tent.

Where are the bodyguards? The Immortals? Where are those incompetent bastards?

The wind was strong now, blowing sand everywhere. He could not see the attackers as they had blindfolded him. He kicked and flailed but they managed to hold on. There was much shouting, but he could not make what was going on. And then just like that, the noise reduced in intensity. He was dropped on the ground—it was hot, but it was grainy and soft. But the sand was no longer blowing on his face.

Someone yanked the rag out of his mouth.

He spit dirt out and gasped. "Who are you?" he shouted, still struggling to see.

There were several men by his side and two near his face, peering down on him.

Why had no one come to his rescue? What was going on?

Then one of the men removed the wrap around his face. Even in the orange haze, where the sun was blotted out by the flying sand, the features were unmistakable.

Babak!

"Hello, noble," he said.

CHAPTER 57

THE GREAT SAND SEA

IMMORTALS

Vyspana, the commander of the Immortals, entrusted with the safety of the most senior men of the contingent, ran out from Aberis' tent in a panic. In his initial reaction to fend off the attack that came from behind him, he had neglected to check his Lord's tent. It was a classic diversion and he had fallen for it. He wrapped a turban around his face and shielded his eyes with his palms. He shouted for his men to group around him. "His Excellency is nowhere, has anyone seen him?" he shouted, trying hard so they could hear him. They shook their head. He had attempted, futilely, to check for tracks near the tent. But the wind was shifting the patterns in the ground, making it impossible to find anything. They had fended off attacks near the officer's baggage train—which was unfortunately lightly guarded, for the thinking was that no one would dare come there. But no one guessed that it would be attacked here, in the middle of nowhere, and during a sandstorm.

It was unbelievable!

He had an idea. He turned his attention to the shadows fighting in the storm. "Capture one of them, don't kill them!"

They then ran towards a group of fighting men. He attacked the first man who was swinging wildly at the soldiers around him. With a single thrust to his back he dropped the man and turned to another. *How many are here?* Then he struck another man running towards a tied camel. The strangely dressed attacker, wrapped in clothes like a dead body, managed to evade his swing in the last minute and the two tumbled to the ground. The sword fell from his hand, and the strong attacker quickly got on top of him. His powerful hands gripped the neck and tried to squeeze. The sand was burning the eyes and making it hard to breathe, but he was an Immortal. Trained in the craft of war. Honed to be a fighting machine. Sand or not, he would prevail!

His arm shot up and punched the attacker on his ribs. The man grunted but did not budge. Vyspana's eyes were beginning to lose focus and the gasping for breath only caused more sand to enter his mouth. With no help forthcoming, he knew it was only up to him. He mustered all his strength and slammed his fist to the attacker's jaw. The man swooned and loosened the grip on Vyspana's neck. In a lightning strike, Vyspana reached to his waistband and pulled out his blessed dagger, one presented to him by the great Cyrus himself, and stabbed the attacker in the neck. The man clutched his neck and fell aside, and Vyspana swiftly rose to his feet and stabbed the man again in his chest. Men were still fighting. He joined a few more, and then heard a commotion as more units began to arrive, providing the necessary reinforcements. He found his lieutenant and screamed. "Get me the archers, now! Have we captured anyone?"

It took a while, but they dragged a man to Vyspana. He too was dressed in this strange way, but he was relatively unharmed. They dragged him to the side and inside a tent so they could interrogate him. There was not much time. The man resisted answering, but after they broke his knees with a heavy bronze rod and punctured an eye, he lost his resolve. The words were simple—Vyspana knew enough to ask simple phrases. "From which direction?" And "Who you?"

The answers came through tortured breaths and plenty of spittle. "That way," the man pointed. He could be lying, he could be truthful, or he might simply not know in this mess—but they would find out. That he was telling the truth was evident in his next answer. "With Pharaoh.

Petubastis."

Petubastis is here?

What a catch! But he knew not to keep his hopes too high. In this gust, confusion, fear, and exhaustion, it was unlikely anyone would be able to find the Pharaoh, even if he was dead and lying somewhere. By then a larger group of archers had arrived and Vyspana prepared to give them orders.

He had an idea.

CHAPTER 58

THE GREAT SAND SEA

BABAK

They lay low behind a dune not far away from the column where the fight continued. The wind was still blowing strong, giving them the necessary cover, even if it was magnifying their suffering. But Babak felt at peace—if it meant his death now, so be it. The man before him struggled with the knots and screamed expletives.

"You fucking coward," Aberis cursed, straining against his binds and spitting at him.

"Brave of you to say that, noble. You really do not know who I am, do you?"

"A coward. A traitor. A scoundrel who spits on his god's face and deceives those who feed him. A diseased dog—"

Babak drove his knife into Aberis' thigh. The sharp blade sliced through the soft muscle and scraped against the bone. The nobleman screamed. His eyes were wild. The pride and hubris in his face were replaced by raw fear. He clutched his injured leg and gasped.

"What do you want?" Aberis asked, but this time his voice was low with agony. Saliva dripped from his lips.

"Can you bring my sons back?"

Aberis stared, uncomprehending. "Your sons? What do you mean?"

"Remember Eshanna?"

Aberis adjusted his position to relieve the pain in his leg. He then reclined on the sandy slope behind him. "Yes. Some little town I had to subdue. We talked about it."

"Do you remember what you did?"

Aberis' eyes opened in realization. "We had to teach the town a lesson. I did what I was commanded to do."

Babak leaned close to the man's face. "Were you commanded to send innocent men, women, and children to the marshes while they were shot at by your archers?"

It took a while for Aberis to come to terms with his situation. And then some more before he realized who Babak was, and what had happened to his sons.

"How could I know?" Aberis began to plead. "It is the nature of conflict. You would not allow such insubordination! Besides, you were in the army. You know how these things are necessary."

"That is what Eribaeus said before I killed him," Babak said. "We fought armed soldiers. We punished mischief-mongers. I never raised my sword at a woman or a child, and I never gave orders for innocents to be slaughtered."

"But your recommendations caused many to die. How can you—"

Babak flung sand on Aberis' face and then smothered him. Aberis kicked around, trying to fight, but he had underestimated how strong the wiry little man was. Then Babak gripped Aberis' neck, squeezing it, and his eyes protruded from the sockets.

"Your desire for governorship will end in this desert."

Squeeze.

"Your cruelty will get buried in this sand."

Squeeze.

"Your army will vanish, and you will be forgotten as a useless, cruel wretch!"

Squeeze.

But just as Aberis' life began to seep out of him, Babak heard soft whistles in the air, faint in the sounds of the storm but distinct, unmistakable.

Arrows!

"Run!" He screamed. And he let go of Aberis and stumbled back. The first set of sleek arrows descended upon them, and one of them punctured Aberis' shoulder, pinning him to the ground.

"This will be the end of you," Babak hissed, staring into the soul of a man that had brought him and his wife so much grief. Aberis only looked up fearfully, his eyes now unfocused and wild with terror.

The arrows kept coming, and some slammed into the Egyptians, throwing them face down into the sand. It was impossible to look up and watch the sky, for the disturbed air obscured all visibility. The wind had died down, causing the dust in the air to slowly settle. The terrifying bolts that rained down from the sky were only visible in their final descent, when it was too late to react. Babak ran as fast as he could—he was dressed for this. The flowing Persian gowns were terrible for the sandy ground. Petubastis had warned him something about a storm. The Pharaoh had forced him to wrap himself tightly with mummy-like bandages and carry a long, slim, bamboo pipe. The pipe would help them breathe if they were buried under sand. This strange attire that he wore made it much easier for him to run and he was thankful for this clever modification. They looked like strange white apparitions running in orange-yellow swirls.

He did not know where he was running or in which direction, for it mattered not. What mattered most was going out of range of the arrows that still glided through the air and fell upon them. And then, just as they began, the whizzing of the arrows stopped. Babak could only make out the hazy outlines of Petubastis' men running around him, and then suddenly, as if ghosts appearing from the air, floating robes materialized from behind a low dune.

Immortals!

CHAPTER 59
THEBES

NEDJEM

"Open your eyes, my baby. Open your eyes," Nedjem wailed. It had now been hours since the morning sun and Amastri had not responded to her mother's words. It was now eighteen days since Babak had walked out the door with the promise of revenge and cure.

And he had not returned—she understood he might need some more time, but time their daughter did not have. Amastri's condition had steadily worsened, and the last visit to the military physician had yielded nothing. The man had asked her to pray five times a day, including both Persian and Egyptian gods, and to pay a shaman to ward off the evil spirits. But where would she get money for all that? What Babak had given her for barter was running out, and Amastri's situation made it even harder for Nedjem to go out and work and earn grain, silver, pottery or vegetables. She was becoming desperate.

Desperate enough to borrow.

She had already met with several men who knew Babak—some were able to give modest loans, some proposed she give immoral favors in return for grain or metal, and most others begged helplessness. She was running out of options.

She was waiting for them to return.

Babak.

Abanare.

Mentu.

Abanare, the dear brother who had loved and watched over her when her father died early. Abanare had spent years in Pharaoh Amasis' court and knew many men who had fled to the western deserts as Cambyses advanced to Memphis. He had connections in Aostris, Horosis, and Ammon.

Mentu. Abanare's son. The sharp, eager boy with much ambition. He saw in Nedjem a mother he never had, and she in him the sons she lost.

Much against her wishes, they had convinced her that she needed them more than ever, and Babak had sat with them before the departure to design their intricate plans. One that might seem fantastically ambitious at first glance. They had left for Horosis days before Babak. In that far town, they said, was a power that could greatly aid Babak in his quest.

But she had heard from none so far. She also had no news at all about the army and where it might be or where last was—except for one little piece of information that suggested that many days ago they had arrived near Horosis.

And now Amastri stirred in her arms. The girl's hands had begun look like sticks and her ribs stuck out in unsightly ways. Her cheeks had sunken to a hollow, giving her a ghoulish look—like the jokes they made about an evil *Baba* with bug eyes and a mile-long nose. What was worrying even more was she had almost stopped eating, and she had to be force-fed milk and grain soup. And then sometimes vomited or lost to dysentery.

So Nedjem sat and prayed again. Who was hearing her cries?

She knew that her child was not immortal, but did she too have to die so
    early?

CHAPTER 60

THE GREAT SAND SEA

BABAK

Babak knew how the immortals were dressed. He had described them and their capability in detail to Petubastis' men. Each warrior was well trained in the arts of the sword, knife, spear, and ax. Many were experts in cavalry though that skill came to no use here. They wore a thick, double-layered light leather cuirass that protected their chest and mid. Bronze plates protected their shoulders.

But in this heat and sand, most had long given up wearing either, preferring to walk unburdened by the additional weight—something Petubastis and his men could take advantage of. But in hand-to-hand they would be exceedingly difficult to defeat.

Which is why they had prepared in a very different way, just in case they were attacked by the fiercest of the Persian army. Even as he ran parallel to the running immortals, he heard a loud sound of a horn. And then to his left, groups of Petubastis' men materialized in pairs. Babak quickly turned left and ran behind them to form a defense line. Each man in a pair held to the end of a thick rope. On this rope was smeared a thick layer of inflammable fat and a malodorous yellow material. The rope burned brightly, creating a band of fire that the men twirled like the fire artists in a court. Only this time they swung and hurled it with great impact. The first few flew in the air and smacked into the oncoming row of the Immortals. The material was sticky and caused the rope to cling to the men. They screamed and flailed about, trying to get rid of it, but their fine gowns, themselves with an affinity for fire, lit up, creating a fiery human torch than ran screaming, blind with agony. The sizzling ropes flew in the hot afternoon air, landing on and near the large group that was now spreading out to escape the attack and circling Babak and the Egyptians. But this was enough to disrupt their rhythm, just as Babak suspected, for not only were many creating a terrifying spectacle running around burning, but the others worried about catching fire. The ground in front of them was now hot, sandy, and lit with flames in many places.

Then came the arrows. The Egyptians had come with a small contingent of archers in reserve, and they now unleased what they had on the Immortals. The bolts struck many in one fell swoop, arcing low in the air, over Babak's head. As quickly as the attack had begun, it had already gone wrong for the Immortals—many who now lay dead either set on fire or impaled by arrows. But they were no cowards—these were men with years of experience in the harshest of places and facing the hardest of men. They quickly retreated and began to form an attacking position. Their swords reflected the fire and the peeking afternoon sun.

Babak noticed that they were forming a wedge, and he knew by experience that this fearsome formation could create much damage. "Spread out," he screamed.

The Immortals rushed towards the Egyptian lines.

This time no burning rope would stop them.

Babak pulled his sword and joined the others—if he had to die now, he would go with honor. The last time he had fought in a battle was many years ago, and he hoped that some skill would return. The first impact on his sword sent him sprawling as a Persian Immortal attacked him from the side. Babak rolled when the sword came down, but when the man tripped on his own robe and fell, Babak turned and stabbed him in the back. The events after that were a blur—the heat, the fire nearby, the settling dust, the sand beneath the feet, and the screams of the fighting and the dying all melded in a cacophony. The swords clanged and blades made the squishing sound as they slashed muscle.

At some point, he collapsed, exhausted and disoriented. His ears rang and he was dizzy—a hellish world swayed and swam in front of his eyes. But soon a man grabbed him under the armpits and began dragging him. Babak fought weakly, unsure if he were being captured or rescued. Then the man leaned closer to his ear and shouted. "Move! Get to higher ground. Babak, move!"

Babak struggled back to his feet. All around him was smoke and dust, and in front was a large, sloping dune, much taller than the rest. The man held Babak's arm and pulled him along as they gasped and made their way to the top. And then the man asked him to descend. They did, and there they found a rocky protrusion, unusual for the land, but present, nevertheless. "Go there. Hide. The storm is coming soon!"

Then the man let go and Babak scrambled on his fours to the outcrop. It was a small overhang, and it seemed worn inside from the wind and sand. But it had a comfortable concave within which Babak could sit. The others had vanished, and he was alone. As he pushed his back to the wall, the brittle layer collapsed, and Babak fell back in. He shouted in fear, but he was in a small cave. When he tried to sit, he felt something brush against his hands.

What?

He screamed. It was almost as if his heart was about to explode.

There, next to him, was a seated, dried body of a man. His desiccated skin had turned black, and whatever garments he had worn long ago had turned to tatters. But curiously, on his sunken shoulder was a worn-out leather bag, still intact.

Who is this? Of all the places...

Babak gingerly reached to the bag and pulled it, and the body suddenly disintegrated into a puff of white bone dust and tissue. Babak recoiled and then gathered himself. It was getting quiet outside, and no one had peeked into his hideout. Besides, the dust in the air still obscured the view which made it safer for him. Babak opened the bag slowly. It was made of tough leather-like material and had many symbols of dolphins and deer on it. The colors were faded, but they still showed through the layers of fine dust.

Where is this from?

He opened the flap and peered inside. What he could make out was what looked like thick, bound papyrus sheets. He was intrigued. A man in the middle of nowhere holding a bag with colorful symbols and documents? It was all too much for him to absorb, coming from a fight to discovering a dead man with documents. Perhaps the gods had a design for him!

Suddenly, a section of the overhang collapsed. Babak felt a sharp pain on his shoulder and a rock slammed to his head. As the world dissolved in darkness, his last image was that day, long ago in Eshanna, when he chased his wife, sons, and daughter, tickling them all.

CHAPTER 61

THEBES

NEDJEM

Nedjem was lost in thought. After the incident at the river, she had visited Sekhet again at her house, but this time accompanied by two hired goons. The woman had cried in fear and begged to be left alone, and that she would never bother Nedjem again. But Nedjem had not accepted the assurances–Sekhet would have to leave Thebes, she demanded, or it would end badly for her. Sekhet finally agreed to leave to her father's house further north. Nedjem had not heard from Sekhet in days–the woman had vanished. Still wary, Nedjem had enlisted Hemmu and her family's help to keep an eye for any other suspicious characters. So far, everything had been quiet. It seemed like her threats to Sekhet had worked, and while she still watched her back every day, nothing untoward had happened. Nedjem's worry now shifted to her daughter. *Are these my child's last days?* She wondered, looking at the girl who now lay almost lifeless on the carpet. She then went back to what she was doing–making preparations for cooking.

There was an urgent knock on the door.

"Who is it?" she asked, worried and alarmed.

"Open the door, my dear sister!" came the voice.

Nedjem was at once shocked and thrilled. *Abanare?*

She opened the door to find Abanare gasping and holding his knees with his palms. Mentu stood behind him, grinning.

Nedjem could not believe her eyes.

Abanare was still hunched. "This boy will be the end of me," he gasped.

Nedjem laughed and hugged Mentu. Abanare stepped in first. He looked at her and his eyes overflowed with affection. Abanare was aware of her struggles. The loss of her sons and now the fate of her daughter had sapped the life out of her. He enveloped Nedjem in his arms and held her as she wept.

But there was no time to waste.

His eyes roamed to the corner of the sparse room. There, on a flimsy blanket, lay Amastri, her eyes closed. Her face was pale, almost as if no blood flowed in it, and a small line of drool showed by her lips.

He turned to Nedjem. "Is she alive?"

Nedjem nodded. And in between her sobs she managed to respond. "I think she is breathing. But she stopped eating two days ago."

Abanare was alarmed. Amunperre had explained in detail the stages of this terrible disease. Unresponsiveness and complete stoppage of food was the last stage—then came death. He rushed to the girl and asked Nedjem to hold her up to her lap. As Amastri's head rested on her mother's chest, Abanare checked her pulse and breath to confirm that she is still alive. After a few agonizing moments, he looked at his sister. "She is alive. Praise be to Amun. He keeps her life in her heart for us!"

Nedjem let out a gasp and clutched her daughter.

"Gently," Abanare admonished her. "I know you have many questions about your husband and his journey, and whether we have the medicine, Nedjem."

She nodded.

"But let us attend to Amastri first. We have the medicine from Ammon!" he said.

Nedjem's eyes opened wide and she relapsed back to crying. Abanare ignored her, for he understood the mother's anguish. He signaled Mentu to come near. "Open the bag. Take two spoons of the powder and mix it in hot water. Now!"

Mentu got to work. He quickly filled a clay cup with water and boiled it over the fire. The priests were insistent that the powder is mixed with water that was thoroughly boiled. "Bad spirits lay await in dirty water," they had cautioned. "When you boil the water, they fly away in agony and seek other sources."

Once the water boiled and bubbled, they waited for it to cool.

"Open her mouth," he told Nedjem. She pried the dry lips open and tilted the girl's neck, and he poured the concoction into her mouth. They had to struggle to ensure the liquid went down and that she did not cough or spit it out. Once the water was in, he gave instructions to Nedjem.

"You must give her this water three times between when Ra dies in the west and is reborn again in the east. And then, during the day, once between the rise of Ra and when he reaches the zenith. And then once between the zenith and when he dies again. And so on, for seven days. She will recover quickly if all goes well."

She nodded. Her shoulders relaxed and she sighed. She had finally reached the end of her grief—her daughter would now return to her or go to the afterlife. There was nothing else they could do.

She fixed her eyes, which now had some life and spark in them, on Abanare. "Tell me, brother."

Abanare asked Mentu to sit by his side.

"Wait," she said. "You must be hungry."

He watched as she fussed over Mentu and cooked some delicious smelling broth—lamb stew with herbs, a Persian dish that they had come to love. She was anxious and desperate to know her husband's fate and how they had engineered this outcome, but she would wait some more.

They ate quietly, relishing the food and filling their bellies. She cast anxious glances at her daughter who was still—as if expecting a miracle.

Abanare touched her arm once. "Be patient." She ate quickly, impatiently, and then she could no longer control her nervousness about her husband's fate.

"What about him?" she said, referring to Babak.

"Your husband is a brilliant but stupid and stubborn man," Abanare began.

CHAPTER 62

THE GREAT SAND SEA

ABERIS

Aberis winced in pain. They had bandaged his injured leg and saturated the deep wounds in his thigh and shoulder with a special poultice which both dulled the pain and, the physician claimed, would heal the wound rapidly. But it had been only a day and his body felt like it had been severely beaten. An excruciating pain throbbed in his thigh, rising all the way to his chest and neck.

Making it hard to breathe.

But he had survived! The bastards had failed to kill him or destroy his army. The captured men had given up where they came from and how to get to Ammon. He had no doubt that this time they had the right directions—he had spared the lives of two men, separated them, and told them— *if your directions do not match, then I will flay your skin, limb by limb, and cut off your digits, one by one, and you will live for days and pray for death.* And so far, a day later, their directions had matched. The army had gently changed its direction from a westbound trajectory to a more north-western angle. It would only be two or three days, the Egyptians said.

This time the army's inexorable march would not be halted. He would fuck the Egyptian gods and priests and burn the entire city. He would kill every man. His revenge would be terrible.

He had to be carried, for he was in no condition to walk. But his orders were clear—move or die alone. The army, finally having received the message that they were now close and that they were headed the right direction, was energized. Their supplies were almost over, water could be managed for a day and no more, and food would be over in two days. But that might bring to the edge and then push them to victory. But they had to rest now, after a brutal day's march.

"Blow horns for everyone to stop. Let them rest and eat."

The four-mile long column finally ground to a halt. Tired men created make-shift shelters using their clothes, for Aberis had ordered them to ditch most of the tents a day before to speed up their journey. They sat in this featureless land. The ribbons on the dunes looked like snakes had slithered in every which way, and the clear deep-blue skies created a mesmerizing contrast to the orange-yellow earth below.

The bearers put Aberis down, and he groaned with discomfort. He was running a fever—his face coated with a sheen of sweat and his tongue coated with patina. He lay on a thin blanket with his head supported by a thick pillow. He had asked to be placed on a slightly higher dune so he could look at the column behind him from a vantage point. An attendant brought a bowl of thin grain soup—a luxury for him and a few others—and provided two hard lumps of bread. He dipped the soup and began to chew on the bread—even that basic staple tasted heavenly, despite the throbbing shoulder and thigh. He looked around and cursed Babak roundly once again.

He would find the man and his family have them tortured to death.

He would make an example of his kind by going after his relatives and his wife's.

What mad man embarked on such a vengeful journey only because of the loss of his sons—something that happened every day! Maybe his bitch wife nagged him to it!

The wind had picked up again. It was not as bad as it was two days ago, but without adequate protection it was annoying to be sandblasted. He wiped his arms and mouth when something far in the horizon, towards the south, caught his attention.

Rain clouds? Here?

It was too far to discern, but a dark patch descended from the sky across a cross-section of the desert. It looked ominous and much denser than the sandstorms he had seen before. He turned to one of his men who was looking in the same direction.

"What is it?"

"I do not know, Excellency."

"Fetch the Egyptians!"

Quickly, one of the captives and a few Egyptians from the baggage train were pulled in. The men came up the dune panting and looking very worried.

"What is it?"

"They say it is a major sandstorm, Excellency. And that it is unlike the others we have seen."

Aberis could not believe what he heard.

What this time?

How many of these did they have to endure!

"What do they mean, unlike?"

"They say these are the storms of god, and they rage with fury like no other..."

The men looked extremely worried and were gesticulating wildly.

"They say we must run and seek immediate protection!"

Aberis looked around him.

Were they mad?

Where would they run for protection?

Any direction he saw there was nothing.

Just a sea of sand.

Not a cliff.

Not a bluff.

Not a bush.

Not a tree.

Where were these idiots expecting they would get protection?

"Run where, you fucking dog! Where? Look around! What should we do?" Aberis shouted. He gasped as any exertion caused the miserable pain to rise through his entire being.

The men stuttered and stammered and one of the bodyguards beat the captive who fell on the ground sobbing.

"They are just mumbling that we must hide."

"Well, we cannot hide. What should we do instead?" Aberis asked, now panicking. Blood coursed faster inside him and his head began to throb. He felt his heart thundering against his ribs.

"They're saying we should try to dig ourselves into the sand, lay low, and protect our bodies with whatever garments we can find…"

Aberis was frozen for a while until one of the officers nudged him. "What do you want to do, Your Excellency? What we do tell the army?"

He looked at the man as if he were mad. "What should we do? You idiot! Tell them to gobble their food and dig up the sand. Prepare me now!"

He felt dizzy and his throat felt like rough papyrus. "Give me some water, some water," he yelled, worrying that when the storm came to him, he may not have any for a while. The worst thing was they were unprotected. In the madness of the last day he had lost his own comforts too. He hoped that his men would not abandon him. Suddenly, Ammon and his governorship felt far away, like a distant bird in the sky, too far to reach.

The orders rippled through the column and soon he could see men frantically digging trenches in the sand, and yet soon as the wind picked up it became apparent that this was another futile exercise. The wind moved sand in a sharp south-to-north direction, hitting them in an angle, and filling up the indentation. His guards had managed a respectable ditch in which they put him. They created a flimsy tent from some of his and many of their robes hoisted on sticks and poles. But the weak and shaky tent wobbled, and the clothes flew away.

Aberis and his men wrapped themselves as best as they could and waited. The ominous shadow grew bigger and bigger, racing at them menacingly.

The storm moved quickly.

And it was a monster.

Far bigger than anything he had ever seen. It was soon looming, reaching from heaven to earth, and blotting the entire view. The dust was deep orange on the top slowly changing to a dark hue at the bottom.

Save us, Ahuramazda!

His eyes were affixed to the mesmerizing sight in front of him. The storm came at them like a hungry beast, devouring everything in its path as the frothing, churning cloud of sand danced its way towards them. The wind had died down, letting the nearby dust settle, but allowing a full and unobstructed view of the incoming terror. It was as if even the wind had bowed to the great monster.

Every man that sat or lay was turned south.

Watching.

Wondering.

Praying.

Many of the animals fought their restraints and ran away.

The others created great ruckus that could be heard at a distance.

The storm's flicking tongue first consumed the tail of the column, and the tiny little spots of men and material vanished. Great swirls of sand rose from the ground, and the wind churned like butter.

O gods of Egypt! We will surrender and return.

Forgive us for our hubris!

Let Ammon live as it always has!

Aberis began to pray with quivering lips, begging forgiveness of gods of all lands. But his prayers sunk in the sand as the storm moved upon them, engulfing section by section—the rear, the remaining Syrian and Scythian lines, the Greeks, the Persians.

The vast vertical column of sand rushed with power. Aberis felt the heat first—as if the front of the great sandstorm had a layer of hot air that pushed forward as it came from behind.

Aberis moaned with pain as he covered his face with a wet towel. His bodyguards vanished from his view.

Cowards! Stay with me!

He felt the air around him get warmed, thicker, and felt the first fine blast of sand.

Please, let this be over as quick as it came!

He begged and prayed.

CHAPTER 63

THE GREAT SAND SEA

THE STORM OF GOD

The powerful storm swept through the unending desert below. The swirling grains, hot and powerful, dislodged great volumes of sand from the patterned ground, creating a malevolent force that bore down on the frightened men below. The incredible power suffocated them with its heat and relentless battering—smashing burning sand on their bodies and attacking every orifice. Men, unprotected for the event, choked and clutched their faces. Animals still tethered pulled and fought until their neck snapped or the rope broke. Men who lay prostrate, hoping to escape the beast, felt the burden of sand building, pushing them further into the ground. A large contingent of Greeks locked their hands like a weaved fabric, and held their shields in front, hoping to face the brunt of the oncoming gust. And yet, the storm paid no heed to their clever postures. The tremendous force, bearing down on them from the heavens, parted them to a man, causing them to fly apart and curl up in self-preservation. The few remaining Scythians, confident in the power of their arrows, shot them in the sky towards the invisible monster, only to see their bolts swatted by the hands of the storm like they were strands of hay. The bolts turned back with lethal force on the men lying below, striking and nailing them to the ground. The intense sand was like a whiplash, blasting them like a million hot needles. Unable to stand or run, they all eventually lay down in surrender, praying to their gods and remembering their loved ones and family, with every man hoping for one thing: divine mercy.

But what mercy would a god offer to an army that sought to burn his sacred temple and kill his children?

As time progressed, the sun was no longer visible to those in the heart of the storm. Even with the glowing orb near the zenith, darkness came below as if it were night. The heat of the ground radiated upwards and mingled with the heat of the whirling sand, which increased in its intensity by the minute. There was no respite to a man or a beast, and any hopes of the storm ending quickly evaporated. Many men, desperate for protection, tried to get back on their feet and formed gangs that would stab the hapless ones still on the ground, and then attempted to use the bodies as shields atop them. With the weight of the dead above and sand heaped upon them by the storm, they suffocated and died themselves. First, they expired by the tens and then by the hundreds, and the long column of fluttering robes and scattered bodies slowly began to vanish under the sand.

Near the front of the column, atop a higher dune, lay a man, writhing in desperation. He tried crawling, braving his injured shoulder and thighs, and he shouted for his bodyguards. But they had abandoned him long ago, for what man served his master who cared none for him and whose service offered no more rewards? His eyes had turned red and bloody. He had rubbed his eyes, causing the grains of sand to lacerate them in an instant, tearing the innards and blinding him. As the weight of the sand began to suffocate him, and his mind became delirious.

He no longer knew what earth was and what was sky.

He saw lights, glorious lights, and then he saw demons, many-headed beings baring their teeth and claws, and then he saw nothing but swirling orange gust. He saw Zeus on his throne, his thunderbolt raised in anger, and by his side the Egyptian god Seth, laughing at him.

He turned on his back to relieve the excruciating pain in his shoulder which radiated to his entire body like a spider web. A blast of sand struck him. The ferocious wind screamed, like a stark raving mad beast, as if to say *look at me, look at what I can do! Look!*

He opened his mouth wide, gasping for air.

That mouth which had ordered so many deaths, which conspired, which laughed at the sorrow of many, which plotted for riches and power.

That mouth which now begged for mercy and water and relief.

And in that mouth went a powerful fist of sand grains, dense and hot. His throat was instantly clogged, and he tried to scream in horror. No sound came out and no air went in. The man began to arch his back and claw his neck in frantic desperation for air, ignoring the exploding agony of his wounds. His bloodied eyes blinked rapidly.

He rolled around, digging his broken nails into the ground, slapping the sand, kicking the air. His attire—that of a noble's—was in tatters, and soon he wore little as the grains battered his bruised skin. The sand gave no quarter to air, and his kicking soon subsided as life slowly seeped out of his body into the uncaring sand. And thus, a man by the side of the *Shahanshah*, the one who held the fates of so many in his hands, simply became a nothing–a spec in the sand.

But not every man fell victim. Far away, further to the southeast, a small band of men led by a Greek captain made their way towards Horosis. They braved the powerful gusts. They looked back at the darkness at a distance. They fell to their knees and prayed. The captain wept with relief and thanked a Persian who had told him to leave the sacrilegious mission. He still felt shame at deserting the army, but he hoped that the gods would forgive him for the choices he had to make.

But no such mercy was forthcoming to the army. The anger of the god was not satiated by the death of the thousands. The storm continued to rage, unabated as the sun inched its way to the west. The dunes that existed hours ago ceased to be, and those that never did came to be, as if by divine order. The column slowly vanished under the sand.

First, the bodies, with their twisted limbs, tortured faces, mouths open in screams and hands still clutching their useless weapons—the swords, the bows, the shields, the axes, the knives, the clubs, the arrows.

Then, the poles, spikes, and the baggage carts with men's livelihoods and valuables. And also Aberis' fantastical treasure—of no use to the gods, and now beyond a man's reach.

And eventually, the earth bore no sign that there were men or their animals here at all.

And on that dead army grew new dunes, like trees on a graveyard. Those dunes grew taller, and they changed shape, and then the entire land looked nothing like it was when that army set foot there.

It was as if the gods would tolerate no evidence of their incursion. When night came and went, and the storm finally gave way to dawn, there was not a sign that here, there was once a mighty King's force, for it had utterly vanished.

And thus did it fare with this army.

CHAPTER 64
THE GREAT SAND SEA
BABAK

The wind howled outside the cave, and fine sand slammed into the walls and sprayed inside. He sat huddled with only ancient bones as his companions. Sometimes he shivered; it was strange, for he was enveloped by heat. The sand first covered his feet. Then it crept up, like a slow-growing vine around a tree. As the gusts continued unabated, the sand rose like water in a well. It covered him up to his waist. He struggled. Sometimes he even tried to pour some out—but he knew it was futile—can a man empty a river with his palms? As time wore, he stared at the ancient bundle in his hands.

What was it?

Who was this man?

How did he come here?

And then he was startled. There was a figure lurking just outside, and then it peered in. It was his wife. She looked so young! Like when they were married. She smiled and showed the baby in her hand. Amastri.

The baby giggled and tried to catch some of the sand.

"No," he tried to shout, but his throat was so dry.

And then just as they came his wife and baby turned into dust and flew away in the wind. He tried to lift his hand and reach to them, but his hands were too heavy. His torso was now in the fine sand which was covering him like a blanket. His thighs felt heavy like a grain sack on them, but there was not much he could do.

And then suddenly there were hands.

Dark, desiccated hands sprang from the ground, growing like plants. They flexed their fingers and they tried crawling his way.

No! What is it—

And the hands vanished. He knew, somewhere in his mind, that he imagined things. In a rare moment of lucidity, he remembered that men who might be readying to die saw those they loved or hated, they saw rivers and forests, they saw strange beasts and glorious lights.

The sand was now slowly inching to his chest and rising to the neck.

He thought of his journey.

How much he had done so fast.

He hoped that Aberis had given up on his mission.

And that he died, not to come back and harm his family.

But then his mind turned to what mattered the most.

His only surviving child—his sick daughter.

Had Mentu and Abanare had reached his wife?

Had the medicines of the priests worked?

Would his loving wife get her daughter back?

Would she survive in Cambyses' world when he was gone?

Questions. But no answers. And then suddenly hundreds of gorgeous butterflies appeared out of nowhere. Orange, blue, green, purple. They fluttered around him and the wings touched his lips. They beat sharply until it hurt.

What?

Those were sand grains.

The butterflies vanished as they came.

He leaned back. Let his head rest on the soft wall behind. He let the light spray of dust fall on his face, and he listened to the soft humming of the wind outside.

He smiled.

And then he closed his eyes.

CHAPTER 65

THEBES

NEDJEM

They had followed every instruction—feeding the concoction through the day and night. Mentu and Abanare had fussed over the girl and Nedjem, helping her clean and care for the sick child.

But Amastri had not moved. Had some color returned to her cheeks? Maybe it was just an imagination. The arms stayed limp and the eyes stayed closed. They had persevered, but how much longer? Despair had begun to set in. After all, no one knew if the girl would survive, and whether Babak was dead or alive. It was the mystery of how the gods determined their fates—the day could end with Nedjem as a widow and childless, or a better fate might smile upon her. Nedjem despaired. She was too old to have more children, and would she now have none after surviving having given birth to three? What cruel fate was this?

Abanare held the girl for the afternoon dose, and Nedjem gently pried the mouth open. They then slowly dripped the liquid down the lips. They held the girl's nose to force the liquid down her throat. And then they gently massaged her throat and chest to help ease it into her belly. Nedjem held the girl and she waited, like she always did. A gentle aroma of lilac floated in the room; they usually lighted up aromatic sticks in the room as an offering to the gods and to reduce the smell of sickness.

And then Amastri let out a low moan and she opened her eyes.

Nedjem almost dropped the girl in shock. Her eyes opened wide and she gasped.

"Amastri!"

Her daughter stirred some more. Her eyes focused on her mother for the first time in many, many days. Her limp arm moved too.

Nedjem was overcome with joy. Tears of happiness sprang from her eyes, and Mentu would later tease her— she was for once short for words. She hugged her daughter hard, and then remembered that Amastri was still weak. She let her go and gently lay her on the mattress.

"Amastri?" She asked again.

Her daughter opened her eyes and she held firm this time. And finally, a small smile escaped her lips. Nedjem began to cry with relief. She let her daughter lie and ran to the idols of Amun and Ahuramazda. Still crying, she lit up two lamps and offered flowers in gratitude to the gods that had brought her daughter back. She thanked her husband, now away in the unknown. Their daughter had returned from the gates of the realm of the dead, but was her husband alive?

Mentu and Abanare were ecstatic. They all sat there by the girl's side, watching. After some time, Nedjem reached out again and held her daughter's hand. Amastri squeezed. There was strength in her hands. Life had returned.

And at that time, far away, in a little cave by the edge of the Great Sand Sea, something stirred under the sand.

CHAPTER 66
HOROSIS

BABAK

Babak groaned in pain. Even the comfortable mattress did little to assuage the misery of a battered body. Each time he moved, agony bloomed from his eye socket and his back felt like someone was sliding sharp blades on him. He had sought refuge in a cave and had emerged from it after the storm abated. Petubastis' spotters had found him lying in the sand, still wearing the bright robes.

But today his mind felt more lucid than ever before. Gone were the nightmares and strange visions. He had prayed when he was awake, and the gods were finally smiling upon him. After days, he could finally reflect on his journey.

How far he had come from that fateful day when his wife burst into the house.

When they spoke of the expedition to Ammon, and that the contingent would be led by the hated Aberis. It was as if the gods had smiled on him and given him a chance to make good on his to promise to his wife—that one day he would kill every man responsible for his son's cruel deaths. It was also mission to prevent bringing down the wrath of Egypt's gods on all of Persia.

He opened his eyes to find Pharaoh Petubastis standing by his bed. Babak knew that Petubastis was pleased with himself. By the grace of Amun, Horus, Thoth, and *me*, Babak mused, Petubastis had hurt the invaders like a pack of hyenas on a foolish lion. There were fifty thousand when they began, and yet now there were none. Cambyses was still on his campaign to Ethiopia, and Petubastis' spies were reporting that the Persian King was suffering there too.

"How are you today?"

Babak struggled to rise from the bed, and Petubastis lay a palm on his shoulder. "I am recovering, thanks to your grace, Your Majesty," he rasped. Babak had lost an eye, was severely sunburned, and had lost movement in his left hand. He knew that Petubastis' physicians had worked for days to bring him back to life. They said that for days he was delirious, and whenever he regained his faculties, he wished nothing but the safety of his wife and child. He had also often mumbled about Mentu and Abanare.

Babak observed the Pharaoh. Petubastis was a powerful man, a renegade, a rebel with ambitions. He was willing to take on the mighty Persian empire. And he had not forgotten to care for a Persian who had helped him. Petubastis had told him that the army had never reached Ammon. And that they had vanished from the earth.

"The storm of god has swallowed the rest of them whole," Senwosret had said.

Petubastis moved closer. "You will be pleased today," the Pharaoh said cryptically. Babak was unsure what he meant. He bowed and looked at the Pharaoh tentatively.

Petubastis then turned to the door and gestured to the guards.

The curtains parted.

Babak gasped.

Nedjem and Amastri!

His wife was radiant. Her smile lit up the room. His daughter, even if still looking weak, held her mother's hand

and looked at him with a twinkle in her eyes. Babak tried getting up but collapsed in pain, but his heart sang.

They rushed to him. *"Baba,"* his daughter said, and knelt by him. His wife prostrated to the Pharaoh first. After all, for her, and for most Egyptians, he was a god. Petubastis lifted her by the shoulders and signaled her to go to Babak.

Babak looked at Petubastis with respect and admiration. "You brought them to me, Your Majesty."

He smiled. "Senwosret would not have it any other way."

Babak bowed to the general who stood quietly by the side.

Nedjem walked to him and sat gingerly. She lifted his head and placed it on her lap. "My husband. All the gods smile upon you."

"And upon you too," he said.

She smelled of rose and jasmine. A heady aroma that Babak had not felt for a long time. He inhaled deeply, letting a sense of happiness fill him.

Mentu and Abanare walked in. Babak tussled the boy's hair. "You are a wonder from the heavens!"

"And you look like a one-eyed ghoul," said Mentu, and had his ears boxed by Nedjem.

Then Babak asked Amastri to come near him. He watched his surviving child with great affection. He asked her to lean forward so he could kiss her cheeks. Amastri smiled shyly. The twinkle was back in her eyes, and she had put on more weight than before. She even wore a pretty little necklace—one that once belonged to Eribaeus, Babak realized.

"Have you been eating well?"

"Yes, Baba."

"Have you been troubling your mother?"

"No, Baba."

"Well, sometimes..." said Nedjem and laughed.

"Have you learned to cook?"

"I will, Baba. And you know what?"

"What?"

"Maman's neighbor, grandmother Hemmu says—"

Nedjem hushed her. Babak laughed—surely there was some history there for him to learn.

And for the next hour they sat and talked.

They praised the beaming Pharaoh and General Senwosret.

They hugged and told stories.

Babak felt tired, and yet his body finally felt alive. A tear fell on his cheeks danced its way to wet Nedjem's lap.

He imagined his sons holding their hands and looking at him from above. Smiling.

He had done the impossible.

CHAPTER 67

ΛOSTRIS, TWO YEΛRS LΛTER

DARIUS

It was late evening and the sun was beginning to set. The battlefield had quietened down. King of Kings Darius, *Shahanshah Darayavahush*, successor to Cambyses, looked around him. To his left were the gentle bluffs, and in front the lapping waters of the serene oasis. But around him were the dead—the last of the Egyptians rebels who stood against him had been finally vanquished.

"We found him, Your Majesty," said one of his generals. Darius walked with the officer, gingerly stepping around the strewn bodies. A thick smell of cinnamon mixed with blood filled the air. They finally reached a dense cluster. It was clear from the pattern of the bodies here that whoever was at the center was important, for heaps lay dead around him, fighting until the very end. In the middle lay a man—stocky, powerfully built. His body bore battle scars and the fatal wounds. But what slew him, as it was evident, were the three arrows still protruding from his broad chest. The face was almost unrecognizable, for blood had spurted from the mouth and nose and crusted all around. But the Egyptian advisors were adamant that they had identified him.

"Pharaoh Petubastis," the general said. He pointed to another man nearby. "And his general Senwosret."

"He fought until the very end," Darius said, with a hint of irritation but with a tone of admiration. The King of

Kings respected those who stood for what they believed in and fought for it. After all, Darius himself, with the blessings of Ahuramazda, had killed Gaumata the impostor, and secured the throne. He was now the ruler of the powerful Achaemenid Empire.

Egypt too was now his.

He turned to his men. "Give him a respectful burial. Let their men entomb him. But his tomb must be hidden and with no inscription."

"Yes, Your Majesty."

"And ensure that the temple of Ibis he supported here is completed."

Darius had heard of valiant stories of this Pharaoh— that he was behind the disappearance of an army his predecessor Cambyses had sent to Ammon. But Darius had to be careful that stories of such heroics were not spread widely, for they may foment new rebellions. He instructed every official and every Egyptian administrator to expunge any accounts from the records, and to maintain that the army was lost in a storm in Egypt.

The King of Kings continued to walk the battlefield. This was an untrained army that he easily defeated, and he could see why. There were the young and the old, youths and the middle-aged. There were even a small number of women. They had faced Darius as if in a suicide mission, and his orders for them to surrender and be allowed to live had gone unheeded.

His eye caught something. He walked to the side, stepping over a headless body. There lay two men—one a strapping youth, and another a much older man. On the boy's neck was a beautiful necklace with the carving of Horus. And from the pose, it seemed like the boy had died trying to save the older man.

Their faces were peaceful in death. It was as if they had embraced each other and chosen to walk the afterlife together.

Darius wondered what their story was.

CHAPTER 68

FARRASIS

BABAK

Babak sat on his porch and watched as his daughter helped his wife with pulling the water from the well. These idyllic days would not last, for *Shahanshah Darayavahush*, King of Kings Darius, would soon leave Egypt in pursuit of other victories. He had recovered quite a bit—though now blind in one eye and having lost most of the mobility in his left arm.

In his right hand he cradled the bundle of papyrus he had found in the cave where he almost died after the sandstorm. *What a mysterious find it was*, he thought. The papyrus was full of writing and diagrams, and yet he was unable to decipher any of it, and neither could a few Egyptian advisors he enlisted. The script was unknown to any, so Babak surmised that it was from a time long ago, from a people that he knew nothing about. He would carry this to his tomb, and perhaps the gods would help him read it in the afterlife.

But for now, he was glad to be alive. Thanks to Ahuramazda and Amun.

And Petubastis.

Babak's life had changed in ways he had not anticipated. First, he spent time under Petubastis' care and advised him on shoring up his forces. Then, he fell out of favor of the Pharaoh for proposing that he seek peace with Cambyses' successor. *Please consider this, Your Majesty*, Babak had begged Petubastis. *Darius is a far more capable commander than Cambyses, and he is an able and kinder ruler. You can remain Pharaoh so long as you submit to the King of Kings.* Petubastis, the hothead that he was, was livid at the proposal and told Babak that he would not execute him only due to his past services. Babak's pleadings to spare a poorly trained army from going up against Darius' formidable war machine had fallen on deaf ears. The Pharaoh had banished Babak who then moved his family to Farrasis and lay low. Once Darius came to Egypt, Babak had sought audience with the *Shahanshah* and received one based on his story that he had advised Cambyses and had tried to save the army from its doomed march to Ammon. With no one to corroborate or challenge his stories, Darius had accepted Babak's version. Babak's goal was to convince the new King to spare Egypt from harsh retribution and help him adhere to the conventions of the land. Darius had done well by this advice: he faced little resistance except for Petubastis, who stubbornly was unwilling to meet any negotiating parties. Meanwhile, his stature growing, Babak had come to an understanding with the priests at Ammon to keep his secret, and in return he would prevent any major structural changes of power in the temple.

So, an uneasy truce fell in place, but whatever distaste to any parties was quelled by the realization that acceptance of Darius would not spill further Egyptian blood. Besides, if the new Achaemenid emperor respected the laws and ways of the land, was there a need to fight him? Especially if Darius allowed most Egyptian officials to retain power and continue to administer their provinces and pay tribute to the King?

The army of Cambyses had truly disappeared. Cambyses himself had suffered more humiliation, forced to retreat due to a similar lack of preparedness for the harsh land in

Ethiopia. He left Egypt to deal with another unrest when he died, leading to Darius becoming King. Amunperre complained that they never found the valuables promised unto them—Babak did not know if Abanare had given them incorrect directions or if the changing patterns of sand had hidden it forever. There were recriminations from both parties, and they had come to an agreement that Babak would secure favor through Darius in return. Babak was never able to go on another finding mission. But Babak was proud of his achievements–he might even describe some of it in his tomb when he died.

Sadness came home once again after Darius defeated the last remnants of Petubastis' army in the battle of Aostris. Mentu and Abanare, faithful and loyal to their Pharaoh until the very end, had lost their lives in the battle. True to his word, Darius had spared the residents of Aostris, Horosis, and Farrasis, and even commissioned the construction of new temples honoring native gods.

He was now the new Pharaoh of Egypt.

Babak and Nedjem had heard that Sekhet, Jabari's wife, had resurfaced in Darius' court as another priest's wife. But she was far away in Thebes where Babak was unlikely to ever set foot, so she faded from memory.

Babak came out of his reverie when he noticed dust rise from the charge of camels.

Darius' men coming towards his house.

He called his wife and daughter to join him.

The elaborately dressed officers, in their green flowing robes and tall Persian caps, approached him respectfully. "The King of Kings asks that you join him in Memphis in twenty days. We go north."

Babak nodded. He then held Nedjem and Amastri close. He looked far into the distance, where the yellow dunes gently melded with the harsh orange ground. He looked into his wife's eyes—and he knew she would be by his side wherever he went.

"Where are we going?" Nedjem asked, and Amastri looked on quietly.

"We go where Ahuramazda takes us," he said, and hugged them close.

THE END

NOTES

Before we even begin—you can now go to https://jaypenner.com/the-whispers-of-atlantis/maps to do a Google maps flyby of all the major locations of this book. Give it a try!

Cambyses' lost army has been a topic of fascination and interest to many. There have been several futile searches for this army, and many speculations as to what happened to it, and if such an expedition even took place. My book certainly touches on some of those theories. Should you be interested, please visit my post on the Lost Army of Cambyses.

Cambyses (*Khambujiya*) was the son of Cyrus (*Kurus*) the Great, the first great king of the Achaemenid dynasty (natively called *Haxamanisiya*). Cyrus expanded his territory and conquered Akkad and Sumer, and was welcomed as the new ruler of Babylon. Cambyses' rule is very poorly documented outside Herodotus' writings, and he was eclipsed by Darius (*Darayavahush*), who succeeded him.

In the book, we see the kings repeatedly pay respect to Ahuramazda, who was the principal god of the Achaemenids. However, we have little evidence as to how much Cambyses invoked Ahuramazda, because his father, Cyrus, barely mentions this god. Ahuramazda became far more prominent in Darius' reign (read the Behistun inscription), but we can make a reasonable deduction that perhaps Ahuramazda's prominence had begun to rise between Cyrus and Darius.

Herodotus does not show Cambyses in good light. Most historians now agree that Cambyses did not kill the sacred Apis bull and may not have heaped indignities on the Egyptians as Herodotus makes it out to be. Now, Herodotus is known to exaggerate details, and it is likely that he was either fed misinformation on Cambyses, or he deliberately chose to misrepresent the rule for he had an ax to grind. Remember that Herodotus wrote about Cambyses almost a century after Cambyses' rule in Egypt. It also appears Cambyses may have been accepted as Pharaoh, so his need to attack Ammon on a slight is also questionable–but then emperors have empire size egos, and one could easily see an angry king sending an army to erase someone because of a perceived insult.

Let us turn our attention briefly to the general understanding of the word "Persian," which applies to modern Iranians. However, in the period that this book is set in, the usage of "Persian" applies more generally to those belonging to the Achaemenid empire–which spanned all the way from Mesopotamia (modern Iraq) to the Indus valley, though the "native Persians" would be from regions in modern Iran.

Now, what about Persian Babak's marriage to Egyptian Nedjem? Well, it is no surprise at all that people of different Kingdoms married for alliances. There are many instances in Egyptian royal rule where kings sought alliances through marriages. You should search for the "Amarna Letters," which offer a fascinating glimpse of royal communications in ancient times. There is speculation that Nefertiti, wife of Akhenaten, may have been a foreign princess. Alexander the Great himself married a Bactrian Princess (Roxanne/Roxana). Alexander's Greek secretary Eumenes married Artonis, sister of a Persian noble. So, it is not a leap of logic that perhaps there may be instances of commoners marrying as well.

Aostris, Horosis, and Farrasis are names used in this novel. We do not know their names during Cambyses' time. All Herodotus says is that the army departed the "Island of the Blessed" but we have no idea what it is. Possibly modern Dakhla, Kharga, or Farafra.

Was Petubastis of this novel real? Well, recently archaeologists found evidence of a Pharaoh named Petubastis, and his base appears to have been the modern Dakhla oasis (the *Horosis* of the novel). He would have lived just around the time of Cambyses and Darius, and one theory is that he ambushed this army and defeated it, and eventually Darius (or Cambyses) hid the truth.

Could a sandstorm have buried an entire army? Some recent simulations indicate that they can be pretty powerful. But bury an army? The world is full of surprises, and perhaps, someday, we will find this army beneath the sands.

THANK YOU

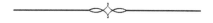

I would be immensely grateful if you could take a few moments to leave a kind review or a rating—these are critical to new and upcoming authors. Thank you in advance! You can also go to https://jaypenner.com/reviews for convenient links.

Grab Book IV: Sinister Sands. Deon and Eurydice from the Atlantis Papyrus are back, and Ptolemy is interested in something that happened in this book! What was in the papyrus bundle? All that and more in Sinister Sands.

When you get to the end, Kindle should present the option to purchase Sinister Sands, which is the next in the series.

JAY PENNER
HISTORY AND FANTASY

Choose your interest! A gritty and treacherous journey with Cleopatra in the Last Pharaoh trilogy, or thrilling stories full of intrigue and conflict in the Whispers of Atlantis anthology set in the ancient world.

THE LAST PHARAOH

WHISPERS OF ATLANTIS

https://jaypenner.com

Printed in Great Britain
by Amazon

78751268R00196